PARTY GIRL

PARTY GIRL

A NOVEL

ANNA DAVID

HC

An Imprint of HarperCollins*Publishers*

PARTY GIRL. Copyright © 2007 by Anna David. All rights reserved. Printed in the United States of America. No part of this book may be used or reproduced in any manner whatsoever without written permission except in the case of brief quotations embodied in critical articles and reviews. For information, address HarperCollins Publishers, 10 East 53rd Street, New York, NY 10022.

HarperCollins books may be purchased for educational, business, or sales promotional use. For information please write: Special Markets Department, HarperCollins Publishers, 10 East 53rd Street, New York, NY 10022.

FIRST EDITION

Designed by Kris Tobiassen

Library of Congress Cataloging-in-Publication Data has been applied for.

ISBN 10: 0-06-119872-2
ISBN: 978-0-06-119872-4

07 08 09 10 11 10 9 8 7 6 5 4 3 2 1

FOR ALL THE PARTY GIRLS OUT THERE—
AND ALL THOSE WHO PUT UP WITH THIS ONE

"Silly things do cease to be silly if they are done by sensible people in an impudent way."

—JANE AUSTEN

"My girl wants to party all the time,
Party all the time,
Party all the time . . ."

—EDDIE MURPHY

1

It is a truth universally acknowledged that crazy things happen at weddings. Or at least that's what I tell myself as my activities segue from outrageous to risqué to downright depraved.

There's the bathroom blow job incident, which I categorize as "outrageous" rather than "downright depraved," solely due to the fact that my eighty-two-year-old stepdad walks in while I'm going down on the cousin of the bride in the poolhouse bathroom. Because of his eighty-two-ness (the stepdad, not the cousin, thankfully), he was prone to more "senior moments" than nonsenior moments—and thus is easily convinced that what had just happened never in fact happened. By the time I'm done talking to him, I've actually managed to convince him that not only was there no blow job, but also there had been no cousin of the bride. I'm pretty sure if I'd kept going I could have gotten him to believe there was no wedding. But the point is, in convincing my stepdad, I'm pretty sure I convince myself. And thus: outrageous, not downright depraved.

Don't bother asking me how I go from sitting next to the cousin and finding him mildly attractive—not gorgeous, just mildly attractive, someone I might have gone out with had he asked me—to kneeling down in front of him while he sat on Mom's bidet. It wouldn't have been my style to have asked, "Care for a blow job in the bathroom?" At least I don't think so. It's possible that after a bottle or so of good wedding champagne, Amelia Stone is replaced by Paris Hilton minus the millions, plus a good twenty pounds, but since my exploits haven't been caught on tape—note to exes, not that I know of—I can only venture this as a guess. I'd like to imagine that I happened to visit the restroom just as he was leaving and that our sudden passion erupted spontaneously. But by the end of the night—well, morning— the whole cousin incident was so comparatively pristine, I may as well have been a virgin in white in that bathroom.

Later, I find myself in the sauna with the groomsmen. It had been my mom's idea, that all the "young people" from the wedding should sauna and swim, but somehow it got down to just two guys and me. By this point, I know that I'm way more than mildly intoxicated, but since technically I'm on vacation, aren't I supposed to be? If I were this drunk in L.A., someone would probably bring out the coke and I'd thus be able to alleviate my alcohol buzz a bit, but parties at Mom's house tend to be pretty short on drugs—at least non-SSRI ones. And since in some ways there's no better high than having two men vying for your attention, I figure it's just as well that I'm not holding.

"I'm going to be graduating in May," Mitch says, as he offers me a sip of his warm Amstel Light. "Medical school has been a bitch."

"Oh, but now you're going to have to do your residency," Mitch's alleged best friend Chris interjects, while interjecting his body into the minuscule space that exists between Mitch and me. "You'll be working, like, ninety-hour weeks for no money."

"Which is so much worse than 'doing your residency' at Paramount for a salary just above the poverty line?" Mitch lobs back, looking at me.

I swear I never get tired of the attention of boys. But I prefer direct attention, rather than transparent male dick-swinging contests. Do they honestly think that the one who gets the last dig in will win my affection? Don't they know that being an assistant and a student, even a medical student, aren't exactly lady-killer positions to be in, and that they should perhaps be digging into their personal arsenals for more compelling things to compete over?

I stand up and they're silenced. "Last one in has to do a shot," I say and before I've even finished the sentence, they're pushing each other aside in their zeal to jump into the pool. I stand at the sauna door, cold air rushing in, their wet towels at my feet. If I didn't know better, I'd swear that the two of them just wanted to have sex with each other.

"Okay, we're going to sleep now," I instruct them, as I try to get as comfortable as I can while lodged between these two guys in a double bed. "Sleep."

I honestly think we're going to bed. Was anyone ever that naive? I can't even sleep on two Ambien by myself, but the birds are dangerously close to chirping—a horrifyingly depressing time to still be partying, as I've recently learned—this is the only bed left in the house, and neither of these guys are in any condition to drive. I turn toward Chris, who's facing the wall. Mitch is on the other side, facing the other wall.

A few minutes pass and I hear Mitch breathing heavily in that way that means he could be asleep. I sigh and feel more relaxed. My insomnia always seems embarrassing, and I'm all too relieved to be able to suffer through it without witnesses. Miraculously, I drift off for a moment or two.

And am awakened by lips on mine—specifically, lips belonging to Chris. My eyes swing open just in time for me to realize that Chris's kissing skills aren't half bad. Some people pride themselves on their gaydars. I pride myself on my kissdar because I can usually tell on sight if a guy is going to be one of those drench-your-face-with-saliva kissers, too-tentative pecking kissers, or a possessor of one of those lizardlike tongues that darts into places it's not wanted. Most guys, unfortunately, fit into one of these categories. It's the ones that don't that drive us mad, in all the good ways. Unfortunately, their kissing skills always seem to accompany a tendency for unemployment, a lack of an IQ, or just a general asshole-ishness. If they could kiss well and also possess qualities that actually made them good boyfriend material, women would probably maim and kill one another to have them. I had assumed that Chris would be some combination of too-tentative and lizardlike—that he'd start out with inappropriate propriety and then swerve into too much without the required sensuality—and am startled to discover that he seems to know what he's doing. He even knows the take-my-face-in-his-hands move.

I kiss him back, enjoying the secretiveness of the act. Despite all their lame competitiveness, despite the fact that Chris is an assistant at Paramount and that he attacks his alleged best friend who's actually doing something useful with his life in a pathetic attempt to win a girl's affection, I'm more attracted to him than I am to Mitch.

Chris is kissing well enough that it's impossible to say how many times we kiss—one time just seems to mesh into another. And then I'm utterly shocked when I feel a hand creeping from behind into my nether region. Had Chris and Mitch, in some sort of a silent pact, targeted my two most manipulatable zones and decided to each work one of them? The thrill of kissing someone while another hand works me from behind is unbelievable. I'm completely getting off on the anonymity of the hand (even though I obviously know whose hand it is) and on this wise solution to all that petty male competitiveness that was going on earlier, until I come back to earth and remember where we are. Which is in the guest bedroom directly below my mom and stepdad's bedroom in their house, which I'm visiting for the weekend to see an old friend get married—not to blow his now-wife's cousin and have a ménage à trois with two of his groomsmen.

"Wait—you have to stop!" I suddenly screech. I jump out of bed and the two of them look alarmed, if not altogether shocked. I grab a pillow off the bed. "I need to go somewhere where I can actually sleep," I say, as if they'd been talking and I was tired of shushing them. Without another word, I stomp off to the den, where I promptly pass out on the couch.

2

Back in L.A., Stephanie asks me about the wedding and I regale her with my exploits. She laughs hysterically, the same way I did when she told me about twisting her ankle while dancing at the wedding she went to back East—at least she thinks she was dancing, as she was actually in a blackout and didn't want anyone around to know so she never was able to determine how it happened. "They should keep us away from weddings—the way we behave is completely foul," she says.

I work at *Absolutely Fabulous*, a celebrity weekly magazine that's basically a glorified tabloid, and Stephanie works one level down, at *American Style*, a weekly magazine that devotes itself to dissecting the outfits and homes of celebrities in minute detail. And thank God for Stephanie. Most of my *Absolutely Fabulous* coworkers are about as cool as Sunday school teachers.

Because of its high circulation rate (five million and rising all the time), those who work at *Absolutely Fabulous* speak of it in the revered tone most might use to describe *The New Yorker*. "We, quite simply, have the best writing and reporting of any magazine out there," our bureau chief Robert likes to say, and we all drink the Kool-Aid. Glimmers of reality peak into that otherwise glorious way of thinking—like the fact that I'm sometimes embarrassed to tell people I work here, that the constant note I'm always given about my articles is that I need to "make my sentences shorter," and that the big joke about the publication is that everyone reads it on the toilet, but it's amazing how convincing a staff of roughly thirty people can be. People seem to stretch reality just enough to motivate them—but it's a little weird, you know? Can't they just say, "When I was little, I didn't imagine that figuring out what Madonna eats would be my living, but hey, this is a successful magazine and someday I may work somewhere else"? I know that it takes a bit of denial for all of us to get out of bed in the morning, but sometimes the people at *Absolutely Fabulous* seem to be swimming in a whole river of it.

Stephanie absolutely hates her job—only works there for the party invites and free clothes, and willingly announces as much to anyone who will listen. Which makes it all the more difficult for me when she keeps rising on their masthead while I stay stuck as a low-level writer at *Absolutely Fabulous*. It's not that I want Stephanie to fail—it's just that sometimes I wouldn't mind if my number one partner in crime were sort of in the same place as I am.

Unfortunately, I seem to inspire a sort of figurative foaming at the mouth from my boss Robert. This could have to do with the fact that I was hired by his second-in-command, Brian, when Robert was on leave, or maybe I just remind him of someone he absolutely hates. I try most everything to turn him around, but when people make up their mind about you, you could save their mother's life and they'd still think you were an asshole. Case in point: Brad McCormick, my high school boyfriend, who hovered somewhere around the five foot four mark during our adolescent relationship. Though he's now about six feet tall—a late growth spurt and, unfortunately, not one I was able to benefit from—to me, he'll always be "little Brad McCormick."

"You ready?" Stephanie asks me on a Thursday at about six. She's standing at my cubicle, workbag slung over her shoulder, flashing the flask that I gave her for her birthday from under her coat.

I used to get really excited before going to premieres. I think I imagined that someone would see me there and discover me for God knows what—I'm not an actress, or I should say I only am in my personal life—but I guess I thought getting discovered for being so utterly fabulous that I would need to be immediately removed from my day-to-day life and deposited into an existence that revolved around being fabulous full time. I think I thought that rubbing up against movie stars would make me happy. But it occurred to me this one night that I found myself in a cigarette-fueled drunken discussion with Jeremy Piven at a premiere. Jeremy Piven didn't seem too happy, so why should I be happy for having had the experience of talking to him all night?

We stop for drinks at some Westwood college bar beforehand. Or, if I'm going to have to be perfectly honest and specific about everything, I should say that Stephanie stops for drinks and I stop for drinks and a few lines.

When I first started doing coke, at parties, it was usually easy enough to count on being in the right place at the right time for a steady supply. But more than a few experiences chatting up thoroughly disgusting men only to learn that they were simply fellow coke-seekers themselves had brought me to a point a few months ago where I finally understood the necessity of having my own dealer. And the sheer joy I've felt over the fact that I can do coke whenever I want because I'm not relying on someone else to get it has made the additional expense seem almost irrelevant.

I wander into the bathroom after a woman with gray hair in a bun leaves, and shut myself in the stall farthest away from the door. Pulling a vial from my purse, I shake some coke onto the window ledge and chop it with a credit card, then take a rolled-up bill from my wallet and snort it up. I hear someone come in and hold my breath while she washes her hands and thankfully leaves, then pour some more coke on the ledge and snort it.

"I still have plenty left," I tell Stephanie as I return from the bathroom and sit down in my swivel chair. The metal taste of cocaine drips down the back of my throat deliciously. Some people say they hate the drip but I love it—that practical evidence that the drug is working its way through my body.

"Nothing could sound more foul," she answers, as she tries to pour some of her vodka tonic into a flask. Stephanie doesn't do coke—she used to have panic attacks and is convinced, probably correctly, that a few lines of cocaine would send her right back there—so I ask her more as a course of habit than as some sick kind of peer pressure.

"Ready?" she asks. I smile, nod, and sniffle so I can swallow and taste more cocaine again.

We walk briskly down the red carpet as skeletal blond actresses—shivering in their summer dresses on this uncharacteristically cool night—smile obediently for the paparazzi.

"Leslie, over here!" the photographers all scream at once at this beautiful blonde who's grinning seductively. The way the photographers are jostling one another and screaming her name with such glee, you'd swear they were trying to get snaps of Julia Roberts, or at least the president or the queen or something. The fact that there are hundreds, if not thousands, of Leslies with bit parts in movies like the mediocre one we're about to see and one, if that, will actually continue to work in Hollywood after this current role, certainly doesn't seem to be at the forefront of the photographers' collective minds. But Leslie handles her moment well.

Stephanie and I decide to make a run for it to avoid being caught in the back of one of these shots. It happened to Stephanie once—a picture of Lindsay Lohan was almost ruined by the image of Stephanie, an extremely unflattering image of her at that, doing a shot with someone the picture didn't capture (that is, me) and the photo ran in about a hundred magazines. Stephanie has yet to live it down.

She takes off at a good pace but I'm waylaid by Leslie, the actress, as she steps backward, lodging her seemingly ten-inch red heel into my big left toe in what feels like an instant toe decapitation—if toes had heads. She starts to trip backward but her publicist catches her, glaring at me for daring to slide my foot under her client's $700 shoe-slash-instrument-of-torture. For an anorexic who couldn't weigh more than ninety-eight pounds, Leslie sure knows how to put some weight into her shoe. Then again, the shoe probably weighs more than her. I limp up to Stephanie, who hands me a bag of free popcorn with butter sympathetically.

"Is it bleeding?" she asks simply.

I shake my head. "Feels more like an internal thing," I answer. "Like maybe she crushed the toe bone. Do toes have bones?"

"Sure," she shrugs. "Hospital?"

"Oh, God, no," I answer as Matt Dillon walks in and waves at me. I wave back until I realize he's actually waving at the manly looking woman wearing a headset behind me. The humiliation and possible broken foot are far from inspiring but nothing a few lines can't fix, at least temporarily.

Unfortunately, the bathroom is stuffed with wannabe actresses who somehow wrangled invites to this and are drowning themselves in makeup and perfume to go sit in the dark for ninety minutes, after which they'll surely have to go through the whole routine again for the after-party. Once the movie starts, I venture back to the bathroom but some security-type woman is lodged there and seems not to be budging. Is she some actress's female security guard? An employee of the movie theater? An insane stalker who somehow got hold of some security-type uniform? I'm certainly not going to ask her. One thing's for sure—she's a buzz killer, in every way.

3

I'm just finishing a "Where Are They Now?" story on Doc from *The Love Boat* when Chris calls.

"What are you doing?" he asks, and I'm not sure if he means right now or in general.

"Trying to live down my post-wedding shame." My answer is partially true and partially a complete lie. I haven't wanted to admit it to anyone, but my mind has been a little fixated on the whole wedding ménage incident, wondering what would have happened had I not freaked out and left. Inappropriate as it was, it *did* turn me on. It also disgusted me, so though I'm a bit excited that Chris is calling, I had also been pseudo hoping that he would crawl under a rock never to emerge, knowing full well that he lived in L.A. and had my number. It probably would have been smarter to make sure that none of my ménage participants lived in my state, not to mention city, but who considers these things at the time?

"Don't be silly," he says. "Nothing to be ashamed of. Just some good, old-fashioned fun."

"Ha." I sort of say it and sort of snort it.

"I've been wanting to call you for a while," he says. "But I didn't want it to be awkward. See, I think you're really cool, and would love to see you one-on-one but . . ."

Just then, the phone is snatched from his hand and I hear Mitch's voice. "I'm in town," he says. "I think the three of us should get together."

Aha. So here we go. The opportunity to see this ménage through has presented itself. As I make small talk with Mitch, I can't decide if this wedding reunion for our triumvirate is a good idea or an incredibly terrible one. *It would make the ménage story even better*, I think.

"Why don't we meet at Jones at 8 P.M.?" I ask rather suddenly, surprising even myself. "If that works for you guys."

"It works for us," Mitch says, not even checking with Chris. "See you then!"

The first lemon drop goes down smoothly, so I follow it with two more. Licking the sugar off my lips, I glance at my cell phone, wondering if I should call Stephanie. She'd actually been so excited by the prospect of my meeting up with my ménage partners that she begged to come along. Not to have drinks with us, mind you—that would be a bit too normal for Stephanie—but to be somewhere in the restaurant so she could spy. I rejected the pitch on the spot but am beginning to wonder if her presence might have been comforting.

But suddenly, before I even have a chance to call her for backup, Chris arrives. Or I should say a guy claiming to be Chris walks up to me. Was he really this short? Did he actually have this much of a receding hairline last month?

"Hi there," he chirps, enveloping me in an awkward hug. Too late, he goes for the cheek kiss but I'm caught off-guard, and he ends up inhaling a section of my hair. Had he developed horrific halitosis since the wedding, or had I just lost my sense of smell that night? I hope my hair doesn't capture and begin to emit his mouth stench. "Mitch is dealing with the valet."

I motion for the waiter before he even sits down. Sipping from my lemon drop, I marvel over how much drunker I must have been than I realized the night of the wedding.

"How have you been?" I ask him as he slides into the booth.

He's looking me straight in the eye and grinning, and the look is altogether too intense. "God, it's great to see you."

I smile, trying to erase the image of him shoving his tongue down my throat from my mind, and take an enormous gulp. "You, too."

My mind is racing all over, trying to figure out what the hell I could have possibly been thinking wedding night. Had I been roofied? But wouldn't I then be experiencing the pleasure of having my entire knowledge of Chris blocked out? I take another sip and tell myself that Mitch is going to show up and make Chris seem better. They had appeal as a duo, not as individuals.

"Hey there," I hear from a deeper voice as Mitch slides next to me in the booth and wraps his hand around my waist so that it rests on my right love handle.

"Aren't you a sight for sore eyes," he continues, looking at me like I'm an enormous sandwich and he's just decided to break his year-long carb-free diet. On my other side, Chris slides in so close to me that his breath seems to replace any oxygen in the vicinity. I notice that Mitch has the crater-faced complexion of someone whose adolescence was defined by acne that he attempted to pick off. I'm suddenly intensely grateful for Jones's dim lighting.

"Drink?" I ask them, motioning for the waiter and they both nod enthusiastically. They're sitting so close to me that I almost feel like we're a single unit. Had they decided ahead of time to act as aggressive as possible or were they both only children who had absolutely no sense of what the term "personal space" meant? There was only one way to deal with this: get wasted and see if they seemed any better.

I stumble out of Jones an hour later, marveling at the fact that my ménage à trois partners had turned out to be so creepy and lame. You're supposed to have a ménage à trois with, like, a member of the Red Hot Chili Peppers or Jane's Addiction and your most outrageous girlfriend, not two dorky groomsmen from a wedding that took place at your mom's house. Why am I always getting everything so horribly wrong?

Just as the valet guy hands me my keys, I hear a guy say, "Whoa—

you're not driving." I look up and see Gus, this slightly pudgy party guy Stephanie sometimes hooks up with. He walks over to me with his friend and snaps the keys from my hand.

I grab my keys back, outraged. "Don't be ridiculous," I say. "I'm fine." My words sound slurred, even to me, which is annoying. Then I drop the keys, which doesn't help my case, but seeing as Gus is the biggest drunk I know, I don't appreciate being judged by him right now.

"I live eight blocks away," I say.

"Most accidents happen when people are within two blocks of where they live." This comes not from Gus but from his friend, a dark-haired guy with a receding hairline and glasses. He holds out a hand. "Hey, I'm Adam. We met at that party in the hills last month."

I shake his hand and nod but have no recollection of meeting him or, in fact, having been at a party in the hills last month. I'm fairly annoyed by his recitation of this fact we've all heard eight hundred times like he's some driver's ed teacher. His overall sobriety bugs me, too.

"Look, you guys, I appreciate your concern but I've got to get out of here." I glance at the valet parker, who's been standing here patiently the whole time. Though he doesn't seem to speak English, the language of you're-too-drunk-to-drive seems to be international. I lower my voice so that he can't hear, despite his non-English speaking. "These two guys I had a ménage with last month when I was at a wedding at my mom's house are inside, and I told them I had to go see a sick friend to get away from them. I really need to get out of here before they come out."

Adam's jaw drops slightly but Gus looks thoroughly nonplussed. Gus turns to the valet. "Her car's staying," he says. "She'll come pick it up tomorrow." Then he turns to Adam. "Can you take her home? I think my E just kicked in."

"You can put it on any station you want," Adam says as he quickly switches the radio from NPR to, essentially, static. "Although I must confess that I like this one, if only because it sounds so much like what's already playing in my head."

I laugh. Even though he's the very definition of holier-than-thou, the guy seems kind of funny. I notice an asthma inhaler sitting in the cup holder, which makes me laugh again for some reason, and then I feel incredibly self-conscious about seeming like a cackling lush.

"Look, I'm really not that drunk." As I say this, I'm looking up at the streetlights, which seem to be blindingly bright and a bit like the strobe lights we used to use for our dance shows in high school, and they make me dizzy.

Adam doesn't say anything. *He looks like such a nice boy,* I think, *the kind my mom would meet and wonder why I didn't like. He must think I'm an outrageous slut.* "I mean, the whole thing I was saying about the wedding and the ménage and all that—I wasn't really serious." I'm not sure why I care so much about what he thinks.

"Hey, I'm not judging." He says it the way that my alleged female friends from high school used to say, "No offense but . . ." In other words, he probably was.

"So, what do you do?" I ask him conversationally, but I kind of know what the answer will be. All of Gus's friends are aspirants of some kind or another—actors, writers, directors, producers, whatever. They tend to, in fact, claim those careers in conversation, even though their rent is paid either by overly indulgent parents or some miserable job waiting tables. After only about a year and a half in L.A., I was already over everyone and their extravagant Hollywood dreams. Don't they realize how few people are actually successful in these careers and that you can't claim a career until you've actually made money at it?

"I'm an actor."

"Really?" I ask. "Been in anything?"

"I had a scene in a Chris Kattan movie," he says, "but it was cut out."

"Oh." I sort of feel bad for him now.

"Right now I'm waiting tables at Norm's."

I feel worse.

"In West L.A."

Oh, dear God. I snap the radio to a random station and the song "Cecilia" starts blaring out of the speakers. I've always loved that song. Truthfully, the name Cecilia has always sounded enough like Amelia for me to sometimes convince myself that the song is about me. I start singing along with it, remembering the drinking game my quad mates and I used to play senior year in college, where we had to drink whenever a singer sang a woman's name. "My Sharona," "Come on, Eileen," "Oh, Cecilia"—we were big into '80s music for some reason.

"Oh, Amelia, I'm down on my knees, I'm begging you please to come home," I sing. God, it feels good to let loose. Adam smiles uncomfortably but I don't care about that or about the legions of people in karaoke bars who have accused me of being tone deaf. Singing this song is the first thing that's felt okay this whole night, besides those lemon drops. I continue to sing for the rest of the car ride, imagining Mystery Perfect Man who seems to resemble Jude Law but who isn't a famous movie star and never slept with the nanny or was married but is just begging me please to come home to him while he's down on his—

"Amelia." Adam is sort of shaking me awake. "Amelia." I open my eyes.

"Whoa," I say. "I was singing."

"You were, but you were also kind of sleeping. It was, to be honest, strangely adorable." Even though he's grinning in a I'm-laughing-with-not-at-you kind of way, I'm so humiliated that I'd rather be under the car than in it. Adam clears his throat.

"This is where you live, right?" As my eyes focus on him, I notice that he looks quite anxious. "Are you okay?" he asks.

I smile brightly, defensively. "Never better." I open the driver's side door. "Thanks for the ride."

"You're welcome."

I step out of the car and onto the sidewalk, almost tripping myself in my Miu Miu pumps as I add, "Even though it was completely un-necessary." I make a mental note not to wear these shoes out at night anymore.

Adam smiles and starts the car. As I watch him drive away, I mar-vel at what an asshole I can be sometimes. Of course the ride was nec-essary. I was a wobbly, dizzy, drunken mess. I'm so focused on beating myself up over being such an asshole that it doesn't occur to me to wonder how Adam even knew where I lived.

4

I'm in Brian's office, griping about how I pitched something to New York that they ignored, but then came up with on their own two weeks later and assigned to someone else.

"I deserved that assignment," I say. People always get on my case for complaining—my mom tells me that my first sentence was actually "It's not fair"—but I've never been good at letting things go.

Brian looks both exasperated and slightly bemused. "Shut the door," he says.

I get up, close the door, and sit down in his fold-out guest chair, moving a stack of still-wrapped CDs to the floor to make room.

"So, why don't you tell me what's really going on with you," Brian says, smiling for the first time since I've come into his office.

Brian has taken this sort of paternal-mentor role with me since I first started, and while my relationship with him is far less complicated than the one I have with my real-life father, I'm never quite sure what Brian wants from me. Other writers tell me that I'm his favorite, but I also feel like he's harder on me than he is on anyone else. Every time I come back from an interview, he peppers me with, "Did you ask them what time of day they were born? And what they excelled in when they were little? And their favorite color?" On and on until he stumbles upon something, usually quite early on in the questioning, that I've failed to ask, after which he proceeds to lecture me about how I have to remember to ask everything because I might not be able to get whoever it is on the phone again. But he also takes an inordinate interest in my personal life—something I invite. I've always been a somewhat compulsive confessionalist—known to confide my life's most intimate details to perfect strangers—and Brian seems to like this about me. I tell Brian about most of what I get up to, but the stories sometimes have to be edited slightly. If my life is NC-17 or R, Brian gets the version that's been specifically edited for in-flight entertainment.

"Been on any good dates lately?" he asks, absentmindedly sliding a Sheryl Crow CD into his computer dock. "Any new boys?"

"An actor," I say, reflecting back on the previous weekend. I don't mention that the actor is someone I met at an after-party and barely remember taking back to my place to make out.

"Really? Has he been in anything?" Brian looks captivated.

"A couple indies," I say, suddenly realizing that I don't, in fact, remember the guy's name. Eric? Seth? Denny? Fuck.

"Think it will go anywhere?" Brian asks.

"Probably not," I say. "The pen I'm holding is probably more intelligent and more stimulating." I realize as I say it that the comment sounds sexual, and I'm embarrassed, more embarrassed than I'd be if I'd been talking to my real dad.

Brian looks even more uncomfortable than me. "I should get back to work," he says, and I scoot out the door, altogether forgetting that I'd come in there to talk to him about work.

Later, I'm sitting at my cubicle regretting those extra two shots of Absolut that Stephanie and I did at Hyde last night when my phone rings.

"Please be someone good," I whisper to the phone, actually believing this will help determine who's calling. When I was little and really into having pen pals, I'd go with my mom to check the mailbox and actually believe that if I wished hard enough, I could control what would be in there.

"Amelia Stone," I say into the receiver, sounding far more efficient than I feel. I used to answer the phone with, "This is Amelia" until I noticed that Stephanie always used her first and last name as a greeting. I decided that's what people who want to get ahead do and have copied it ever since.

"Hey, it's me," a male voice says.

I know exactly who it is but absolutely hate it when guys start phone conversations this way—unless, of course, it's a guy I'm sleeping with, but somehow those guys never seem to do it. "Who is this?" I ask coldly.

"It's me—Chris. How are you?"

Why Chris has taken to calling me regularly I cannot imagine. I'm not sure which surprises me more—the fact that he continues to call me when I'm nothing but rude in response, or the fact that he actually is trying to make *a girl he met through a ménage* into his girlfriend.

"What do you want?" I want to ask but I'm too chickenshit so instead I settle on, "What's up?" in an I-couldn't-care-less tone.

"Not that much. Just the end of another long, busy week. My boss has been, like, a complete nightmare. Claiming I'm not giving him messages because some agent didn't call him back and he's completely paranoid. He can't accept the fact that his ideas just aren't . . ."

Chris continues to drone on ad infinitum. Does he honestly think I give a fuck about what he's saying? More important, does he really think this kind of rap is the way to woo a girl?

"Look, things are really crazy here right now," I say to get him to shut up. Even though it couldn't be further from the truth, it's my permanent excuse, my go-to line whenever I want to get off the phone—which means, essentially, that Chris must believe my workplace is balls-to-the-walls craziness at all times.

"Oh, of course," Chris says, sounding apologetic. "I was just wondering if you wanted to come with me to a Rob Thomas concert on Thursday?"

Think fast. "Thursday? Oh, yeah, that's the night I have to work late."

"The tickets are free—I got them through work." He's clearly not going to make this easy for me.

"That's great, but I think things are going to be pretty crazy around here for a while."

"But what about dinner? I mean, you have to eat, right?"

What can I say to this? And why can't I bring myself to ask him to leave me alone because he reminds me too much of how out of control I can be, and inform him that I wouldn't hook up with him again even if I was on a hundred hits of Ecstasy?

"Look, I have to go," I say, and I hear him trying to say something in response but I cut him off. "I'll talk to you soon."

I slam the phone down, wondering why I always seem to attract guys who are gluttons for punishment.

5

"Can we please concoct some reason we have to move in here?" Stephanie asks as we gaze out at the Pacific Ocean on a clear, perfect night.

We're in the backyard of this completely grandiose $20 million Malibu mansion where Gus is staying for the time being. Words cannot describe how ostentatious this place is—there are about twelve bedrooms, a sauna, a freaking room for "wrapping presents," no joke—and it's right on the PCH. But it seems even more enormous than it actually is because of the fact that it has no furniture.

"Anthony's parents were busted for embezzling," Gus had explained as he showed us the infinity pool, which spills into a Jacuzzi big enough to fit a football team. "Honestly, I don't know the entire story, but as far as I understand it, they went bankrupt, the bank took their furniture, and they're planning to unload this to the highest bidder. Anthony was supposed to be showing the place but the whole thing bummed him out so much, he took off for New York."

"So you're house-sitting?" I'd asked him, inhaling on my cigarette. Gus is always lucking into the plushest situations. I swear, the people who live the best in Hollywood are the nonworking grifters, since they're usually attractive enough to convince horny producers to loan them their Range Rovers or charming and calculating enough to befriend a guy whose parents need someone to show their $20 million Malibu spread. The worker bees, those watching their youth drift away as they do coverage, place calls, and write "Where Are They

Now" stories on Doc from *The Love Boat*, are the ones who seem to live the grifter lifestyle.

Now that I've gotten a look at the place, I'm incredibly pissed that I haven't called my ever-reliable Mexican coke dealer Alex. Stephanie has brought along her friends from college, Jane and Molly, both of whom do coke, but we'd been so rushed—wanting to get out here before the sun set—that we neglected to bring the evening's most necessary ingredient. Maybe I've watched *Less Than Zero* too many times but as far as I'm concerned, the sole reason for palatial Malibu mansions to exist is so that coke can be snorted in them.

The tacky, probably embezzled extravagance surrounding us seems to be having the same decadent influence on Stephanie as it's having on me. "Hey, Gus, do you have any Jägermeister?" she asks as he turns the Jacuzzi on.

Gus goes inside to check as Adam and two other guys I've never seen before walk out to the backyard.

I wave at Adam and he walks right up to me and leans over to give me a hug. "It's good to see you, Amelia," he says, and I smile. I'm a sucker for people saying my name. Call me an egomaniac, but no one ever says anyone's names anymore and it makes me feel good to hear mine.

"Hey, thanks for the ride home that night, Adam," I say. "Sorry I was a little out of it."

"Are you kidding?" he asks. "I got to watch you 'sleep sing.' I should be thanking *you* for exposing me to something I'd never known was possible."

I can't help but laugh. Something about his tone—slightly nebbishy, mostly bemused—puts me oddly at ease, and I think about how much cooler he is than I realized as he introduces Steph and me to his two friends. When they go back inside, Stephanie turns to me.

"He's oddly sexy," she says and I nod. "And I think he likes you."

I consider that, and then shrug. "Too bad I'd never date an out-of-work actor," is all I say.

*   *   *

A good three hours later, we're all draped on these ticking fabric—covered couches in the sitting room off the kitchen. Gus has thoroughly abandoned any notion of making us continue to go outside to smoke, and Amstel Light bottles are being transformed into ashtrays as the bottle of Jager gets passed around. I'm the good kind of drunk—definitely more than buzzed, but not slurring my words or being a fool—so when Stephanie's friend Jane brings up the idea of us all playing "Truth or Dare," I declare her a genius and personally convince everyone in the assembled group that they have to play. I always love games where I have to reveal something highly personal to a group of people, but then again, I've always been something of an emotional exhibitionist.

Gus starts off by asking me if I want truth or dare.

"Truth," I answer, relishing the fact that everyone's watching me come to the decision, even though people are sort of having their individual conversations.

"Have you ever fooled around with a girl?" he asks, and the entire room goes silent.

"No," I admit, actually feeling slightly ashamed of my conservatism. Basically every girl I know has slept with a girl, whether it was a "college thing" or "just a wild phase," and I've never even come close. My college roommate used to say that we were a couple of years too old to have been a part of the trend, and that about two years after we graduated from high school, adolescent girls started madly messing around with their girlfriends. "Lesbians have hit on me, but never the cute ones."

"So you're saying you would if she was hot?" Gus asks.

"Hey, no double questioning," Gus's friend Dan—a guy with an enormous dimple in his chin—interrupts. "My turn."

Gus shrugs, as he takes a sip from the passing Jägermeister bottle.

"Amelia, truth or dare?" Dan asks.

"Dare."

He looks from me to Jane, who happens to not only be a gorgeous, statuesque blonde, but also openly bisexual. "I dare you to make out with Jane."

I turn to Jane, half embarrassed and half excited, and she's smiling at me. That song "I Kissed a Girl" flashes through my head, as well as an image of Portia de Rossi. I move my face in close to hers and hesitate.

"Don't be scared," Jane smiles.

And I just dive in, touching her lips with mine tentatively, then retreating and returning, opening my mouth a bit wider and allowing her tongue into my mouth. The greatest shocker of all is that this doesn't feel any different from the lifetime of experience I've had kissing boys, although Jane's lips are perhaps the softest I've ever encountered and she tastes slightly minty. With the crowd quite literally fixated, Jane and I continue to kiss for a good minute or so. And then I pull away and can't look at her.

"How was it?" Gus asks, and I find myself blushing.

I glance at Jane shyly. "It was nice?" I say, and Jane nods.

"Want to go in the other room together?" This is Dan, who seems way too determined to have this happen. But the truth is, though kissing her felt amazing, what turned me on far more was the excitement of the crowd watching.

Then it's Molly's turn, and she dares one of Gus's friends, a guy who's been sitting rather silently in the corner, to show us his dick. We all sit back and prepare for him to pull some floppy thing out of his jeans for a second, but suddenly Mr. Diminutive leaps to his feet, takes his penis out, and starts performing some kind of incredibly disturbing little jig, shoving his hairy thing in each of our faces. And while yes, it's not infinitesimal, the guy isn't so huge that such a genital dance might be justifiable, if such things could be justified. As he begins to circle the group for the third time—shoving his dick as much at the guys as the girls—I start to literally feel sick to my stomach. *He gives us exhibitionists a bad name*, I think.

Minutes later, this guy, Eddie, passes out under the couch but the game continues. Molly is doing a striptease from the kitchen counter. Stephanie is putting ice on her nipples. Gus is revealing to anyone who's listening that he slept with a transsexual in Tijuana. The entire game is essentially verging on pre-orgy. Never one to stand on the sidelines too much, I start doing a sort of impromptu striptease by the fireplace while everyone else in the room is gathered in various places doing their own drunken form of expression.

I know that removing my top as a party trick is supposed to reveal that I have no esteem or am slutty, but the fact is I'm quite proud of my naturally voluptuous boobs, which I feel I've earned. All the silicone and latex girls didn't have to deal with being teased ruthlessly by Joe Ford for having "boobies," or have to accept the fact that "braless" was just not going to be a part of their vocabulary, even at age twelve. Is it so wrong that my boobs want a little validation now? My stomach, however, is absolutely from hell. No amount of treadmill time or crunches seems to have an impact on this potbelly of mine. I'm sort of drunkenly pondering all of this, as well as the fact that I never really related to that book *Are You There God? It's Me, Margaret*, even though I probably read it close to fifty times, when I notice that Adam—who's been a somewhat reticent participant in all the Truth or Dare shenanigans—is watching me. I grow horrifically self-conscious, feeling suddenly like any buzz I possibly had has definitely evaporated, and quickly slide my shirt back on.

"Show's over," I say to him with probably more hostility than he deserves, seeing as I was the one performing the spontaneous striptease at a party. But he doesn't respond and just smiles at me. The smile makes me feel bizarrely comforted, and I find myself flopping onto the pillow next to him and lying down on my back.

"What are you smiling about?" I ask him.

"I was thinking about this." He reaches out and pats my tummy, still smiling, and I'm horrified and offended by the fact that he's noticing and calling out my most shameful body part, rather than praising my two most revered.

I sit up quickly. "And what were you thinking about it?" I ask coldly.

He doesn't seem remotely thrown by my cold tone, and I like that he's not backing down the way I thought he might. "I was just thinking how much I'd love to sit and rub it—away from all this. I was thinking how wonderful you'd probably be, completely sober, without all this insanity, by a fireplace, and how much I'd like to be there with you, rubbing your stomach." As he's talking, he's slowly trailing his fingers over my tummy, and for once the stomach from hell doesn't feel enormous and omnipresent, but sweet and somehow sexy. I wait for Adam to apologize for being so forward, or for me to ask him to take his goddamned hand off me.

"Hey, wait a minute," I say, suddenly sitting up when I remember how he seemed to know exactly where I lived when he dropped me off that night. "How did you know my address?"

He smiles, looking embarrassed. "Oh, God. Here's where you become thoroughly convinced that I'm a stalker."

Suddenly, I'm very intrigued. "What are you talking about?"

"It's nothing, really. Just a few days after I met you, Gus and I were driving around West Hollywood and he mentioned that you lived nearby. I asked him where and we drove by your place. But I swear I'm not a bunny boiler—in fact, I had one myself as a kid."

I laugh. "You have a good memory," I say.

He smiles again. "For some things." He pulls a pillow under his head and lies down, then grabs another pillow and motions for me to lie next to him. I do and he smiles confidently, reaching his hand back to my tummy and starts slowly caressing it again.

Such surreal things happen during crazy, drunken nights that I often wake up the next morning not quite sure what really occurred and what I've dreamt. *I must be dreaming*, I think as I smile at him while he rubs my stomach, because I abhor sentimentality and this is definitely verging on sentimental.

*　*　*

I guess I fall asleep for a little while because the next thing I know, Stephanie is shaking me awake and telling me that we're leaving.

"Leaving?" I croak. "Christ, what time is it?" I sit up quickly and see Gus and Adam playing cards across the completely trashed room. Adam smiles at me shyly, and as he does, I realize I was dreaming about him, only he was my best male friend from college and we were in love but also flying—and, well, you know how crazy dreams are.

"It's four," Stephanie says, sounding so sober that I immediately know I can't convince her she can't drive. "And I have to sleep for at least a few hours if I'm going to be able to go to that event tonight and get my article done by the next day."

Event tonight? Article? Tomorrow and the day after? Jesus. Before I even have time to resent Stephanie for dosing me with so much reality, she literally yanks me to my feet.

"But Molly . . . and Jane . . ."

"They're in the car passed out," she says, suddenly the very model of a Stepford wife, only with three wayward girls in place of a husband. "Come on."

Adam stands up, as if he's going to either try to stop us from leaving or at least try to hug me good-bye and ask for my number, but then he sits down again. It's kind of a relief because my breath probably smells like a hundred drunkards smoked several hundred cartons of cigarettes over a period of a year inside my mouth. But I have to admit I'm a little disappointed. Maybe I was imagining this guy had a crush on me. Then again, that whole speech about my rubbing my tummy, while original, was surely his lame rap. I mean, he did get up and leave me passed out on the floor without even thinking of putting a blanket on me. I'm about to say something to him, something cutting just to show him that I couldn't care less about him, but Stephanie grabs me by the hand and starts marching me out before I have a chance.

"Thanks, Gus!" she yells. "Call me if you want to hook up at an after-party tonight!"

*　*　*

I sleep most of the drive back to West Hollywood, only waking up when we stop so that Molly and Jane can pee. Though my throat feels like someone carved their initials on the side of it, I open the extra pack of Camel Lights I'd left in Stephanie's car, wordlessly handing cigarettes to Molly and Jane when they get back in the car.

"This is disgusting," Molly says, taking a long drag.

"Horrible," Jane agrees.

"It's making me nauseous," I chime in. We continue to smoke.

"Me, too," says Molly.

"Not me," says Jane. "But I almost wish it would."

Stephanie glances in her rearview mirror so she can look at Jane and Molly in the back. "I'm sorry, but I will never understand the compulsion to take a burning stick and *suck on it*, especially when it doesn't even do anything to you. I can't imagine anything more foul."

"There's no rest for the truly sick," I say, and Molly laughs so hard she ends up throwing up out the window.

After Stephanie drops me off and I start walking up the building's entryway to my apartment, it occurs to me that eventually we all get old and die, and the sadness I feel over this thought seems wholly debilitating. Sometimes I just become so overwhelmingly depressed by my thoughts—like when I'm watching movies from the '70s and '80s and they're starring and costarring people I've never heard of, and they're directed by people whose names don't even sound vaguely familiar, and I think, *These people were once this town's big deal. They ate at all the right restaurants, and got invited to all the right parties, and had their names in* Variety *and were adored, and I've never even heard of them, and now they're gone and who the hell cares about them today?* When I used to say things like this, my college roommate would tell me I sounded tired or hungover, and I should never come to massive conclusions about life when I'm tired or hungover, and alcohol is a depressant, and blah blah blah. I'm thinking about this and about how much it sucks that my college roommate and I had that falling out so she's not around to say things like that anymore.

The cats moan in their catlike way, seemingly berating me for leaving them alone for the past thirty or so hours while I got drunk and kissed a girl and did an impromptu striptease at a party. I feel so depressed, I know that throwing their food in a bowl and diving into bed is all I can manage at the moment. Someone told me at a party recently that L.A. is number seventeen on the list of most depressed cities, based on the number of prescriptions for antidepressants and the number of days people say they're depressed in a calendar year. I don't think he told me what the sixteen depressing cities that preceded it were, but I know he said Laredo, Texas, was supposed to be the happiest city on earth. I feel too depressed to have a cigarette and ponder moving there, and that seems like the most depressing thought of all.

6

When I wake up later that afternoon, things seem a bit brighter. One of my cats is sitting on the pillow next to my face and she looks so adorable and innocent, I realize I can't be as despicable a person as I feel like. I mean, I could still be horrible and have a cat like her, but she surely wouldn't choose to sleep right next to me if I didn't have some redeeming qualities.

I come as close to bouncing out of bed as a person with a significant hangover can, and feed the cats. Sometimes I feel like my life is made up of the act of pouring dry food into bowls and scooping wet food from cans on top of the dry food, and then the things I do in between doing that.

"I know it's late for breakfast," I tell them in my cat voice after glancing at the clock and seeing that it's 4 P.M. "Let's consider this brunch." Then I realize I've become someone who's perfectly comfortable talking to her cats in catlike voices, and wonder if I'm slowly losing my mind.

I light a cigarette and pour five scoops of coffee grounds into my one-cup coffee press while I boil the water but I don't feel like I have the patience to let it seep, so I just stir and gulp it down. As I feel the caffeine hitting my central nervous system, it occurs to me that I haven't checked my home or cell messages in something like two days. Somehow this gives me a great surge of optimism, which is further enhanced when the woman's computerized voice informs me that I have three new messages. *I am loved and adored*, I remind myself.

"Hey, it's Chris," I hear, and am so annoyed that my voicemail had the audacity to count this as an actual message—and not, like, a submessage—that I delete it before he gets much further.

Second message: "Hello, Amelia, it's your mother," I hear, and her voice makes me feel so automatically guilty that I want to curl up in the fetal position and never get out. "Your dad is extremely upset that you haven't called him, and he wants me to tell him why. What should I be telling him?"

I delete that message, feeling tears springing to my eyes. My mom hasn't been married to my dad for over seven years, but in some ways, she's as married to him as ever. Even though he left her in the midst of one of his affairs, when Mom met my stepdad and fell in love, Dad decided he'd made a crucial error and wanted Mom back. Mom isn't going to go there again but she acts like she's still married to him by having dinner with him once a week and trying to coax me into seeing him. But he's angry and sad, so I stay away, and Mom guilts me for it. I'm not sure who's the bad guy and who's the good, or if the words "good" and "bad" are even relevant here, and I'm not remotely in the mood to ponder it. I delete her message before it's done, also.

Message number three: "Hey, it's me again," I hear, and recognizing Chris's voice immediately, I toss the phone across the room so that it smashes into the wall and the piece of plastic holding the battery in breaks in two. Amazingly, Chris's voice withstands even that. "I'm wondering if you'd want to, I don't know, hang out," he's saying. I realize I have to get the hell out of my apartment immediately if I'm going to be able to get through this day without massively suicidal feelings overtaking me, so I smash out my cigarette, put on my gym clothes, and drive the three blocks to the gym.

"How's it going, Amelia?" I hear, as I'm running on the Stairmaster, with the latest issue of *Absolutely Fabulous* propped in front of me for reading material, and Eminem's anger blasting into my ear through my headphones. I look up and see Chad Milan, a talent agent I met like my second day in L.A.

"Got any plans for tonight?" Chad asks, and I shake my head and remove my headphones, accepting the intrusion.

"I had a really late night last night," I say when I realize that it's Saturday and Chad is about to jump to conclusions about my pathetic lack of a social life. "What about you?"

"Dinner with Sam and the guys and then we're going to Doug's party in the hills," he says. He references the party like he assumes I know about it, so I act like I do. Chad continues to talk to me about where they're going to dinner (Woo Lae Oak) and why Doug's having the party (he was just made VP at Warner Brothers), and I'm so busy wondering why I get invited to so few parties that I barely notice that Chad's stopped talking and his face wears the expectant look of someone who's just asked a question.

"I'm sorry?" I ask.

"I just asked if you'd want to go to dinner next Saturday."

I feel unprepared for the question, and immediately conflicted. I couldn't in a thousand years see myself hooking up with Chad, but how the hell do I work that into a casual conversation? How come other women seem to know how to say, "Actually, I don't see us having a romantic connection" or some such?

"I'd love to," I say. "That sounds great." It occurs to me that maybe being taken out by a nice but dull agent may be exactly what I need. I don't even think I'm lying to myself when I tell him that I'm looking forward to it as I leave the gym a few minutes later. *I mean, that's seven whole days from now*, I think. *Who knows how I might feel then?*

Even though working out usually enlivens me, I'm still sluggish after the gym, so I decide to stop by Kings Road for a cup of the strongest coffee in town. I notice Brian sitting at one of the café's outdoor wooden tables as I approach the coffee shop.

"What the hell are you doing here?" I ask. Brian lives in the Valley.

He gestures to a tall, lean, adorable man with dark brown hair sitting with him. "Amelia Stone, Tim Bromley," he says, and then adds, "Tim's the editor of *Chat*, in from New York. And Amelia," he turns to Tim and smiles, "well, you've just been hearing all about Amelia."

"Indeed I have," Tim says in an upper-crust English accent as he shakes my hand, and I try to look completely cavalier. *Chat* is a sort of combination of *Vanity Fair* and what *Playboy* used to be, and it wins national magazine awards while also managing to have millions of readers. I know exactly who Tim Bromley is, though inconceivably the fact that he looks like a male model had never been made clear. And I certainly didn't know that Brian knew him, or that one day I'd stumble upon them having coffee and apparently discussing *me*.

"Uh-oh," I say with what I hope is a charming smile. "Should I be worried?"

"Not at all," Tim says, as he pushes one of the iron chairs toward me and I flop into it. "Brian was simply telling me that you're constantly regaling him with outrageous stories about your personal life."

"Oh, was he now?" I ask, mock angry but secretly thrilled. I know that I probably should feel betrayed because God knows I've told Brian some incredibly intimate things that I never imagined him passing along in casual coffee conversation but something about Tim is making me too thrilled with the attention to care. "What can I say?" I shrug. "They're all true."

Tim smiles. "So have you gotten up to anything interesting lately?" he asks, and I find myself launching into the story of last night and Truth or Dare, complete with the details about the dick that was shoved in my face repeatedly, the girl-on-girl kiss, and the out-of-work actor wanting to take me away from all this and rub my stomach. Somehow, nothing I'm telling them sounds depressing and tragic anymore, but exciting and dramatic, a night in the life of a spontaneous party girl with outrageous and decadent friends. It's amazing how my perception can shift so thoroughly when I get the slightest glimpse of how other people are seeing something. And I don't know if it's the material I have, the fact that I feel like I'm walking through glue today and am therefore less self-conscious, or that Tim's smile is as white and bright and non-British as a Midwestern picket fence, but I find myself embellishing the stories a bit as I notice that and Brian and Tim are eating up every word, laughing hysterically the whole time.

Brian drains his coffee and turns to Tim. "What did I tell you?" he asks.

"If anything, you *under*sold her," Tim replies.

I'm reveling in the feeling I have right now, of all this attention on me, and feel their validation washing over me like a Jacuzzi stream would on aching muscles. And then I suddenly panic, positive that I'm going to say something utterly inane that will screw up this fabulous impression I've managed to make on Mr. Debonair Hot Shot Magazine Editor. I realize I have to get the hell out of Kings Road before Brian and Tim discover just how backward and unimpressive I am. I glance down at my wrist and pretend I'm looking at a watch even though I've actually forgotten to put it on today.

"Would you look at that, I'm late!" I say, instantly shooting to my feet.

Brian and Tim look surprised by my abruptness, but before I can even begin to analyze that, I start making my way toward the door.

"Good to see you, Brian! Nice to meet you, Tim!" I sort of shriek as I knock into a Kings Road waitress.

"She never even got coffee," I can hear Tim say in his crisp English tone as I scatter away like a complete freak. *I should probably talk to hot men only while intoxicated,* I think as I rush back to my car.

I wake up the next morning with the sense of purpose that anyone rising before noon and without a hangover on a Sunday morning must feel before remembering that I told Brian I'd go to this NBC party

tonight. Brian tends to pass party invites along to me when he doesn't
want to go, using phrases like "really good career opportunities" and
"important just to get out there and network." The parties always
sound terribly exciting at the time—and I always feel flattered that
I'm the one he wants to go in his stead—but the day of, I always regret
having said yes.

Part of the problem is that invariably you have to go to these
things alone. When you're at Brian's level, you get an automatic plus
one; but when the invite's been transferred to me, somehow that extra
space they would have had at the event evaporates, and I'm left
circling the room endlessly, constantly pretending I'm looking for
someone specific when really I'm just seeking out anyone I know or
someone who looks friendly enough to approach.

As I glance at the invite for the event—which will be held, as all
of these things seem to be, at one of those glamorous but nondescript
Culver City hotels—a feeling of dread threatens to overwhelm me.
Why did I tell Brian I'd love to go to this? What made this sound good
at the time?

I put the invitation down and remind myself to think positively.
Who knows what could happen here? I could meet a television producer who could decide I'm far too interesting to be wasting away at a
cubicle desk and create a show around me. When you live in L.A. and
aren't physically deformed in some way, everyone always asks you why
you're not trying to be an actress. Theatrical though I am, I always felt
that I didn't have the struggle to be an actress in me—I mean, I feel
shitty enough without lining up with a bunch of bitchy anorexics to
compete for one line on Grey's Anatomy. No, I'd decided that if acting
was going to be in my future, it would come to me because I'd been
discovered like Lana Turner. Then I'd be able to have an assistant deal
with the stalker-type calls from Chris. A fabulous party is probably just
what I need.

*   *   *

As I'm getting dressed for the party—the one little black dress that doesn't seem to attract the piles of cat fur that the others do, arch-abusing Jimmy Choo's—I remember that I still have a stash of Alex from last weekend tucked into an envelope in my sock drawer. I'd for-gotten all about it before Gus's get-together, and the sudden realiza-tion that I have some coke feels like the best epiphany I've had in weeks, if not ever. *It will be a perfect pick-me-up for the event*, I think. *Just the added boost I need to be the schmoozing powerhouse journalist of Brian's dreams.*

I grab the envelope, which contains coke inside one of Alex's infa-mous Lotto tickets—his signature coke-holder because everyone in L.A., even the Mexican drug dealers, has to add an ironic twist to everything—tap the powder out onto a CD case, and use my Gap credit card to chop it up on my coffee table. I start to roll up a dollar bill before remembering that I'd recently bought straws in order to avoid trying to pay for things and having all my bills emerge from my wallet folded a billion times and sprinkled in white powder.

Grabbing the package of straws, I slide one out, cut it in half, and snort the four lines quickly, feeling the drip down my throat and ex-citement coursing through my veins.

One of the cats jumps up on the table and starts swishing her tail over the CD case that still has a thin layer of coke on top of it, enough for a small line. In my more paranoid moments, I think that my cats know that I'm doing coke, and are hell-bent on keeping Mommy from cracking out, but right now I get that she just knows that I'm intently focused on something that doesn't involve petting her or opening cans of her food, and she wants to know why. I pick her up and place her on the floor, but she jumps back onto the table and knocks the CD case completely over, scattering bits of the powder into the off-white carpet. I feel crushed by this disaster and utterly convinced that every-thing I do always ends in this kind of catastrophic disappointment, and there seems to be only one way to cushion this realization.

When I pour out my next two lines, I decide that I'm going to make them extra thick but I make them so thick that they essentially kill my entire supply. I light a cigarette and lodge it into the silver *Vanity Fair* ashtray that I swiped from a book party at Kelly Lynch and Mitch Glazer's house.

I feel infused with somewhat manic energy and suddenly decide that I should spritz on enough Marc Jacobs perfume to give off just a whiff of it, transfer the contents of my frayed brown bag to my fake Frada nighttime one, and get out the door within the next three minutes. But between the spritz and the purse transfer, it occurs to me that I've done enough coke now to have to be concerned about a comedown, which—if I'm to trust my powers of estimation combined with my body's consistency when it comes to drug reaction—should occur sometime after appetizers are being served. *I'll just have to drink my way through it,* I decide. I only call Alex when I'm partying with friends so I certainly won't be paging him to come meet me at some phony Culver City event.

If I were to do that, it would mean I had a problem, I think, and remind myself that I'm acting like an amateur and I'm perfectly capable of doing a little coke and then going to an event. "I wouldn't be so paranoid if I didn't have these thoughts," I say out loud, but then realize it's the other way around.

My paranoia has developed legs and possibly arms too by the time I valet my car. I try to shrug it off as I approach the bar with faith that a screwdriver will bring me back to "happy buzz" mode. The drink goes down smoothly and I realize that this had been my problem—I'd just been missing my lubricant. I decide to do a lap to look for anyone I know.

I pass Tori Spelling (regaling a group of men with some story about her dog) and Bill Maher (ogling an Asian woman's breasts, to her seeming delight) and the stylist Philip Bloch (talking about how he picked Halle Berry's dress the year she won her Oscar) during my cir-

cle of the room before finally coming upon a face that's familiar because we actually know each other: Brett Lawson from Sprint, who
gives free phones to celebrities and other allegedly influential people
but never to me. It's not so much that I want one—I actually have a
BlackBerry that I'm more than happy with—but I always want to be
deemed important enough by him to receive the offer. He's sometimes
extremely nice to me and sometimes a bit cavalier, depending on if
he's talking to someone less or more important than me at the time, so
interactions with him always feel a bit like a worthiness test.

"Brett!" I say and he gives me the cheek kiss and then goes in for
the other side. The two-cheek kiss seems to be sweeping L.A. lately.

"Amelia, do you know Trent?" he asks, nodding his head in the direction of a tan, gelled guy that I can tell is gay and also a publicist before he even opens his mouth. Trent and I shake hands as Brett
explains that Trent works at Sony, after having been Pat Kingsley's assistant for six years.

I start to ask Trent about upcoming Sony releases, but when I see
that Trent and Brett seem to be far more interested in each other than
they are in talking shop with me, I realize I've tripped into The Void,
and there won't be any finding my way back tonight.

The Void is what can happen when you're on a little too much
coke and a silent, paranoid, and completely insecure personality
usurps the bubbly, impassioned, talkative one coke is supposed to give
you. In this state, all I can think about is how uncomfortable I sound
and how disinterested people seem to be in me. I've tried to escape the
void with more lines, but moods, as most anyone who's done drugs can
attest, can be impossible to shift once you're high.

I make a sudden decision to exit the premises immediately, skip
out on dinner, and let my tablemates endure the empty seat. I bid
Brett and Trent good-bye, but they're too busy talking at each other to
even hear me.

*　*　*

The next morning, I'm walking up to my cubicle thinking about how exhausted I am despite my ten hours of Ambien-induced sleep when I see Brian scribbling a note for me with one of his Sharpie pens.

"Looking for me?" I ask.

He seems incredibly harried. "Yeah, I was just leaving you a note. We have to talk."

"Why?" I ask, instantly paranoid.

"I'm worried about your lack of professionalism," he says, as if he were saying he was worried the office coffee wouldn't be strong enough. Doesn't he understand how abrupt he sounds, how horrifying this is to hear? Doesn't he know that my heart has instantaneously started beating faster than it has during any coke binge? How can he go from being my biggest fan, raving about me to charming British editors one day to taking on this stern, humorless boss role the next?

Brian folds his arms, the bottom of his white button-down unearthing itself from the top of his jeans. "What happened to you last night? Melanie McGrath left me a message saying she thought she saw you walk in but by the time the dinner started, you were AWOL."

"I felt sick," I protest somewhat weakly, and remind myself that this isn't in fact an outright lie. For dramatic effect, I add, "I threw up all night."

"Amelia, you went in my place. If you felt sick, you should have at least introduced yourself to the publicist and told her how sorry you were that you couldn't stay for dinner."

I glare. "Maybe I didn't want to get her sick."

"Save it, Amelia," he says. "And please don't let that happen again."

I begin to feel thoroughly irritated with Brian. "Stop lecturing me," I say, and then, probably too late, I add, "please."

Something about our conversation reminds me of interactions I've had with my dad.

"You *need* a lecture," Brian sneers, and I feel myself about to fly into a rage.

"Enough!" I say. "Will you please leave me alone so I can try to feel better?"

Brian just looks at me and shakes his head. "Get it together, Amelia," he says as he walks away.

7

While I really did convince myself that Chad Milan could seem sexy and appealing over dinner, this possibility has completely evaporated before we've even ordered appetizers. I'm not sure if it's the way he's tasting the wine (swilling it around his mouth and closing his eyes pretentiously) or the fact that he's declaring *The Da Vinci Code* the best book ever written, but I literally want to reach across the table, put my arms around his neck, and squeeze tight. I absolutely hate it when I feel like people, particularly men, aren't acting like themselves but like someone they think you'd like. What's further annoying me is his insistence on touching my arm or leg whenever he makes a point. As he tells me how thrilling it was the first time he saw his name in *Variety*, I realize that he's not doing anything that terrible, that he's just being exactly who he is.

"Look, Chad, I wanted to make something clear," I say, after taking a gulp of wine for liquid courage.

He looks up expectantly: every guy knows this kind of introduction, and that it's time to stop talking about the thrill of getting your name in the trades and pay attention.

"I . . . I . . ." I want to be able to say, "I only think of you as a friend" but I can't seem to get that sentence out. Because the truth is I don't think of Chad as anything even close to a friend. And besides, I'm sitting here at The Little Door, a decidedly romantic restaurant, splitting probably a $75 bottle of wine with him. And, though I'm going to do the after-dinner wallet reach, I'm going to expect him to pay and be horrified if he has the audacity to accept my offer to go dutch. So what should I say to him—that I only said yes because I couldn't think of a reason to say no, and besides, I'm so terribly lonely that at least this "date" would help me believe I'm not completely cut off from the human race?

"I'm not really ready to get into anything now," I manage.

I expect Chad to have that disappointed-but-hiding-it look that most guys get when they understand that they're out roughly $200 and probably aren't getting laid. But something seems to have been lost in the translation, for Chad's smile widens.

"See, that's what I love about you."

"What?" This is so not good.

"You're so straightforward, so direct," he says. "Most women don't ever say what they mean but you always do."

I've often been commended for this quality, which usually confuses the hell out of me, as I almost never say what I mean. If, comparatively speaking, I'm clearer than other women, I feel truly sorry for the male race.

"I'm not sure if I'm being direct enough—" I start to say but Chad cuts me off.

"You were perfectly direct. And the last thing I'd ever want to do to you, or any other woman, is rush her. We're just here to get to know each other better." He ends that ridiculously optimistic response to getting blown off by holding up his glass and motioning for me to pick up mine. "Cheers?" he says.

I dated a guy in college who was obsessed with cheering. Coffee, glasses of water, milk—every liquid short of spittle was worthy of making a special moment out of. And, well, I've just never really been a "Cheers" type of person.

But, what are you going to do? I tried to explain my feelings to Chad but his blinding insistence on his ability to agent me over to his side means my point hasn't a hope of getting through. So, as far as I'm concerned, I've done my part and can now eat and drink guilt free.

What's another hour of my time? I lift my glass and clink his with a smile.

"Cheers," I say.

As Chad pays the check—the-move-the-bill-to-his-side-and-shake-his-head-as-I-start-to-object move—I start worrying about how I'm going to get out of this night's good-night kiss. No matter how many people tell you that just because a guy's taken you to a nice dinner, he doesn't think you owe him some tongue at the end of the night, those few moments of horribly awkward conversation about how delicious the chicken was or how early yoga starts tomorrow morning say otherwise. As I'm debating whether it might be less awkward to simply make out with him for a minute and get it over with, Chad suggests we go somewhere else for a drink.

I shake my head, calculating that if I have to make small talk for another hour, I may peel all of my cuticles off my fingers out of anxiety and general unhappiness.

"What about Guy's?" Chad asks, hitting a soft spot. It's the one bar in L.A. that I actually like and it's so tough to get into that being a girl doesn't even help. "I'm on the list." I'm sort of surprised that Chad has the cachet to pull off Guy's, but I shouldn't be. The doorman probably dreams of being the next Johnny Depp, and is under the mistaken impression that Chad can help make that happen.

During the car ride over, Chad gets on his cell phone, which would normally horrify me but I'm actually grateful to the person on the other end of the phone for saving me five more minutes of pretending to seem interested. It seems to be another agent on the phone, because I'm hearing Chad talk about Ashton and packaging fees and Orlando Bloom in a way that I can tell he thinks might impress me. And, truth be told, if it were a guy I was attracted to, it might well have.

When we pull up at Guy's, Chad hands the car over to the valet, and an enormous black burly doorman opens the velvet rope and waves us through. I spy my friend Bill Kirkpatrick at the bar, with an assortment of shot glasses filled with various and sundry liquids in front of him. Bill and I were good friends in college but for some reason we don't ever hang out in L.A., which is unfortunate, seeing as he's the only friend from college that I'm still in touch with. So Bill is a major breath of fresh air after two hours of Chad Milan. I poke Chad's arm and point to the bar.

"That's my old friend Bill," I say, starting to step through the throng and in Bill's direction.

"I know Bill Kirkpatrick," he says. A pause, and then, "I hate Bill Kirkpatrick." There's always the chance of this with Bill, as he's never afraid to piss people off.

"A girl I dated was two-timing me with him," Chad continues, glaring at Bill.

"That sucks," I say. "Oh, well." I know this is a coldhearted response but the truth is, I need a break from Chad and this discovery seems to provide it. Particularly when a guy in a three-piece suit—clearly another agent—slaps Chad on the shoulder by way of greeting.

"I'm just going to go say hi to Bill," I tell Chad as he starts chatting with Three-Piece-Suit Guy. "I'll be over there." Chad nods as the other agent guy hands him a cocktail.

Then I make my way over to Bill, who glances past me, toward Chad.

"Oh, God. Please don't tell me you're here with Chad Milan," he says. Bill likes to act protective of me, but the way he typically expresses this is by telling me that the guys I hang around with are complete idiots. "He's such a tool."

I don't refute the statement and Bill slides down a stool to make space for me at the bar, nodding his head in the direction of a guy whose back is to us. "I'm here with my friend Rick. We're matching each other, shot for shot." Bill gestures to the shot glasses, most of which are still full. Just then, Rick turns around and I realize with a jolt that Rick is Rick Wilson. As in Rick Wilson, the former child star who I'd been almost preternaturally obsessed with in eighth grade.

"You're Rick Wilson," I say, before I can help myself. With famous people, you're supposed to act like you don't know who they are or, if you happen to, that you're not all that impressed by what they do but are quite interested in getting to know what they're really like as a person. When it's an extremely famous person, it's easy to remember this. But if it's someone decidedly less known, I get initially confused and think I actually know them. I once saw Gregory Hines walking down the street in New York and greeted him with a "Hey, how are you?" because I thought for that minute that he was, like, one of my grade school teachers.

Rick, for his part, looks altogether thrilled to be recognized. It's actually possible that he hasn't worked since the mid-'80s. "I am," he smiles, tiny but perfect teeth shining under his full lips. "And, though I don't recognize you, I wish I did," he says. He leans past Bill to brush my cheeks with his lips. Bill glances from Rick to me.

"Shot?" he asks, but before even waiting for an answer, he slides one over to me and one over to Rick. Somehow when Rick says "Cheers," it doesn't bug me.

And that's around where everything starts to go slightly hazy. Or maybe it's after the second round of shots, or the third. All I know for certain is that eventually we make our way through the glasses on the bar that had once been full. The bar gets extremely crowded and then it seems to thin out. I wonder why Chad hasn't bothered to come over to where I'm standing and decide that he's being really rude. Bill helps support this theory.

"He brought you here and doesn't even have the balls to suck it up and come over and have a drink with us?" he asked. "What a tool."

Rick nods, continuing to make heavy eye contact with me. And then I come up with the ideal solution for getting out of kissing Chad Milan and into kissing Rick Wilson.

"Why don't I tell Chad I looked for him everywhere but couldn't find him?" I ask Bill while Rick is in the bathroom. Guys isn't exactly a massive nightclub—it is, essentially, one room—but Bill nods supportively.

"You should," he says. "Rick is definitely into you. Just call Chad when you get home and tell him that when you couldn't find him, you got another ride home."

I'm not sure exactly how this plan is communicated to Rick but the next thing I know, I'm making my way toward the bathroom, being careful to make sure Chad isn't looking in my direction, and then out the back exit, where I then crouch by the side of the building like I'm the female James Bond or something.

"Let's get you home." Rick smiles as he walks outside. Grabbing my hand, he leads me to a black BMW parked in the back and opens the door for me. I slide in and unlock his side, remembering that some guy once told me that he knows a girl is going to sleep with him if she unlocks his door. Rick notes that his door's unlocked with a wink at me as he slides into the driver's seat and starts the car.

"Are we all clear?" he asks. "Any sign of your guy?"

I look around and see only valet parkers.

"I think we're good," I say. "But just to be safe . . ." I slide down the seat, so that my legs and butt are on the floor of his car and my head is on the seat. From this angle, I can't help but notice the bulge in Rick's jeans. He glances down at me noticing, and winks. I laugh, and continue to when he looks around, jokingly furtive, as we pull in front of Guys and out onto Beverly.

"I think we made it," he says, pretending to wipe sweat from his brow. "It's not always easy to escape from the claws of a smarmy agent."

I slide back onto the seat and sit up straight. "Well, this damsel formerly in distress is quite grateful for your help in the matter."

When we pull up in front of my building, he immediately starts looking around for a space. "Do you need a permit to park here at night?" he asks.

I hadn't had any intention of actually bringing him inside my apartment. Call me a tease—and believe me, many have—but if I like a guy and think we have a chance of actually having a relationship, I won't do anything more than kiss him, unless I'm severely impaired to the point of near blackout.

"You don't need to park," I say. He looks annoyed.

"Should I leave the car running?" he asks, and I reach over and turn the ignition off as an answer before leaning in for another of those fantastic kisses. Fairly quickly, we're making out passionately and, as I alternate between breathing into his ear and kissing his neck, it occurs to me that Rick could be the answer to all my dreams.

Pulling away, I ask in a low, sexy voice, "Are you seeing anybody?"

He looks so horrified, you'd think I'd just asked him if he masturbates about family members. "Whoa—mood killer," he says, leaning back and immediately pushing the cigarette lighter in.

"I wasn't trying to kill the mood," I say, kicking myself for my timing, and yet snuggling up next to him and grabbing another Marlboro Red from his pack. "I was just curious because I think you're cool." As soon as it's out of my mouth and surrounded by nothing but silence, I realize how lame this sounds.

Rick lights his smoke, takes a drag, and exhales. "I don't have a girlfriend, if that's what you're asking."

I smile and drag on my cigarette, as Rick unleashes a torrent of non sequiturs about a girl he was seeing who was always ruining what they had by trying to make the relationship more serious. He says the word "serious" the way a vegetarian might say the word "steak." I'm sitting there and smoking and regretting having launched him on this entire line of thinking, when I hear him muse, "Don't you think it's interesting that the word for someone being sent to an insane asylum—'committed'—is the same as the word for being in a serious relationship?"

I nod, for the first time wondering about the decision-making ability I've displayed in the past few hours. Though this anti-relationship rant has helped to make his feelings on the matter abundantly clear, I wonder if he still likes me, if we're going to date, or if my Rick Wilson experience is going to prove to be as ephemeral as his successful Hollywood career. Glancing at my watch and discovering that it's one thirty in the morning, I decide it's time to cut my losses.

I lean in quickly for a kiss and then I retreat, saying, "Ask Bill for my number if you want to reach me." I open the passenger side door, get out, and steady myself on my Miu Miu pumps, just as Rick is saying—mostly, it seems, to himself—"Jesus, you're just about the most abrupt chick I've ever met!" I smile as I slam the door shut. I like being called "the most" anything, even if it is something as unexciting as abrupt.

The next morning, I wake up at about six and can't fall back to sleep. I'm utterly useless on days like this. I know some people get tired but I get literally insane. My IQ probably drops a hundred points, I have trouble seeing clearly, and the only thing that gets me through the day is the thought that at some point all this torture will be over and I'll be able to get in bed and sleep.

Since I'm up and have a good two hours before I'd even think about leaving for work, I decide to hit the gym. Maybe I'll sweat the exhaustion out of me—ridiculous logic, I know, but I told you I can't think straight when I'm in this state.

At the gym, I force myself onto the treadmill. The place is completely empty, which doesn't ever happen to gyms in L.A., what with exercise addiction being so rampant. It must be a Jewish holiday or something. I'm so out of it that I barely notice when someone else comes into the gym. Then I look up, catch this person's eyes, and immediately pray for a time machine and the opportunity to be anywhere else.

"Hi, Chad!" I all but scream to Chad Milan in such a fake-cheerful voice that I'm immediately shocked it's come out of me. My head races through some shadowy reflections of coming into my apartment this morning after Rick dropped me off and rubbing moisturizer on my chapped chin. Did I freaking call Chad the way I'd planned to, or did I pass out before getting to it? Suddenly, I'm positive I did. I remember almost fainting with relief when I got his voicemail. All of these thoughts zip through my mind in the amount of time it takes me to smile winningly and ask, "Did you get my message?"

Chad nods and stops beside my treadmill. "Yeah, I did," he says. "And forgive me for not calling you back afterward."

I'm about to tell him that it's okay when he walks over to the Stairmaster and adds, "It's just that since I'd gone outside to find you and saw Rick holding your hand and leading you to his car, it somehow made your message about how you'd looked everywhere for me seem less convincing." Then he gets on the Stairmaster and starts it up. And I say nothing. There is no retort. There is just Chad Milan, an empty gym, and my utter horror. Chad doesn't say another word, and even in my state of complete and utter humiliation, I admire him for having the balls to put me in my place like that. *Now I actually understand why a girl might be attracted to him,* I think as I slink out of the gym moments later.

8

My first instinct when I see Stephanie standing at my front door, swigging from her flask with Jane in tow, is to tell her that I don't feel like going out tonight. I just feel off—more so than usual—and could probably use a quiet night at home. But for some reason this thought doesn't even make it out of my mouth.

"Ready to pre-party before Steve's?" she asks and I nod.

Steve Rosenberg parties tend to be massive gatherings of successful studio executives, directors, and B-list actors at his enormous house complete with basketball and tennis courts. There's no way tonight can happen without Alex.

"Want some Mexican food?" I ask Jane, who knows that "Mexican" refers to Alex's coke, whereas "Italian" means getting it from this wannabe former wise guy named Joey. "Breaking the fast" is code for scoring from Vera, this Jewish woman whom I met at a party. But since Alex is the only one of the three who delivers, he tends to get the bulk of our business. Jane nods, so after giving each of them an Amstel Light, I page Alex. My mouth literally starts watering after the beeper pause when I punch my digits into the phone and press pound and I think I can actually feel my serotonin levels rise as I hear the long beep that tells me my phone number has been read. People's anticipation of coke can be so Pavlovian that I know a guy who says he has to go to the bathroom as soon as he calls his dealer since the coke he buys is always cut with baby laxatives.

At seventy bucks a pop, Alex provides the best deal in town for door-to-door service but his coke sometimes tastes and smells so strongly of gasoline that, as it makes its way up your nose and begins its drip down your esophagus, you can't help but envision the tanks it was stored in for its trip from Mexico. Inevitably someone will always complain when we're doing Alex that they feel like they've strolled down to the nearest 76 station and started inhaling directly from a pump and someone else usually points out that inhaling gas probably isn't that much worse than inhaling pure cocaine.

Alex is as timely as ever, and twenty minutes to the second after he returns my page, his Toyota Tercel pulls into my building's driveway. I have about ten neighbors who could look outside and see me doing my deal with Alex—he pulls up, I hand him an envelope filled with $140, usually in twenties, and he hands me a similar envelope, with two grams, each folded neatly into Lotto tickets—and during my more paranoid moments, I'm convinced that my neighbors make a sport out of watching me buy my drugs and secretly gossip about what a bad person I am. It has to be obvious—I mean, who else but a person buying drugs would exchange envelopes with a Mexican guy she never speaks to?—but either they don't find my behavior all that notable, aren't watching me, or simply don't care because no one has ever uttered a word about it or wandered out while Alex has been there and gazed at me suspiciously.

Inside, Jane and I each chop up lines from our separate bindles as Stephanie busies herself playing with my makeup. Stephanie's relationship with our coke snorting is sort of the same as the one my parents have with my smoking. It's done—rather blatantly, as a matter of fact—but it seems to still go unseen. As I watch Jane roll up a twenty, I pack up my supply for the night. I usually carry the coke I bring out with me in a bullet that's attached to my car key chain—such a ridiculously asinine move in terms of getting busted that it's probably akin only to keeping a beer holder on your steering wheel—but I couldn't resist its cool practicality when I saw it for sale at the Pleasure Chest.

We do our lines in silence while Stephanie drinks until Jane says that the gasoline smell is giving her a headache and Stephanie suggests we get to Steve's before it gets completely overrun by fake-titted aspiring actresses looking for their next casting couch.

The party is even bigger than I expected it to be, and during the initial circle that Stephanie, Jane, and I make around the indoor and out-door bar areas, I feel my skin tingle with excitement over all the prom-ise the evening holds. I remember how much that tingle kept me going when my love affair with partying started back when I was a sophomore or junior in high school. It would build from a sense of ex-cited anticipation I usually had the day of an event—anticipation that was typically far more enjoyable than the actual party—and grow as I strolled around a place, marveling at all the potentially exciting things that could happen to me that night.

Somehow, seeing the odd celebrity—Nicky Hilton talking to a stylist I once interviewed, Colin Farrell laughing with Selma Blair as they wait in line for the bathroom—only enhances my excitement. If these celebrated people could go anywhere they wanted to and they chose to come here, "here" must really be amazing. It's usually not until a good hour later, when I realize that nothing's really happening and probably won't that the inevitable depression—as heavy and over-the-top as my previous elation—sets in.

At least we have pockets full of Alex to help us through those periods. It can be challenging to do coke at parties, considering the complications: not showing judgmental nonimbibers that you do it while also not giving it away to the free riders who like to hit you up and ask if you're "holding" or who gather in the bedrooms, knowing those are the number one choices for people looking for special party rooms. Jane and I opt for the roughly thirty-minute-interval bathroom break routine. There's nothing that screams "we've just been doing drugs" louder than two girls emerging from a bathroom together, usually sniffling, after having held up a line for longer than it could possibly take them to pee, but it usually seems like the lesser of several evils.

Jane and I seem to be doing a solid job of not letting each other get too paranoid or sensitive or unable to communicate with other people, and I find myself intensely grateful for her companionship. I marvel at those people who seem able to cruise through a party solo, who don't need a friend by their side to help them deal with bitchy women or cute guys that ignore them. Without a wing-woman, I tend to fall apart.

Stephanie handles big parties completely differently. She basically goes in search of liquor and boys and disappears entirely, only to emerge hours later with her lipstick smeared. Tonight is no different, and by the time Jane and I are on our fifth bathroom visit, we've completely lost her. Gus and his friend Dan wander in and Jane and Dan go off to smoke pot—a drug I've yet to see the appeal of.

Gus and I move onto the impromptu dance floor in Steve's living room. 50 Cent's song about wanting to unbutton my pants just a little bit is blasting from Steve's enormous Bose speakers as Gus and I start dancing alongside a slew of drunken William Morris assistants.

"God, this song makes me want to have sex," I say to Gus, and he smiles, nods, and moves closer to me.

And I guess if you want to be annoyingly accurate, you'd probably say that Gus and I start dirty dancing. Nothing insane—it's not like we're all but having sex with our clothes on or anything—but yes, it gets a little intimate. But that isn't really the problem. The problem is more that Gus starts kissing me and I kiss him back.

We're kissing for maybe a minute or so when I look up. And that's when I see Stephanie standing at the door staring at us with this completely devastated look on her face. And, even in my not terribly sober state, I realize that for all that she talks about how she doesn't really care about Gus and they're just "friends with benefits" and all that, she's devastated. And I should have known—it's my responsibility as her best friend to translate what she says into what she means. I pull away from Gus and motion for her to come over.

"Steph, there you are!" I say like I've been looking all over for her and not swapping spit with her sometime fuck buddy.

There's something different in her face than I've ever seen before. See, Stephanie is just about the most tolerant person I know—she's put up with my moodiness and crying jags and negativity like no one else I've ever met—and no matter how inappropriate my behavior has been, the look on her face is always one of forgiveness. But now she's gazing at me coldly, like I'm someone she doesn't understand or have any interest in tolerating. Obviously, if I'd been thinking—if I hadn't been high and liked the song and the feeling of connecting—I'd have realized that Stephanie probably wouldn't have liked the idea of my kissing Gus. But somehow I never seem to understand these things until it's too late. She gives me the world's nastiest glare and starts walking down a staircase. I follow her.

"Steph! Wait! Can I talk to you for a minute?" I yell as I run after her. Gus is right behind me.

Stephanie looks past me to Gus and says, "You're coming with me." She grabs his hand and leads him outside and I'm left standing there alone, feeling even lower than the dirt they're probably walking on.

And then I'm wandering around the party by myself, with the distinct feeling that Stephanie, Jane, Gus, and Dan have all left together and are currently talking shit about me. But maybe the coke has made me paranoid? After a solo coke bathroom visit, I start to think that this may be the worst night of my life and I should probably just try to find a ride home and call it a night.

But when I get outside, I realize that utter mayhem seems to have broken out on Temple Hill Drive, with cops flooding in, drunk people pouring out, and the odd random person showing up a bit on the late side. I get carried along with a crush of people the cops are kicking out, and realize that although everyone looks familiar, none of them are my friends. Depression and something worse—panic—starts to take over me.

As I stand there looking for someone—anyone—I know, Adam walks by.

"Hey!" I scream excitedly, grabbing his leather jacket.

"What's going on here?" he asks as he gives me a hug.

"Cops are breaking it up, I've lost everyone I know and it's been invaded by agents' assistants," I explain, gesturing toward the mayhem at the front of the house. "Why are you so late?"

"I just got off my shift," he says, and I'm reminded that he's an out-of-work actor, someone who deals with things like shifts and punch cards and tips. But I'm so grateful to see someone I know—even if it is someone who abandoned me by the fire and then didn't say good-bye to me in the morning the last time I saw him—that I force my judgmental side to relax.

Adam takes a look at the people milling around and suddenly says, "This looks a little like what Sartre might have created if he was crafting my own personal version of hell. Want to get out of here?"

I bring him back to my place because there doesn't seem to be anywhere else to go at two on a Saturday night-slash-Sunday morning, feeling optimistic again because the possibility still exists that tonight can be salvaged.

"Be right back," I trill, leaving him petting one of my cats in the living room, and make my way to my bedroom. *I hope he's sort of out of it and just thinks I went to the bathroom,* I think as I remove a framed print of Gretna Green—procured during a trip to England with my family like a decade ago—off the wall and pour some Alex onto its glass surface. I snort four lines quickly, then slide a bit onto my index finger and over my top gums for what my friend Lisa used to call "Numb-y Gummy" when we'd find her dad's coke in high school. I light a cigarette and feel the coke flow through me as I make my way back to the living room, where Adam is continuing to pet my cat.

"I'm mad at you, you know," I say, as I make my way over to where he's sitting and join him.

"Mad at me?" he asks. He motions for my cigarette and sits up. "Why?"

"Why? Well, after telling me you wanted to take me away from our sordid Hollywood scene, you left me alone, without a pillow and blanket, by the fire, and then never even said good-bye to me when I left," I say, amazing myself at how casually these details are rolling off my tongue. I don't tend to be a fan of making myself vulnerable but then again, Alex has a way of making me forget about things like that.

"Oh, Amelia, Amelia, Amelia," he says, leaning back on the couch and suddenly wearing a sweet smile. I notice that his ears are bright red. I wonder if I've made him incredibly uncomfortable.

But then he looks at me confidently, right in the eye. "I held you as you fell asleep but then you pulled away from me and onto the floor," he says. "I tried to tuck a pillow under your head and a blanket over you but you pushed them away. And then"—he takes another drag off my cigarette—"I watched you sleep, and thought about how it was one of the most beautiful sights I'd ever seen."

It's such a genuine and sweet thing to hear from a typically sarcastic person that I literally don't know what to say. I wonder for a second if I ought to mention the whole making-out-with-Gus incident, but I love the feeling flowing through me so much that I don't want to do anything that might make it go away.

So I just move closer to him and he puts his thick hand on my knee and we start talking—about nothing in particular but at the same time pretty personal stuff. It feels a little like how postcoital pillow talk is supposed to feel but never does—complete with the passing of the cigarette back and forth. I notice for the first time that he has one of the deepest, sexiest voices I've ever heard as he tells me how much he hates working at Norm's Deli and how much it sucks to see this completely talentless but attractive guy he knows get called into auditions he'd kill for. We discuss how depressing Hollywood parties can be, and I explain to him how much trouble I have with my friendships. The whole time we're talking, I'm wondering if he's thinking about kissing me.

I don't mention to Adam that I'm jetting to my bedroom for regular intervals of coke because I feel utterly certain he'll judge me, and we seem to be getting along so well that I don't want to risk putting him off. My next trip to my bedroom and inhalation of four lines, however, puts me a little on edge and I find myself rambling more manically than usual when I return. I suddenly see myself as an outsider, or a movie camera, might capture me, telling some incredibly pointless story about how I may or may not have a hostile relationship with the gossip columnist at work. *I need to chill out*, I pep talk myself, then immediately wonder again if Adam is thinking about kissing me.

And then I basically lose patience with wondering, and lean in to kiss him myself. Call me a feminist but I've never much seen the point of always waiting for guys to make the first move. Adam returns my kiss with far more passion than I'm expecting, and I'm suddenly literally dizzy as we continue to make out. The word "swooning" travels through my mind, as does the phrase "weak in the knees." I'm not exactly sure what he's doing but Adam has somehow found a way to access something apparently deep inside my larynx that is turning me on more than anyone ever has before. I wonder if I'm literally ever going to be able to stop kissing him. As I start to feel my chin tingle with that raw-verging-on-scabbed feeling I always get when I'm making out with a guy who has stubble, Adam suddenly pulls away and looks me directly in the eye.

"Wait a minute . . . have you been doing coke?" he asks. He says the word "coke" the way I might say "coconut," something I hate, and I become immediately anxious, like he's a cop and I'm being put through a sobriety test.

"What are you talking about?" I ask him but I'm really just buying time, wondering what the hell I'm going to say.

"I can taste it on you," he says, and I disentangle myself from him entirely, lean back on the couch, and light a cigarette using a funky lighter I got at the Pasadena Rose Bowl flea market. I exhale deeply. I had no idea someone else could taste coke on you if they were kissing you, and I immediately start thinking of all the other men I've made out with while I've been wired who never said a word about it. Were they simply not familiar with the taste or did they just not want me to stop?

I cop to what I've been doing, both because it's evident I've been thoroughly busted and because I've always been an atrocious liar. Adam doesn't ask any more questions, but the moment is gone and my panties have become about as dry as the Sahara during the stress of The Inquisition.

And then things are completely, horribly awkward. He says that he should go because he has a lot to do tomorrow, even though he'd been telling me like ten minutes earlier that he had no plans at all.

"But I'll call you," he says, as he stands up.

I write down my number, even though I feel like we're both just going through the charade of polite behavior and he doesn't have any interest in calling me, because I'm an out-of-control girl who secretly does coke while she's making out with someone. Then I walk him out, where he leans in and gives me a quick and absolutely rudimentary peck on the lips. He folds the piece of paper with my number written on it in half, and puts it in his jeans pocket.

"I'll call you," he says again, but when he walks down the driveway back to his car, he doesn't look back once. I go inside and tears start streaming down my face. I'm not sure if it's because I feel rejected, because there's no more Alex left, or because I know that it's going to take several vodka shots and at least four Ambien to get to sleep and that even still, I probably won't be slumbering until long after the birds have started in on their oppressive morning chirping session. Or maybe it's all those reasons. I chug from the bottle of Absolut I keep in my freezer without even chasing it with Diet Coke.

I get to work on Monday with every intention of going downstairs to apologize to Stephanie. During my Sunday of only occasional consciousness—I'd opted, after being up for a few hours, to take more

Ambien and sleep the whole day through—I'd come to the conclusion that heavy partying was really beginning to have a negative impact on my life, and that I was going to cut back on drinking and stop doing coke altogether. Stephanie, who I'd heard make more than a few of these apologetic declarations herself, would have to understand.

But I also have to do a story on Ken Stinson, this incredibly cheesy actor who's going to be playing Hercules in some terrible-sounding movie you couldn't pay me $1,000 to see, and I decide that I should do the story first so that I can be more relaxed when I talk to her.

The story is for our "Most Beautiful People" issue, and though he's not remotely beautiful and the editors are clear on that, everyone knows that they don't actually pick the most aesthetically pleasing famous people—just the ones coming out in movies and TV shows the readers will flock to.

His publicist Amy connects the call and Ken tells me all the basics—no, he doesn't go in for things like facials, he works out because he loves it and not for vanity—and when it's over, I ask him if he has a childhood friend I could interview for terts.

Terts are tertiary comments from people who know the source well, and though *Absolutely Fabulous* typically likes to use terts from other bold-faced names, they allow us to use "civilians" for our special issues. So Ken, after confirming his height (five foot eleven) and weight (two hundred pounds exactly), gives me the name and number of his best friend from high school, back in Kalamazoo, Michigan.

The high school friend—a real redneck-sounding guy named Chuck—seems sweet and genuinely proud of Ken's success. He laughs that before Ken became "an actor stud," he was a dork "just like the rest of us."

I transcribe and start writing the piece with the speed of a madwoman, noting that the height-and-weight stats Ken gave me conflict with the DMV records we always check them against. He must have thought that five foot nine and 180 pounds simply wasn't "Most Beautiful People" material. Granted, he could have lied when he gave the DMV his stats, which could of course mean he's even shorter and scrawnier than that, but there's only so much a reporter can do.

And then, when I'm putting the finishing touches on the piece, I get an e-mail from Stephanie, which has the formality of an Ed McMahon Publisher's Clearinghouse notification. *Dear Amelia,* I read, my heart racing. *I'm sorry to have to write this note but I just don't think I can continue to be friends with you. I think you can figure out why. Best of luck in all your future endeavors—Stephanie.*

Tears start pouring out of my eyes before I'm even aware of them and I have an urge to take the computer and toss it on the ground. She can't be friends with me? She thinks I can "figure out why"? Jesus Christ. Who the fuck does she think she is, e-mailing me a goddamn friendship rejection letter like I've interviewed for a job she's not hiring me for? You'd have thought Gus was her husband the way she was carrying on.

After a few minutes, though, I feel strangely calm. If I'm going to be thoroughly honest, I've been getting sick of Stephanie lately— she's been a lot harsher and less comforting of late and I'd been starting to wonder if maybe we didn't have as much in common as I used to think. Other people seem to have these friends that they've known since they were like in the playpen, or at least that they went to high school with, but I'm not very good at keeping those people around. Old friends never seem as exciting and cool as the new ones and Stephanie—who I met a year and a half ago, when I started working at *Absolutely Fabulous*—had seemed rather exciting for a while. *But I'm not going to let her make me feel guilty for the rest of my life,* I think, and decide to play her cold game, too, and not even respond to the e-mail. If I see her in the elevator, I decide, I'll be cordial but distant.

I write the Ken Stinson piece in record time and the New York editor e-mails me back within minutes to tell me how thrilled she is with my work on this—an altogether unprecedented event. A few minutes later, Brian walks in smiling, saying the New York editor was just raving to him about my work, and hands me a piece of paper. I glance down at it and see that it's an assignment to interview Kane—a British singer who specializes in inexplicably popular adult contemporary music and tends to date actresses.

"You're giving this one to me?" I ask, surprised. Within the world of *Absolutely Fabulous*, this is a choice assignment and would typically go to a more senior-level reporter who specializes in music.

"Yeah, I figured he'll like you," Brian smiles. I tell myself that my luck has clearly turned and things are going to start getting better from now on. Names like Rick, Gus, Adam, and Stephanie sit lodged in the back of my mind, threatening to fill me with self-loathing, but if I can keep busy enough, I know I can ignore them all for the time being.

9

I read everything I can find about Kane on the Internet and then go to meet his manager—a dour woman with a sensible brown bob—in the lobby of the L'Ermitage hotel. She escorts me up to the seventh floor without saying a word, silently leading me down a hall and opening up a room, where Kane is waiting.

Though not by anyone's standards attractive, Kane nonetheless radiates massive amounts of star quality—or perhaps it's the gleaming diamonds in his ears and around his neck. He stands in the middle of the hotel bedroom in a white linen suit, wearing a beaming grin.

"Come in, come in," he says, leading me through the room's sitting area and into the bedroom, then shutting the door. To his manager, he calls out, "Janet, we'll call you if we need you."

I feel immensely relieved to be rid of the grim, personality-less manager—every now and then you'll encounter a rep who insists on sitting in on the interview, which is about as nerve-racking as the notion of a parent sitting in on an adolescent's date.

Kane settles his enormous frame onto the queen-sized bed, his white boots dragging dirt onto the down comforter, and pats the space next to him. "Come join me in bed, darling," he says, his rather lovely British accent making the sentence seem less like a sexual come-on and more like a sensible suggestion.

And, truth be told, either one is fine by me. Getting a flirtatious rapport going with people I'm interviewing is one of my tricks of the trade—my other main one being confessing intensely personal information to subconsciously motivate them to do the same. It also doesn't exactly hurt my ego if a guy significant enough to be interviewed by *Absolutely Fabulous* flirts with me.

So I climb onto the bed willingly, just a tad nervous that Manager will come in and catch me, the allegedly professional journalist, in this compromising position. But I soothe my nerves about this by being extra vigilant with my questioning, and Kane compliments me on both my questions and my overall personality.

Then again, at a certain point it becomes clear that Kane is complimenting me on just about everything, and the conversation is turning into something more akin to a date than an interview. "I don't have any brothers or sisters, do you, Beautiful?" he lobs back at my sibling query, and though I'm happy to answer him, I'm also quick to point out that *Absolutely Fabulous* readers don't give a rat's ass about the details of my life so we might as well focus on him.

"Look, don't worry so much about your article," Kane says reassuringly. "We'll make it great."

"We haven't even talked about your first album yet," I protest.

"Look, I have an idea," Kane suddenly says, rather abruptly. "Why don't we finish this interview at my house?"

"Really?" Brian had told me that Kane didn't allow reporters there.

Kane glances at the door and then back at me. "I just didn't want a whole slew of photographers traipsing through, but you could come," he says. "I think it would make your story a lot better."

Glancing at him, lying on his back with his heel crossed over his knee and looking quite pleased with himself, I quickly weigh the pros and cons. Pro: I could do a kick-ass story, wowing Brian and everyone else that I was able to talk a source into an at-home interview. Con: He could be a date rapist. But this is unlikely. Additional con: It's definitely possibly unprofessional. I think of Cynthia Jordan, an *Absolutely Fabulous* coworker who's so serious and by the book that she probably would have marched right out the hotel door and over to a sexual harassment complaint center if Kane had suggested to her that she interview him while lying next to him in bed. And then I think about how much I dislike Cynthia, and how dull her life seems.

"What time tomorrow?" I ask.

"Seven P.M.," he answers quickly. And then, after glancing in the direction of the sitting room, he says, "Love, don't mention this to Janet. Why don't I just give you my address and we'll plan to see each other tomorrow?"

After I say good-bye to Kane—a kiss on each cheek, in front of a scowling Janet—and start to make my way through the lobby, it occurs to me that a screwdriver would taste good. I don't have to be back at work for the rest of the day—Brian had suggested I go home after the interview and just start transcribing—and the truth is, I feel a bit self-satisfied after scoring the follow-up at-home interview with Kane for tomorrow. I briefly wonder if Kane and I are going to fall in love and entertain other couples at dinner parties at our English country-side estate (or the house in Spain that he mentioned repeatedly during the interview) and laugh about how we met back when I was a reporter for *Absolutely Fabulous* and I interviewed him.

As I walk up to the bar, I feel a tap on my shoulder.

"Well, if it isn't Amelia Stone," says the perfectly accented British voice belonging to Tim Bromley. He grabs my hand—yes, grabs my hand—and gives me a kiss on each cheek. I am doing damn well with the Brits today.

"Amelia, this is John Davis," Tim says, motioning to a not-at-all-cute grayish guy with a paunch. I shake John's hand as Tim gestures for me to join them at the bar.

Tim orders a screwdriver for me from the waitress, but before I can tell him that this is exactly what I was going to order, he says, in that delightful British sardonic tone of his, "John may not look impressive, but he is."

John smiles at Tim good-naturedly. "Gee, thanks, Tim." He's just way too American and not cute and a bit old for me to care about anything he has to say, until he then remarks, "You should hear how Tim talks about people who don't sign his paychecks." I give John my friendliest smile.

"It's true," Tim shrugs, and then winks at me. When a cheesy guy winks, it's cheesy. When a charming British guy winks, it's heart-meltingly adorable. "John may *seem* down-to-earth—he is, after all, sitting here getting quite blotto with me—but don't be fooled. He's *Chat*'s publisher."

Publishers are never terribly interesting—I'd honestly rather lick paint than be invited to lunch with the *Absolutely Fabulous* publisher when he's in from New York—but they are The Bank. "Are you in from New York, John?" I ask. Playfully, I add, "Or should I call you Mr. Davis?"

John smiles and insists that I only and always call him by his first name, and then launches into some story about the movie he watched on the plane coming out here. I notice that Tim is observing my inter-action with John approvingly, and suddenly I feel grateful for John's presence. Something I learned back in high school was that it's easier to make a guy like you if you can reel in his friends, or if you can per-form your humor-and-flirt routine for a crowd. I'm calmer with two people than I am with one—being alone with somebody tends to make me terrified that I'm going to run out of things to say. As I listen to John talk about the movie he watched in his room here last night— this guy sure likes movies, and boy, can he ramble—I think about how much more comfortable I am being around Tim this time than I was when I first met him. I'm still wearing the attention I was getting from Kane like a protective coat, and am feeling like the very epitome of a Sexy Woman Who Has to Fend Off Advances from Her Interview Subjects on a Regular Basis.

As if on cue, Tim asks, "And what brings you to the L'Ermitage this afternoon?" I swear, he can make even dull questions sound charming.

"I was actually interviewing a musician," I say, and then, after glancing around the bar area, determining that neither Kane nor his sour manager are in the vicinity, and lowering my voice anyway, I proceed to regale them with the story of my recent interview—complete with the bits about being invited into the bed and his suggestion for a follow-up interview tomorrow at his house.

"You are too much!" Tim exclaims, looking absolutely delighted. "You do realize that these things don't happen to normal people?"

Since there's almost nothing I'd rather be less than normal, I feel utterly thrilled.

"I hope you don't think I'm horribly unprofessional," I say.

"Absolutely not!" Tim says.

"You should use what you've got," John adds.

I continue to revel in my impressive story and their reaction to it for the next half hour as I finish my screwdriver. Just as I'm thinking about how much I want a cigarette and am wondering if I can tell Tim Bromley I smoke because surely the British don't have the same closed-minded attitude about cigarettes that overly health-conscious Americans do, he glances at his watch and tells me that, regretfully, he and John have to meet some advertisers for a drink across town in twenty minutes and that they should probably be on their way. I love the way he says "regretfully"—it almost makes up for the fact that he's leaving.

"Do you have a card on you?" he asks, and as I literally feel my heart alight with delight, I realize that I ran out of cards a few weeks ago and still haven't gotten around to ordering more.

"I don't," I say. "But why don't I write my information down?"

He smiles and slides me a napkin and a ballpoint pen, and I write down my work number and e-mail address. Then I add my cell phone and put a little "x" next to it. *Subliminal message that will make him think of kissing when he looks at it*, I think.

The next day at work, I rush over to Brian's office to gloat about my follow-up interview with Kane, and he asks me when I'm going over there.

"Three o'clock." Even though I'm meeting Kane at 7 P.M., this an-swer just comes out of me, probably because I know that if I tell Brian the truth, he'll get the wrong idea. I make a mental note to leave the office at two thirty to perpetuate this lie.

Rather than saying anything, Brian just hands me a sheet of paper: an assignment to interview singer-songwriter Linda Lewis.

Now I'm a little too cynical to get my panties all in a twist over in-terviewing any celebrity but from the moment I heard Linda Lewis's song, "Sinner," on the radio—on my way to work after a coke-fueled night—I felt inspired. It literally made me go from feeling somewhat suicidal to powerful, and right then I decided that Linda Lewis was going to be the Next Big Thing. Of course, I've been convinced of that many times during my *Absolutely Fabulous* tenure, only to be ig-nored by the New York editors, and then watch the person become ridiculously famous, and not be remotely interested in being profiled in *Absolutely Fabulous* or any magazine besides *Vanity Fair*. I'd also had my misses—people I declared were going to be the next Angelina Jolie or Steven Spielberg who ended up barely causing a ripple—but I was always convinced that if *Absolutely Fabulous* had profiled them back when I suggested they should, those people would have been su-perstars, too.

But thank God for my ADD—I took the test and literally have it, but "a mild case that doesn't conflict with my ability to live normally," according to the shrink, meaning I don't get Ritalin, which is proba-bly a good thing, based on what I've heard about how fun it is to chop up and snort. I'd pitched Linda Lewis to the New York editors ages ago and forgotten all about it. It's always shockingly wonderful when the New York editors approve something—like finding $100 in the jeans that went out last year and you stopped wearing. *I am so turning my work troubles around*, I say to myself as I run from Brian's office back to my cubicle.

I call Linda's publicist, Tina, immediately, and she screams with excitement when I say that *Absolutely Fabulous* wants to profile Linda. But as I'm explaining the requirements of an *Absolutely Fabulous* profile—she has to talk in some kind of detail about who she's dating, and we'll print her age and check it with the DMV—Tina gasps.

"Oh, Linda doesn't say her age," Tina says. "She really thinks of age as just a number."

Oh, God. Something I learned on my first story here is that it's the people whose ages we care about the most who think "age is just a number."

"Can't you make an exception in this case?" she asks. I tell her I don't know but doubt it, put her on hold and then call Brian on the other line and say Linda's rep is kicking up a fuss about us printing Linda's age.

"Tell her if she doesn't want us to print the age, there won't be a piece."

Returning to Tina's line, I repeat Brian's words.

Tina sighs. "Maybe she can be convinced," she says. I put her on hold and switch back to Brian.

"Maybe she can be convinced," I repeat.

"Hmmm," Brian says. "If the publicist is hesitant now, we might be better off dropping this one."

"But Brian—"

"You'll get another good assignment soon. Seriously, I'd just forget it."

I hang up the phone and decide that Brian's wrong. Linda can be convinced, and I can be the one to do it. I need to kick some ass at work, and I just know this is the story that's going to allow me to do it. I call Tina and tell her we should go ahead and schedule the interview and we'll just work out the details later.

My other line clicks in as I set a time to meet with Linda at her West Hollywood house but I ignore it until I notice that the person is devil-dialing me—that is, letting the phone ring and ring, hanging up when they get voicemail, and calling right back.

"I better see who's stalking me," I say to Tina. "Thanks for everything." I hang up with her and answer the other line.

"Amelia, this is Amy Baker, Ken Stinson's publicist." With a start,

I realize the "Most Beautiful People" issues are out today. I haven't even had a chance to see them yet.

"What's going on, Amy?" I ask but I can already tell something's wrong. Celebrity publicists only have two tones—happy, when you're doing the story on the client that never gets any press, and pissed the rest of the time—and she definitely is giving me the latter.

"You're going to need to print a retraction on the piece," she says. "You got his weight and height completely wrong, and you completely misquoted his friend."

She's speaking to me the way one would talk to a very small child or incredibly stupid adult and I immediately start panicking. I'm always half-convinced I'm screwing everything up, and feel entirely vulnerable to this attack since I haven't seen the issue.

"Amy, let me just take a look at the piece and give you a call right back," I say, placing the phone down before I can even hear her objections. I rush over to Brian's office, where the new issues are stacked, grab a copy, and sprint back to my cubicle. I can hear him asking, "Is everything okay?" but I ignore him.

Opening the issue to the page featuring Ken Stinson—man, is he *not* beautiful—I look at what we've listed as his height and weight and remember that he'd given me different numbers than the DMV had listed for him. Ha! I feel a rush of simultaneous redemption and outrage over having been accused of making a mistake when I didn't.

And then I examine his friend's quote: "He was a dork, just like the rest of us." And I know without even having to call Amy back exactly what happened. The slightly scrawny and definitely short Ken Stinson opened up his issue of *Absolutely Fabulous*, excited to get his ego fed by relishing over his placement in an issue with actual beautiful people when he noted that his height and weight weren't the figures he gave me. Reading further, he saw his friend's quote, and, rather than laughing at it the way any person with normal self-esteem would, he got pissed, called the friend to vent, and the friend simply claimed he'd been misquoted.

I call Amy back and explain the "mix-up" about Ken's weight and height, and assure her that I have the tape with Ken's old friend's quote. Even though I know I'm right, I'm semi-hysterical and guilty over Amy's accusation, kind of like how I always feel like I've stolen something whenever I see a sign in a store that says they prosecute shoplifters. And being right while feeling guilty is never a good combination for me.

"If you'd like to avoid these types of exchanges in the future, I'd advise you to tell your clients to be honest when they're being interviewed, and not pass on the phone numbers of friends they're not comfortable with speaking on their behalf," I say.

"Excuse me?" Amy says after a hostile pause. "Are you trying to tell me how to do my job?"

The fact that she's getting snippy with me, rather than apologizing for accusing me of making mistakes when I hadn't, pisses me off even more.

"It seems like in this case, you need to be told," I snap back.

"Jesus Christ," she says, and just as my blood starts pumping for a real knock-down-drag-out fight, she slams the phone down and I'm left hanging. I'm always so surprised when I get hung up on that I'm usually still holding the phone by like the fifth time that computerized female voice informs me that if I'd like to make a call, I should hang up and try again. I'm tempted to devil-dial Amy right back to yell at her for hanging up on me but part of me knows I've just done something terribly wrong.

Everyone who does celebrity journalism knows that personal publicists in Hollywood are insane, and that the important thing is to act like they're not. Brian told me this on my second day at work, after a publicist called and yelled at me for telling him that the Jim Carrey write-around story I was doing was a cover story, even though I'd never said any such thing. *Would you let a crazy woman yelling at you on the bus make you cry?* Brian asked at the time, and I shook my head, even though this fictional crazy woman probably would make me cry

and anyone who has to ride the bus in L.A. should surely be continu-
ously crying anyway. Tears start to stream out of my eyes, which I don't
really understand, seeing as I'm the one who won this fight.

I decide to pull it together and not go running to Brian and tell
him about what a crazy bitch Amy was to me. So I spend the rest of my
time at the office that day blasting Kane's and Linda Lewis's music
from my computer CD player and thinking about how it's a shame
that Amy Baker doesn't understand how important I am—that I hang
out with important British magazine editors and am invited into the
homes of extremely famous musicians, even when they've already de-
nied the magazine that right.

10

Kane has one of those video camera doorbell things that everyone who makes more than half a million dollars a year in L.A. has, where you look into this black box—which surely distorts your face completely, like a rearview mirror—and the person decides whether or not to let you in. *I'm a potential appetizer being displayed before actually being served*, I think as I smile self-consciously into the camera.

"Hello, there!" Kane's exceedingly recognizable voice booms as he buzzes the door. I push it open and see Kane standing on a porch at the top of a flight of white stairs overlooking a tree-filled garden. A man sits strumming—or maybe tuning—a guitar on the couch on the porch and Kane casually introduces me as I walk up the stairs.

"Greg, Amelia. Amelia, Greg." Greg gives me a simultaneous nod and smile, managing to wordlessly communicate the fact that he thinks I'm Kane's plaything for the night and thus not worth shaking hands with, or even acknowledging for more than about half a second. The fact that Kane doesn't introduce me as "Amelia from *Absolutely Fabulous*" is also duly noted. Whether Greg is an assistant, guitar tuner, band mate, or roommate is likewise not addressed.

"Would you like tea?" Kane asks as he leads me into his gadget-filled kitchen. He opens a drawer that seems to contain every type of tea known to man, and even some that probably aren't. People from England are way too damn obsessed with tea.

"Do you have anything a little . . . stronger?" I ask, feeling corny and like I'm reciting dialogue out of a made-for-TV movie starring

Tori Spelling. "A beer? Or a drink-drink?" It hadn't even crossed my mind that he wouldn't offer me a real drink, even though this was a follow-up interview and all. Of course, I interview people when I'm stone cold sober—most of the time, anyway—but this situation was already feeling like it was veering into decidedly un-interview-like territory and I was thus feeling like a drink was sounding mighty appealing, if not downright necessary.

"I'm afraid I don't, Sweetheart," he says. "But I can make you a strong tea."

Kane whistles as he throws a tea bag in a ceramic mug and holds it under a boiling water faucet, motioning for me to sit down on the couch in this sort of sitting room off the kitchen. The whole place is loftlike and open, so I can hear Greg playing chords like he's sitting on the same couch.

"So, we didn't really get into too much detail about your childhood," I say, as Kane sits down next to me. He sighs and I don't really blame him. What he had said had sounded intensely depressing—Dad abandoning the family, Mom drinking heavily, the usual ingredients of a tragic childhood—and I'd been so uncomfortable about having to make him pontificate about these things yesterday that I'd changed the subject altogether. But such details are Absolutely Fabulous's bread and butter so I know there's no avoiding them now.

I notice that Kane is glancing at the tape recorder rather incredulously, like he hadn't actually expected for me to bust it out. Am I the stupidest person alive? Does everyone know that "follow-up interview at my house" is actually code for "come to my fancy house and fuck me"?

Don't get me wrong. I really don't have any problem with sleeping with him, at least in theory. But there would be plenty of time for that later, after I'm able to get him to reveal personal, painful secrets in what would go down in history as the preeminent Kane interview.

"Look, Kane, as I told you before, I'm going to need to talk to some of your friends—famous friends, if possible—about you for the story," I say. Most celebrities are usually fairly quick to offer up the phone number for their sister or Bruce Willis or Andy Dick or some other random celebrity they consider a friend. But Kane had kind of ignored the question when I'd asked him about this yesterday. Now, though, he smiles and says he can get me in touch with Joni Mitchell and some backup musician.

"But you're being so businesslike now," he smiles. "I'll get you those numbers. Call me tomorrow or the next day and I'll make sure you get in touch with everyone you need to."

I realize that no digits are going to be forthcoming now, so I get busy asking some of my questions, and Kane answers them—the same sort of stock, unspecific, guarded responses he'd given me the day before—while at the same time distracting me from what I'm trying to do.

"You know, you're one of those girls that gets more beautiful the more I look at you," he says, just after I've asked him if he ever speaks to either of his parents anymore.

I put the tape recorder down. "Thank you. That's very sweet," I say, silently begging my ego not to take over and start gunning for more. "But I'm curious . . . when was the last time you talked to them?"

Kane smiles at me, somewhat dreamily, moving so close that his face is right next to mine. "I'm serious, Sweetheart. Some girls look spectacular at first but then their features start to look rather plain after you've gazed at them for a while. Yours are the opposite. You look more stunning every second."

I glance down, officially distracted now, and the next thing I know, Kane's big, wet lips are brushing up against mine. I look up, shocked, even though I've been half expecting this the whole time.

"Kane!" I say, moving away from him. It's the only word I can think of.

He reaches out to massage my shoulder. "I'm sorry, darling. It was terribly rude to do that without asking. I simply couldn't help myself."

"Look," I say, shifting uncomfortably so that I can take a swig of cold tea for placebo-like liquid courage. "I'm attracted to you, but I also have a story to do, and I really need to deal with the former before I can even address the latter." I like the way that comes out. Official, yet alluring.

Maybe at another time, or with another guy, I could toss the tape recorder to the ground, not caring if it busted wide open, and let him seduce me right there on this very couch, but my desire to really turn things around for myself at work is looming so heavily on my mind and I know I can't afford to fuck this up.

Whether or not I'm actually attracted to Kane isn't something I've examined much. He's bright and shiny, like all celebrities, and so I can't quite be myself—whoever that is—in front of him. I feel the same way I did when I met Oliver Anderson at a party and then drove to another one with him, making out in his Porsche at every red light: I could basically hear myself talking, like I was an invisible person in the car who was listening to the interaction and quite impressed with how Amelia Stone managed to attract the attention of someone so sought after while simultaneously concerned that she was going to say something any moment to screw it up and make him realize that inviting her into his orb was a mistake.

Kane seems satisfied with what I've said and pats my hand platonically, almost condescendingly. But he's still smiling. Then he glances at the clock and mentions that it's getting late.

"I should probably be going," I say.

He nods, stands up, and walks me out of the house, onto the front porch, past the still-tuning Greg who doesn't bother to say good-bye and to my car that's parked at the curb outside his front door. Giving me a kiss on each cheek, he smiles.

"Good night, darling," he says. "Drive safe."

I smile back. "So I'll call tomorrow to get those numbers from you?" I say, more as a question than a statement.

He takes a step back and it's so dark that I can barely see him anymore. "Yes, darling," he says. "Good night now."

*   *   *

Linda Lewis's publicist calls me on my cell the next morning and asks if I can do the interview that day at noon. Since she lives near me and the office is across town, I call Brian to let him know that I'm going to prep for my interview at home and come into the office later.

"That's fine," he says, sounding completely distracted.

"I did my follow-up with Kane," I say, wondering why I'm bringing up something I don't even want to talk about.

"Good, good," he says, and I can tell there's someone in his office that he wants to talk to more than he wants to chat with me.

I don't want to let him go without some guarantee that he's back on my side again. "By the way, I ran into Tim Bromley yesterday," I say.

This fails to captivate Brian. "Did you? Tell him hello," he says. Bastard's not even listening to me.

I decide to give him a test to see if he's paying even the slightest bit of attention. "So, I'll see you tomorrow, then," I say, even though I'd said I was coming in this afternoon.

"See you tomorrow," he says and hangs up the phone.

Staring at the phone, I think about how much I'd like to call Stephanie and tell her about the Kane experience, and about Linda Lewis and inadvertently getting the day off work, and then I feel myself starting to get sad.

Whatever, I think, as I put on Linda Lewis's CD and blast "Sinner" as loud as I can. Maybe Linda Lewis can be my new best friend.

"It was tragic," Linda says, her features scrunched together as a tear falls out of one of her eyes and hits her lap. "I was devastated."

And so there it is—my first interview subject to cry in my presence. I had just innocently asked her about the cat she references on the fourth song on her CD; it turns out Daisy was run over by a car, and next thing I know she's crying. It's not like I'm angling to be the next Barbara Walters, or that making people cry has been some kind of a career goal, but you have to admit that you're probably doing something right if a subject's tear ducts are activated when you simply ask a question. I kind of want to hug her, but after last night's brush with Kane's lips, I feel distinctly aware of that reporter-subject line and how much I don't want to cross it.

I gently lead Linda back to happier subjects, like the moment she got signed by her record label, when she first heard "Sinner" on the radio, and how it feels to be getting the acclaim she so clearly deserves. She cheers up and regales me with anecdotes and thoughts that I completely relate to—like her take on authority (that she doesn't have the instinct that other people do to respect the people in charge, and it's always getting her in trouble), feelings about her sexuality (just because she embraces it doesn't mean she's not a feminist) and San Francisco ("overrated"). I feel like most of what she says could have come directly from my mouth. *Jesus, I'm developing a platonic crush on this woman,* I think as she tells me that she so likes the taste of salty and sweet together that when she's feeling particularly indulgent, she'll throw Milk Duds into her buttered popcorn at the movies—something I've been doing since about the age of ten.

"Me, too!" I shriek for about the thirty-ninth time during the interview.

"Amazing," Linda smiles. "We're very connected."

She actually cares about what I have to say, I think, *unlike other people I've interviewed who pretend like they do but are just planning when they can stick a tongue in my mouth.*

And I'm so enamored with everything she's telling me that I let some other things slide, like the fact that she's closed off most of the rooms in the house and won't say whether or not she's married. I figure I'm getting such amazingly descriptive answers from her on all kinds of other topics that it will more than make up for some of the other odds and ends the story may lack.

I save the whole age question until the very end, starting it off the way I always do when I suspect it might be a sensitive topic.

"So *Absolutely Fabulous* is completely obsessed with putting people's ages in every piece," I say.

Linda's lids fly open and she looks at me with wild eyes. "I never say my age," she says.

"Oh, so Tina didn't say anything to you about this?" I ask, even though I know the answer. Damn publicists. Linda shakes her head.

"Well, I told her on the phone that this was pretty important."

Linda seems really cold suddenly, not at all the evolved and loving being she'd been a few moments earlier. "I never say my age," she says again. "Just tell your editor I wouldn't tell you."

I take a deep breath. "That's the thing about *Absolutely Fabulous*," I say. "They don't accept answers like that. We're not *allowed* to let people not answer questions."

"That's ridiculous!" she snaps, and then, realizing how harsh that must have sounded, she smiles. "Fine. Just tell them I'm thirty-something."

"If I don't get an exact number, they'll just look it up from DMV records." I say this in a really low voice that some might label a whisper. But the woman has the aural capabilities of a trained dog.

"DMV records?!" she shrieks. "Is that even legal?"

Smiling at her, I think how much I hope that this ridiculous age issue isn't going to cause a permanent fissure in what I'd imagined would be our lifelong friendship. "Look, I'm on your side about it," I say. "I think it's ridiculous. But *Absolutely Fabulous* has all these policies that people just end up adhering to." I smile again. "You look amazing," I say, but not in a way that might make her think I'm coming on to her. "And really, age is just a number."

Glancing down at the ground, I think about how much this situation calls for a cigarette. When I look up again, I see that Linda has tears in her eyes again. This time, I'm a lot less thrilled.

"You can't let this happen, Amelia," she says, suddenly reaching over and grabbing my hand. "I can't have people knowing my age. I'd rather have the piece not run than have it say my age."

*   *   *

While I'm interviewing Linda, Brian leaves me a message informing me that my Kane piece has been moved up in the rotation schedule, and that I need to be able to turn it in in the next twenty-four hours. His voice is distant, which definitely doesn't help cushion the news that I'm going to have to stay up all night if I'm going to be able to make this happen.

Luckily, Alex is as available and ready as usual. And, also as usual, he's a stickler about his two-gram policy. If I'm alone, I usually only want to do one gram—and yet, if I have two, I will do two. Surely Alex has all this figured out. But since, for a drug dealer, he's extremely reliable, I always buy the two grams and then try to hide the second one from myself so that I don't do them both in the same night. But I can never think of a hiding place that's good enough for me to be able to forget about it, which is probably because my apartment is about the size of a postage stamp.

Alex makes his delivery, and I give him the crisp bills still warm from the ATM, slide the folded-up Lotto tickets into my pocket, go upstairs, and lay the coke out on a Jay Z CD. I don't have the butterflies and sense of anticipation I usually have before doing coke because the night doesn't hold the intrigue and promise of a typical night out. It's just, I decide, a necessary work enhancer. Sure, I could just drink coffee, but the problem with coffee is that it doesn't keep me interested in what I'm doing. Somewhere into transcribing the second hour of the Kane tape, I'd probably find myself too bored to keep going. But coke has a way of making whatever I'm doing seem infinitely more interesting than it actually is. *I'm doing this to save my career*, I say to myself as I roll up a dollar bill—I'd tossed out all my straws in a moment of remorseful horror at the state of my life during the depression that hit after the Steve Rosenberg party night—and do my first few lines.

I type so much that my neck starts to ache from sitting at my com-

puter for so long and I know that I should take a break and at least
stretch a little bit, but I get into this compulsive cycle where I'm playing the tape and typing, taking breaks only to snort more lines and
light the occasional cigarette. And then, just when I'm nearing the
end of the second side of the tape, I realize I'm a little *too* wired. My
heart is racing like I've just finished a one-mile sprint and my mind
feels jumbled and a bit unsafe.

Knowing that the coke could capture and hold onto this mood,
the way it did when I had to ditch out of the NBC event before dinner, I take a deep breath. I'm not willing to surrender to the too-wired-
feel-a-little-nervous-wonder-if-I'm-going-to-have-a-heart-attack state,
which can basically only be handled with a handful of Ambien and
several shots of vodka to move the unwinding process along before
the Ambien starts to take effect, and sleep. *I can't let this happen,* I pep
talk myself. *I have a story to write, and it's going to be the best fucking
story* Absolutely Fabulous *will ever see.*

I get up to chug some Absolut, and at the last minute decide to
chase it with a Diet Coke. All goes down smoothly, but for a tiny gag
at the end. I burp, loud. I feel better, calmer—like I just sneezed or had
an orgasm.

Which makes me remember that the best way to come down just a
little is to masturbate. I mean, I hate to be overly graphic or make anyone uncomfortable here but if *your* heart was racing and you were feeling like you were maybe teetering on the edge of a mountain and
could fall off, wouldn't you think about masturbating?

I retreat to the bedroom and plug in my Magic Wand. The thing
is mammoth and manages to penetrate my potentially coke-dulled
nether region, making me come in under a minute. And the vodka-
and-Wand combination actually works—I feel immediately better. I
charge back to the living room, leaving the still-plugged-in Wand on
my bed because I know I might need it again later.

*   *   *

The birds have already been through their incessant chirping routine and my next-door neighbor has long since left for work when I'm putting the finishing touches on my Kane piece. It has parts I'll need to fill in later—like the tertiary comments from his friends—but I've done everything I can for the time being. This tiny part of my brain is in complete hysteria about having to call Kane and act like a professional journalist—that is, someone he didn't kiss the other night—but I'm so wired that this anxiety manages to sort of stay on the periphery of my thoughts.

See, the thing about a coke all-nighter is that you partially feel amazing, like you could conquer the world, while on the other hand you know that what's going on is incredibly fucked up and you should just acknowledge what you're doing and start sleeping it off. Since duty calls, however, I make an effort to stay with the first feeling.

A couple of lines get me through the car ride, and once I'm at work I know that I have to call Kane sooner rather than later and also know I need some powder encouragement to do it. Waiting until I'm sure that no one is about to go into or out of the bathroom, I storm in there, enter a stall, sit on the toilet, and lock the door. Not sure if I want a bump or an actual line, I sit there for about half a second but then panic and decide that it's less risky to do a few lines because that means I won't have to duck into the bathroom as often. I tap some coke out of my vial onto my left hand, pull out an already-rolled bill and snort it down. That goes well, so I do another.

When I leave the bathroom and make my way back to my cubicle, I see Brian approaching. Even though I know there's no way any white powder could be lodged under my nose, I can't help but panic and imagine that some has appeared in the three seconds since I left the bathroom.

"Problem, Amelia," he says. *I'm so fucking busted*, I think. "Kane told you he was single, right?"

I nod. He'd offered this fact up literally seventeen times.

Brian tosses a photo on my desk—a picture of Kane making out with a skinny blonde. "This was taken at the American Music Awards last week," he says. Pointing to the blonde, he asks, "Who is she?"

"I don't know, Brian. He told me he wasn't dating anyone. And just because they're kissing doesn't mean they're, you know, dating." All-too-familiar shame courses through my veins. Kane is obviously a complete player. How could I have thought for a second that he was interested in anything more than just sleeping with me?

"Look, if the camera got it, we have to address it," he says. "You told me how well you got along with him. Just call him up and ask him."

I nod. "Sure. No problem," I say as Brian walks away. Before I lose my courage, I start dialing Kane's cell number. Relief floods me as I realize that I'm getting his voicemail, and I struggle to make my voice sound singsongy and light. "Hey, Kane. It's Amelia from *Absolutely Fabulous* here. I just wanted to say thanks so much for the other night. Oh, and I have a few follow-up questions for you. Also, if you could get me the numbers of those people I can interview about you, that would be great." I hang up the receiver, hating the fact that I'm now covered in a cold, clammy sweat. But the message was perfectly appropriate, I decide. If the blonde from the picture hears it, she'd never suspect that his lips had touched mine.

Of course he'll call me back, I say to myself. *How could he not?*

The afternoon isn't a soothing one. A few more trips to the bathroom have made me so jumpy that every time my phone rings, I quite literally spring about five feet into the air before picking up the phone and trying to sound as calm and collected as possible. Of course, today it's only the second- and third-rate publicists who have called—benign, sycophantic ones offering me opportunities to write about products and people the magazine wouldn't even consider.

Sometime after lunch, I start to accept the fact that Kane may not call back, so I dial his manager. To my surprise, Janet is nice. When I

explain that I have some follow-up questions and also need to interview a few of Kane's well-known friends about him, she tells me she'll
get right back to me. I debate running to the bathroom for a quick
bump but decide against it, and less than a minute later, she calls back.
But she doesn't sound quite as agreeable now.

"Look, I just got off the phone with Kane and he told me to tell
you he's done answering questions for you," she says.

"I'm sorry?" I say and even though I am, I'm using it here to act
like I'm surprised by what she's saying, even though I'm not.

"He also told me you came to his house?" This is more an accusation than a question, and I want to reach through the phone wires and
slap the bitch. You'd think I bought a star map and showed up there
like a stalker from her tone.

"I did go there," I say. "But—"

"Please don't go to his house or call him anymore," she says. "We
don't want you interviewing anyone about him. And, as for the
woman in the picture, she's just a friend."

Janet hangs up before I even have a chance to respond and I sit
there for a moment—stunned and yet determined not to give this
British cheeseball singer who makes elevator music any of my tears.

An hour and a few more bathroom trips later, I decide that I can't
handle a face-to-face interaction with Brian so I e-mail him and explain that I can't get the Kane questions answered or terts. No excuses, no explanation. And then I just sit there. Despite all the PR
about coke making you energetic as hell, sometimes it can be completely immobilizing. As I continue to stare at my computer screen,
Brian e-mails back.

So we'll kill the piece, the e-mail reads. Not I know you tried or How
could you let this happen? Although it seems like Brian has given up on
me, I feel inordinately grateful, like I just talked my way out of a
speeding ticket I clearly deserved, and all the more determined to win

my way back into Brian's good graces by saving my Linda Lewis story. I haven't even been given a deadline for the piece yet, but if I finish it as quickly as possible and then turn it in early, he'll have to be impressed.

First, of course, I have to deal with this ridiculous age issue. Glancing at the original assignment sheet, I see that Bruce Young, a New York senior editor, is going to be editing the piece so I decide to call him directly. Brian and Robert always tell us not to bother the New York staff with inane questions, but since my question isn't inane and I haven't called a New York editor in the year and a half that I've worked here—I've only talked to them when they've called me to go over my articles—I tell myself that this time it's okay as I dial Bruce's number.

"Bruce Young," he says into the phone, sounding harried.

"Bruce, hey. It's Amelia Stone in L.A."

"Who?" He sounds frenzied and annoyed.

"From the L.A. office. A staff writer."

"Oh. And?" Christ. I know editors aren't renowned for their interpersonal skills but can't he make more of an effort to be gregarious?

"Look, I'm doing the reporting on the Linda Lewis piece and—"

"Are we doing a story on her?" he asks, cutting me off.

"Yes, it's on the schedule," I say, marveling at his incompetence. "You're listed as the editor."

"Oh, okay. So what about it?"

Something inside warns me not to continue with what I'm about to do but I feel strangely powerless over my ability to stop now.

"Look, here's the thing. Linda won't say her age—"

"She has to say her age. It's company policy." The guy clearly has no issue with repeatedly cutting me off.

"I know, but here's the thing. The interview was amazing. I mean, she *cried*. She talked about stuff she swore she'd never tell anyone. I really think it could be an outstanding story." I'd normally never use the word "outstanding," but Bruce seems like the kind of guy who might respond well to it.

"So go find out her age. Call the DMV."

"Well, she said she'd rather have the story killed than have her age run, and I just—"

"So let's kill the story. Or, if we've already photographed her, let's not waste valuable film and a photographer's time. Just find out her age and print it. Screw what she wants. Personally, I think she sucks, anyway. I mean, 'Sinner'? Are you kidding me?"

Even though Bruce is insulting Linda, I feel like I've been slapped in the face. For a brief second, I want to be outraged by his ridiculous lack of empathy for the human race but the truth is, my outrage seems, like most things, to be all about me.

"Well, it's a ridiculous policy," I snap after a stray tear manages to escape from each eye.

"Excuse me?" For the first time in the conversation, I seem to have inspired something more than an indifferent response from him. I'm about to respond with a snippy explanation for exactly why I feel the policy is insane when suddenly Brian appears at my cubicle.

"You need to come to Robert's office," he says. He has this look on his face that I've never seen before, like he's somewhere between scared and furious.

I nod at him that I'll be there in a second, hoping he'll walk away so I can finish my conversation with Bruce.

"Now!" Brian yells so loudly that I jump out of my seat and about three feet in the air.

"I have to go," I say to Bruce and hang up, not even waiting to hear if he says good-bye. I suddenly know exactly what's about to happen and start passionately wishing for that mammoth earthquake everyone says is going to come and wipe out all of California.

"Follow me, please, Amelia," Brian says. The word "please" sounds formal and uncomfortable coming from him.

As I follow Brian down the hall, heads poke out of office doors and then back inside. Nosy motherfuckers. Brian bypasses his own office, me just a step behind, and walks straight into Robert's. It's only my second time in Robert's office and I'd forgotten just how austere and uncomfortable it was. I sit down on the corner of a brown couch while Brian sits opposite me in a cushioned seat that's the same color. Robert leans back in his Herman Miller chair. Nobody says a word and for one brief, horrific second, I think I'm actually going to have to be the one to start this conversation.

"We know what you've been doing today," Robert finally says, staring at the ground.

"In the bathroom," Brian, who now looks pink with anger, adds.

"Apparently you weren't very subtle," Robert says, his gaze still fixated on some small stain in his carpet. I'm about to defend myself, to tell them that what I've been doing today is practically *de rigueur* in Hollywood, but I seem to have lost the ability to speak.

"And do you know how much trouble you've gotten us in lately, Amelia?" Brian continues, looking like he literally might cry. "This thing with Amy Baker. What the hell did you say to her?"

I should have known that anorexic, soulless wench would call someone above me to complain, I think. I'm about to defend myself and explain that she was the one who falsely accused me of misquoting people, but I seem to have lost the ability to speak or even, for that matter, focus. I try to keep my mind on what's going on in this room but my head seems to have other ideas.

"And this ridiculous drama with Kane—telling me you're going there during the day for a follow-up interview when really you were going to his house at night!"

Janet is a scum-sucking whore for telling on me, I think. I don't say anything.

"What were you thinking?" Brian asks but it's the very definition of a rhetorical question because it's perfectly obvious he's made up his mind about me and nothing I have to say will make a damn bit of difference. I'm feeling light-headed and sort of confused. *Am I being fired?* I wonder but then tell myself, *I can't be fired because this job is the only thing I have. I have no friends. No boyfriend. No family here. Nothing. And this is a town that forgets about people who have nothing.*

This is just a warning, my head tells me. *If I was going to be fired, they would be really nice and apologetic and tell me they were sorry things didn't work out. People feel bad when they fire you.*

I force myself to tune into what Brian is saying.

"—one thing if it was just a drug problem—"

A drug problem? I think. Christ. I need a pick-me-up one damn day and suddenly I have a "drug problem"?

"—but we've given you, frankly, more chances than you deserve—"

More chances than I deserve? I think. How the hell should they know what I deserve?

"—attitude problem—"

Now that was something I'd been told since I could remember. Whenever I got upset when I was little and cried, my dad would laugh and call me his "little actress." He'd call me a petulant princess, and Mom, thrilled to see her always-depressed husband actually smiling, would laugh, too. There were entire car trips to Tahoe where I'd be crying and my parents would be laughing at me. Later, Dad would summarize the incident by saying that it all started because I had an attitude problem.

Focus on what Brian is saying, I tell myself, *before it's too late.*

I look up and concentrate very hard on not crying. Brian seems to have stopped talking. I notice that Robert's lips are moving but it's very hard for my brain to comprehend the fact that he's talking to me because of his utter focus on a piece of lint on the ground. But when I tune in completely, there's no mistaking his words and what they mean.

"We'd like you out of here within the hour."

I nod, and somehow make it out of his office without allowing even one droplet to leave my eye.

The next thing I know, I'm at my desk, packing my files into a box someone had placed next to my chair. Christ, had the entire office been told I was going to be fired before I even knew?

As I copy all my files, delete everything else on the hard drive, and take pictures and notes off the cubicle walls, I marvel at the fact that not one of the spineless assholes I work with is going to come over and tell me they're sorry and what's happening isn't fair, the way they did when this nerdy guy, Raoul, was fired a few months ago. It's true that I wasn't exactly friends with any of them—Brian was actually the only person I really talked to here—but you'd think that an iota of human compassion might penetrate one of their superficial hearts. *What do they think, that getting fired is contagious?* I wonder as I grab unused notebooks, packs of Post-it notes, and packets of Uniball pens, and toss them in my to-go box. *Consider this my severance package,* I silently tell the halls of *Absolutely Fabulous* as I pick up the box. The coke I've been ingesting over the past twenty-four hours has definitely drained from my system, leaving me depleted and dry, but my desire to get the fuck out of this building somehow overrides my comedown. I make my way to the elevator, pray not to run into Stephanie, and eventually make it to my car, where I collapse in hysterical sobs.

Then I remember that Brian and Robert or anyone else from *Absolutely Fabulous* could come down to the garage and see me like this, so I force myself to get it together enough to drive. Somehow I make it home, where I walk inside and straight to bed.

//

"It's completely unfair," I say to Mom. "I mean, I could probably sue them for wrongful termination." I don't mention anything about the coke, because I don't see how it's any of her business, and just tell her I was fired for having an "attitude" problem.

"Oh, honey." *Oh, honey* is about all she's said during this incredibly unpleasant conversation. Lately I've been having this feeling that I've stopped disappointing Mom—that, in fact, she's resigned herself to the fact that I'm always going to be sharing disappointing news—and so she just sounds sad and I resent her for this.

"Everything's going to be fine, Mom," I say. "In fact, things will be better than fine." I'm having this conversation on absolutely no sleep since yesterday, after getting home from work, passing out, then waking up and calling Alex, I'd proceeded to stay up all night with a gram while listening to this Black Eyed Peas song over and over. But obsessively playing the song had actually sparked some mind expansion of sorts, wherein I'd realized that the publishing world simply didn't appreciate my gifts and it was time to find a place that did. "I'm beginning to think, like, screw the magazine business," I say to her. "Maybe I should get into the film business, you know? I am, after all, in Hollywood."

Mom "Oh, honey"s me a couple more times and doesn't provide any of the comfort, I think, that a mother should. No proclamations that I was surely right and Brian and Robert were wrong and declarations that no one should undervalue her baby, who was clearly so special. "You better call your dad to talk about money," she eventually says before we hang up. "And let me know what happens."

The truth is that I'm a trust funder. The only thing is that Dad convinced me to sign the trust over to him and Mom when I turned eighteen and was supposed to get it. So, in theory, Mom and Dad share the responsibility, but Mom essentially relinquished all decision-making power to Dad so he decides if I ever get to see any of the cash. The fact that the money is technically mine—and I won't get the bulk of it until I'm like forty-five or something—usually feels like a moot point. Convincing my dad that I need and deserve some of it has to be, I think, more challenging, and surely more guilt-inducing, than earning every penny.

But now, of course, I don't have the option of earning it. *I'd like to work*, I think, as I dial Dad's number. *But they won't let me.* As I explain to Dad what happened—the version he gets is that I was fired even though I was doing a really good job because my two bosses were complete pricks—I promise myself that I'm going to make it through this entire conversation without crying.

"So, there's no chance they'll change their mind and take you back?" he asks.

"Haven't you been listening, Dad?" I wail, incredibly irritated with him for not keeping up with the story. "I wouldn't *want* them to take me back. In fact, I'm getting out of publishing and into the film business."

He sighs. "How much do you need to live?" he asks, ignoring my film business plan altogether. "What's your budget?"

Dad's always asking me annoying questions about my "budget"—about how much I spend on dry cleaning and renting movies and other things—and it tends to depress the hell out of me. It's so anti-life—this insistence he has on counting up every penny even though there are so many of them.

"Just send me a couple grand and I'll start looking for a new job today," I say, and for some reason this makes me want to sob. *I'm such a piece of shit*, I think. *A good-for-nothing spoiled brat who can't support her-*

self at an age where most people are married and self-supporting. Dad doles out a lecture on the importance of valuing money, promises to send a check in the next couple of days, and I'm able to get off the phone before the wracking sobs start.

I get into crying for a while, burying myself under my covers with a box of tissues to blow my nose into and watching my pillows get drenched in snotty, teary—and I have to confess, even slightly bloody—liquid. But then I remember that I don't need to be depressed because I can just do a bump or two and that will make everything okay.

Just a little bit, I think as I get out of bed and walk over to my purse, *to keep me motivated today.* I pull out the enormous plastic bag filled with coke, take the Gretna Green picture off the wall, pour it out, chop it up using my Macy's credit card, and inhale. I feel immediately better and decide that I'm going to make better use of my time than I would if I hadn't been fired and still worked at *Absolutely Fabulous.*

I e-mail a girl I know who's an assistant at UTA and ask her to send me the job list. UTA is one of the big agencies in town and for whatever reason, they have a list of the unannounced industry jobs available. In order to see it, you need to know someone who works there, and so the lack of availability of the job list to the general populace serves as its own screening process. *It wasn't announced—I just found out about it from the UTA job list,* I've heard people say. I was, I decide, going to be one of them.

I do a line and then, in what seems like minutes, the UTA girl e-mails me back. I print up the job list and start highlighting the positions that sound appealing, taking only one break to snort up a few more lines. Even though I already did assistant duty—slaving away as an editorial assistant at a parenting magazine in San Francisco—I realize that if I'm going to take the film business by storm, I'm probably going to have to start at the bottom. And the UTA job list provides many different opportunities to do just that: *Mailroom clerk at William Morris,* one listing reads. *Second assistant to top-notch producer with Sony deal,* reads another. And then my eyes catch on a listing that seems tailor-made for me: *Part-time personal assistant for Imagine executive Holly Min*, it says. *Ideal for writer or actor needing extra cash.* I think I've seen Holly Min's name in the trades before. And, as I focus in on the words "ideal for a writer," it occurs to me that what I should probably be doing is writing screenplays of my own.

Think about it. Everyone in this town, down to the guy who bags my groceries at Gelson's, is a "screenwriter." They all lug their laptops to Starbucks and register their scripts at the Writer's Guild and talk about their "second act problems," even though none of them are actual writers. Most of them will even admit as much. *Oh, I'm not really a writer*, I heard a guy say at the premiere of his movie. *I just had a great idea.*

Well, I *am* really a writer. I wrote short stories from the age of about twelve on, majored in creative writing for Christ's sake, and have logged time as a professional journalist at two different magazines. *I'll show these wannabe writers how it's done*, I think, imagining my life as an aspiring writer working for Holly Min. I would schedule her meetings—when she, Ron Howard, and Brian Grazer would meet with Russell Crowe or Tom Hanks or whomever—and read her scripts for her, and over time she'd realize that the comments I gave her about the various scripts she was developing were more intelligent than anything in the scripts. *This girl's the real thing*, Holly would say one day, grabbing my hand and bringing me in to meet with Ron Howard. *This is the mind we need to tap.* Ron would value Holly's opinion so much that, on her word alone, he'd beg me to write something that could inspire him. I'd hesitate for just a second, and then blushingly admit that I actually had been working on a script. Holly would wink at me from across the room because she, of course, would have already read this screenplay, declared it brilliant, and planned this reveal. I'd pull a copy of the script out of my chic Coach briefcase bag (which Holly would have given me when she realized after a few weeks of our working together that her life had never run more smoothly) and leave a copy with him. I'd go to Starbucks with Holly, where we'd smoke ciga-

rettes and make plans to start our own company based on her produc-
ing acumen and my writing talent and by the time we'd return to the
office, Ron would have finished reading, declared it a masterpiece, and
offered me a million dollars—or maybe, like, $750,000.

I call Holly's number, and speak to her assistant, Karen. "I'm actually going to be doing the interviewing for Holly," she says, "because
she's just too busy."

That makes sense, I think, as I try to suss out if Karen and I are
going to be friends or if she's going to be resentful over Holly's clear
preference for me. "Great," I say. "Can I fax you my résumé?"

"Oh, there's no need," she says. "But I'm meeting with people
today. Can you come in around three?"

After making the appointment, I gaze into my closet and try to
figure out what outfit would impress Holly the most. My eyes dart
quickly from tank tops to dresses to jeans and I realize then that
I'm quite wired and should probably chill out on the coke until
after the interview. I can't very well be ducking into Holly's private
bathroom—I'm somehow positive she'll have one—for a bump if I
start to come down during my interview. I pick out a conservative
brown dress, but can't stop staring at my closet once I notice how
fucked up the paint job around it is. It's the same off-white, cruddy
color that decorates the rest of the room—and, in fact, the entire
apartment—but while repainting the apartment has always sounded
entirely insurmountable, repainting my closet some cool, dark color
sounds absolutely within the realm of possibilities. *If I get the job*, I
decide, *I'll celebrate by painting my closet tonight.* Feeling more motivated than I have in ages, I decide to hit the gym for a long workout
and then a steam—which will surely deplete all the drugs from my
system—before heading over to the interview. *I should get fired more
often*, I think, as I open my exercise clothes drawer. *It does wonders for
my motivation level.*

*   *   *

"Wow! *Absolutely Fabulous* magazine! Are you serious?" Karen asks, widening her eyes. "That's so cool! Why would you ever want to stop working there?"

Karen, a slightly overweight Valley Girl, is, I quickly determine, no match for me. Before I've even handed her my résumé and explained my desire to start working part time so that I can dedicate the rest of my time to my screenwriting, she's telling me how perfect I seem for the job. When I mention that I recently left my writing gig at *Absolutely Fabulous*, the girl practically has a conniption fit.

"I want to be one of the people doing things, not one of the ones who writes about them," I say. When she nods sympathetically, I make a mental note that I should remember this line for future challenging conversations with Mom and Dad.

"I totally hear you," Karen says. "But working at *Absolutely Fabulous* would have to be, like, so cool and, like, a dream job. So I totally admire you for leaving that to do, like, this."

I feel my nose starting to run as I smile and tell her that *this* sounds like a dream job.

"Well, before you decide that, let me tell you about it, she says. "You'll be taking care of all the details of Holly's personal life: food shopping, picking up dry cleaning, and walking the dog. Walking the dog is, like, the main thing, actually. Her boyfriend gave her this Doberman pinscher and she was so excited, but then she's at the office 24-7 and never has time for it! I was finally like, 'Holly, man, you need another assistant.' "

I nod at Karen and smile, knowing that Holly's not going to need Karen's inane advice anymore now that she can have mine. Holly's life sounds stressful and glamorous and since I plan to make part of her life my own, I decide that I like everything that Karen's saying. I figure, groceries today, scripts tomorrow. I keep nodding, while Karen tells me about how I'll get $10 an hour and I should invoice Holly once a month and walk the dog at least every day and the whole time I'm wondering why she's talking to me like I have the job when I'm

not even sure we've started the interview. I'm tired so I zone out a little bit while Karen rambles, and I allow my eyes to fixate on her fleshy
cheeks as she explains how Holly likes things done. The cheeks stop
moving at a certain point and it takes me a second to snap out of the
zone I've gotten into.

"So that's it," Karen says, looking at me kind of strangely. "Could
you start today?"

"Today?" I ask, positive that I missed something crucial. "You
mean, I got it?"

"You got it!" she exclaims, standing up and reaching out to pump
my hand. "Congratulations!"

Landing the job right then and there wasn't something I'd bargained
for, and being given keys to Holly's house, her grocery list for the
week, and the name of her dry cleaners without ever meeting the
woman herself was likewise something I hadn't quite anticipated. But
I'm so high off of the ego boost of getting the first job I interviewed
for—a job off the UTA job list, no less—that I decide not to let any of
this bother me.

I chain-smoke as I drive to Holly's house in Carthay Circle, but
when I get to the address I've written down on Imagine letterhead, I
think I must be in the wrong place. It's this barf-colored tract house,
not exactly the kind of place I'd think a producer for Imagine would
live. Inside, the floor-to-floor carpeting and low ceilings are, in fact, so
reminiscent of the first apartment I had after college that it actually
makes me feel like where I live isn't all that bad. *But she probably owns
this, so it's a good investment,* I tell myself as I try to ingratiate myself
with her growling, unpleasant dog.

I grew up with golden retrievers and like dogs in general but
Doberman pinschers, I realize as I nervously let Tiger out of his cage,
sure are big, mean, stern-looking things. When Karen had asked me if
I knew how to walk and "take care of" a dog, I'd nodded vigorously

because I figured only an idiot didn't know how to deal with dogs and besides, I'd grown up with dogs my entire life. But the dogs we'd had just ran freely around the neighborhood, where people didn't seem to use words like "leashes" and "pooper scoopers." All too late, by the time I'd already gotten to her house, I realized this chick was expecting me to pick up the dog's shit. *Artists have to make compensations along the way*, I tell myself as I slide a leash on Tiger and lead him outside. Brad Pitt, I seem to recall hearing, dressed up in a chicken suit and handed out El Polo Loco flyers when he first moved to town.

So I take Tiger around the block, marveling over the fact that walking a dog isn't as much fun as it sometimes looks like it is when I pass people doing it in Runyon Canyon. Of course, the depressing, utterly unpopulated streets of Carthay Circle don't exactly make for impressive scenery. And Tiger isn't, of course, a very furry, warm, or even especially cute animal. It feels, actually, more like walking a sort of surly, serious old man than walking a dog, and I'm utterly convinced that I'm somehow doing it wrong. Does it hurt them if you pull on their leashes? Tugging Tiger along, I imagine accidentally snapping his neck and having to explain to a tearful Holly that I just didn't know you were supposed to let dogs lead.

When I put Tiger back in his cage in the kitchen—is it normal to keep dogs in cages? How come we never did that with our dogs at home?—I realize that my enthusiasm for my new life is flagging. *I need to treat myself to a little of my stash*, I think, as I glance at the vial I'd remembered to put in my purse before I left for the interview.

Even though I'm obviously the only one there, I slip into Holly's bathroom to lay some coke on my hand and snort it up. *I know this is the wrong way to start working for you*, I silently tell Holly as I snort. *But making me pick up shit and keeping your dog in a cage is wrong, too.*

Feeling inspired again, I decide to do a little more, then bid Tiger good-bye, lock up, and realize that I'm not up for doing Holly's grocery shopping or picking up her dry cleaning just now. Karen had, in fact, told me I simply had to do it "later," and she hadn't specified whether "later" meant later today or simply later in the week. With the coke now flowing fully through my veins, I decide that I need to do something for me, and that painting the closet would really be a way to embrace this new turn my life was taking.

So I start driving toward the paint store on Beverly. I'd never really fancied myself someone who was capable of doing things like painting. But now, I was beginning to see, anything was possible. I was, after all, on my way to becoming a screenwriter with a deal at Imagine. I needed to prove to the universe that getting fired and landing this new personal assistant job was a good thing, and if I painted, I'd prove that I was now more productive than ever. Tomorrow, I decided, I'd start working on my script.

As I park, I realize that I'm incredibly exhausted and jittery. But the thought of giving in now—going home, getting in bed, and sleeping this whole thing off—doesn't seem within the realm of possibilities so instead I go inside and tell a guy who works there that I want gray paint.

He starts bringing out little paint cards with all those different shades on them, asking me if maybe I want a silver-gray or even a greenish gray, and I want to snap his neck. Doesn't he understand that the exact nuances of color don't matter, that people only debate between mauve and taupe and baby blue because they don't have anything better to do?

"I just want gray," I say, with barely simmering rage. He eyes me nervously, then says he'll go and mix the paint for me. As I wait for him, my nose starts running and I reach into my purse for one of the wads of Kleenex that I thankfully stashed in there this morning. I wonder if the guy knows I'm high and isn't in fact "mixing color"— what the hell does he need to mix if I've just picked a solid gray color anyway?—but calling to report me somewhere for something. I pick at my cuticles and then file them down with a nail buffer I keep in my purse for this very purpose until he returns—it could be twenty minutes later or it could be two hours—with a can of the paint.

"Do you have paintbrushes?" he asks, and I feel certain this is a test. I shake my head and he picks a paintbrush off the shelf behind him and places it next to the can of paint on the counter. He rings everything up and I pay him with as businesslike a demeanor as I can muster. *I dare you*, I think as he hands me my change, *to think I'm crazy or weird or on drugs*. But he just smiles and tells me to have a nice day.

Both painting and writing get put off for the next week or so as I fall into a routine of sorts—going to Holly's, walking Tiger, picking up his shit and pretending it's not happening, then coming home and doing some Alex while I figure out my life. I keep telling myself I'll start my script just as soon as I finish reading *Us Weekly*, but somehow I never seem to finish reading *Us Weekly* or, if I do, I'm too high by then and need to do something else to come down, like take a bath or a shot or a ride on the Magic Wand.

Finally—I think on a Thursday but it could actually be a Friday—I get fed up with myself. I glance at my laptop, which is on my book-shelf lying on top of my Hollywood biographies, then walk over and get it out.

Even though I've read only a few scripts and don't really have any idea what I'm doing, I just start writing. I already have Final Draft software on my computer so the dialogue I'm coming up with looks so much like an actual script that I'm instantly motivated. I start crafting a character named Melinda who's misunderstood and unappreciated and fired from her magazine job. I smoke and do lines and write and think that if I keep going and don't go to sleep for the next week or so, I could have my script completed and dropped off at Holly's office in under a month. I have this vague notion that I should probably plan out an actual story but decide that it's better to just go with the flow and see where it takes me. I can imagine my quote in *Variety* about it. *I started typing and the story just flew out of me*, I would say in the article that would detail the bidding war that had ensued over my script.

And there's no denying the fact that I *am* flowing. I'm on page fifteen when I hear my next-door neighbor leave for work the next day and when I take my midday break to go to Holly's, I've written almost thirty pages of what I'm convinced is snappy, smart dialogue. *Why, I wonder, doesn't every Hollywood screenwriter just use coke as a way to expedite the writing process?* As I place the coke-covered framed picture on the top shelf of my closet so that my cats can't knock it over while I'm gone, I wonder if maybe they all, in fact, do.

After walking Tiger and depositing him back in his cage, I decide that I'm not only going to write my script in a month but also paint that damn closet. Back home, I pull the paint and brush out and just start slopping the stuff on the front of the closet. Too late, I realize that I probably should have taken my clothes out before I started painting and also remember that you're supposed to lay tape around the area you're painting so that you end up with a straight line. Ah, well. After removing most of the clothes and tossing them into piles on the ground, I decide that I like painting—something about dipping the brush in this mess and then using that to change the way the closet door looks is quite soothing. And I've always loved the smell of the stuff.

I'm obsessing over the paw prints that one of my cats has tracked through the unpainted bottom part of my closet when the phone rings. Because of the clothing piles all around, I have to toss the paint brush into the can and then dart through the piles like an army recruit on a training course before I can even glance at caller ID and decide if I feel like answering. I see that it's Karen from Holly's office and get the phone just in time.

"Hello!" I all but sing into the receiver, realizing too late that my hands are covered in gray paint, which is now decorating what used to be a pink phone. I've done more coke than I ever could have imagined was possible in the last couple of weeks but the only impact this seems to have had on my job with Holly is that I've stopped picking up Tiger's shit. The residents of Carthay Circle, I've decided, can sully their shoes in it every day for all I care. But I've been almost obsessively checking in with Karen, reporting on completely fantastical interactions Tiger has allegedly been having with a neighborhood basset hound, chatting about how adorable the animal is and just generally trying to sound the way I think a brilliant, soon-to-be famous screenwriter should. Part of my act involves never letting on that I have caller ID and thus making her believe that I always answer the phone like I'm as cheerful as a midwestern schoolteacher.

"Amelia?" she says. "I have Holly for you."

I can't believe it. My first interaction with the woman who's become sort of larger-than-life—with her dog cages and assistants who hire assistants and barf-colored tract house—in my mind.

"This is Holly Min," she says, and for a second I'm confused. Am I calling her or is she calling me? Everything has seemed so surreal lately, like it's all coated in a thin layer of gray paint, that I keep finding myself confused like this.

"Hi, Holly," I say with exaggerated cheer. "It's great to finally hear your voice."

"Oh, you, too," she says. "Listen, do you have a minute to talk?"

This is what I've been waiting for—the conversation where we discuss how I shouldn't be doing her errands and picking up her dog's shit but, in fact, writing screenplays that she can produce or, at the very least, having coffee or drinks or lunch with her. Yet the timing of this seems strange, since she couldn't possibly be aware of how special I am yet.

"I understand from Karen that I'm paying you $10 an hour to walk Tiger," she says.

"Yes." This is not how I expect the conversation to start but I hide it well.

"And are you walking Tiger for a full hour?"

"Well, no." I know as soon as it's out of my mouth that this is the wrong answer. Why the hell am I afflicted with this ridiculous instinct to tell the truth at the most inconvenient times?

"That's what I wanted to discuss," she says. "I was thinking . . . if I'm paying you $10 an hour to walk him and you're, say, only walking him for twenty minutes, then you're being paid for forty minutes of time that you're not earning."

My right nostril runs and I wipe it. "But you live twenty minutes from me, so even if I walk him for only twenty minutes, it still takes me an hour." I don't want to be argumentative with my mentor/producer/savior but I'm also dimly aware of the fact that I don't like where this seems to be going.

"I get what you're saying," she says, rather condescendingly. "But—well, you know that I work at Imagine, right? And I get paid to work here. But Imagine doesn't pay me for the time it takes me to get to work and home. Are we understanding each other?"

"Um . . . I think?"

"Good," she says. "Karen has been telling me how great you are so I'd hate to lose you over something like this. So, how's this? You get $10 an hour, starting from when you report to work. If you only walk him for twenty minutes, you get a third of that. We'll be working on the honor system, of course."

Glancing around my bedroom at the clothes in piles; the only partially painted closet; the gray paint spilled on the floor; and my shaking, half-gray hand with its bloody cuticles clutching the phone, I find myself nodding. "Sure, Holly," I say, feeling like I'm about to hang up the phone and never speak to her, Karen, or the fucking dog ever again. "That's fine."

I hang up and toss the phone across the room, where it lands in the middle of the paint can, splattering more gray everywhere.

Dusk. I've always hated the word, and the time of day. They say that people get depressed at the time of day that they were born but I was born at 9 A.M. and usually feel okay around then, if I happen to be up. It's the evening hours—where the day isn't quite over and the night hasn't quite begun—that kill me.

Even though I seem to have lost whatever powers of estimation I may have once had, I'm guessing that it's been a few hours since Holly and I spoke and I've moved to the living room, where I seem to be unable to move. I've had to pee for at least an hour, but either my appendages have lost their ability to follow through on directions from my brain or the messages are getting lost in the translation because I just continue to sit there. I've been steadily doing coke for God knows how long and not moving.

I'm wired to the gills, I think, borrowing the expression from this militant lesbian I overheard one night and feeling good about it, the way I always do whenever I manage to hear a figure of speech and then use it as my own. And then I think, *What the hell does that even mean? Fish have gills. Am I so high that I think I'm a fish? Or am I so high that I've grown gills?* I think about this as I do more coke and don't pee.

At a certain point, I realize I'm shivering and have the distinct sensation that it didn't just start. Is it possible to get hypothermia inside a heated Los Angeles apartment? I shake my vial onto the CD case in front of me. *Fucking hell,* I think. *I can't be out.* I don't want grams and grams more—just a few good lines to get me over this shaky, immobilizing state I'm in.

And then I come up with a new plan. I manage to stand up—it's not so difficult once I convince myself that my very survival is dependent on it—shuffle to my bathroom, open my medicine cabinet, and swallow five Ambien before I can freak myself out with thoughts of what combinations of cocaine and sleeping pills can do to people. Total unconsciousness is my only desire. Not for the rest of my life, mind you—just until I can feel a little better. I drink a bottle of Arrowhead to make sure the sleeping pills flow as far into my system as they possibly can, lie down on my bed, and wait to feel exhausted. Nothing happens so I go back to the living room, light a cigarette, and wait some more. Ambien is usually amazingly sharp in its ability to knock me from complete consciousness into serious REM—while not as drastic as an anesthetic, a close second—and I always revel in that split second where I slip from life to a place that's temporarily problem free.

But this time, the Ambien does nothing. It seems, if anything, to make me more alert. I've been taking a lot of it lately, more than I'm prescribed, but my doctor is so clueless about how bad my insomnia is that he actually tells me to cut the pills into quarters when they don't even do a damn thing unless you swallow at least two or three of them. Lately, though, two or three hadn't been guaranteeing sleep the way four or five did. I never bothered to explain this to the doctor—he would surely just launch into a lecture about how I need to be more careful—so I usually just tell him I've been traveling and lost the rest of the bottle on my trip when I need refills early.

After about twenty minutes, or maybe two hours, I realize that my body simply isn't going to be coaxed into anything akin to sleep. I seem to have perfectly regained the use of my limbs, however, and as I stomp into the kitchen to get out my last pack of Camel Lights from the carton I bought last week, I decide I want to be around people. The idea is both radical and terrifying, and when I discover that the carton is actually empty and I already smoked the last cigarette from what I thought was my second-to-last pack, I feel even more convinced that companionship will be my salvation.

I decide to walk to Barney's Beanery, this bar down the street that was built in like the 1920s and looks it. When I get there, I make my way directly to the bar, where I ask for an Amstel Light, a shot of tequila, and a pack of Camel Lights. I'm so eager for the tequila that I don't even wait for the goateed bartender to deposit salt and a wedge of lemon: I just shoot it down and chase it with a long gulp of beer. And then I scan around the bar, noticing a table filled with these big, brawny guys wearing USC shirts and hats. My eyes dart around furtively, first to the other side of the bar, then to the people gathered around the karaoke microphone, then to a group of girls making their way in through the back door. Eventually, I leave the safe perch I have at the bar and, deciding that the most practical move for me right now is to look around for someone who has coke, start walking from table to table.

I go up to the USC table; tap a tall, kind of pale guy on the shoulder; and ask him if we met through Gus. I know we didn't but I can't think of anything else to say and I need something.

He shakes his head but smiles. "Is Gus your boyfriend?"

Now it's my turn to shake my head and smile. "I don't have a boyfriend," I say.

The guy introduces himself as Simon and asks if I want to sit down.

"Why not," I say, as he moves over. "My friends aren't here yet." *Technically*, I think, *I'm not lying.* None of my so-called friends *are* here.

Once I slide in, Simon's friend returns with shots of Goldschlager and I expertly bullshit them about how Goldschlager actually contains specks of gold from the days of the California gold rush. It's something I remember some guy telling me in a bar in San Francisco when I was too drunk to tell him that I thought he was full of it. But Simon and his friends—a Josh, a Todd, and, I think, two Johns—seem to buy it and next thing I know, I'm chatting reasonably comfortably with them and we're all exchanging anecdotes about getting busted for drinking in high school.

As I finish up a story about getting drunk before performing in *Hair* my junior year, Simon returns from the bathroom, leans over, and whispers in my ear. And I know before he opens his mouth exactly what he's going to say. I swear, I'm better than any drug-sniffing trained dog when it comes to zeroing in on the nearest users in the vicinity.

"I left a few rails for my friend on top of the windowsill over the first stall in the men's bathroom," Simon says as he winks at me. "Why don't you take them?"

Simon's being so generous that I decide I can absolutely forgive his terrible Guess jeans and cheesy wink. I nod and slide out of the booth silently.

I've used men's bathrooms about three thousand times in my life—all those times they're empty when the women's one is full—so I know how to just stroll in there as if it's the most normal thing in the world. The bald guy peeing in the urinal doesn't seem to have as much experience with this as I do, however, so he looks at me in shock, but I shrug, whisper, "The women's line was too long," lock myself in the first stall, see the lines on the sill above, and wait for him to leave. As soon as he's gone, I take out a rolled-up bill, stand up on the toilet, and inhale the lines. Instant relief, or at least something like it.

Once I'm back at the table, though, something strange starts happening to me: I sort of lose the ability to speak. One second I'm fine and the next I can't seem to form words. It sort of reminds me of how I didn't feel like I could move earlier, but this seems more alarming because there are other people around, people who will be expecting me to behave normally. Luckily, Simon doesn't seem to notice. He's telling stories and his friends are laughing and I want to laugh, too, but I feel nauseous and overwhelmed and like my head is maybe caving in on itself, though I'm not really even sure what that means. My head pounds and I want to lie down, even though I don't really feel tired.

"I don't feel well," I manage to get out.

Simon nods, as if this is par for the course. "Falling into a K-hole?" he asks, conversationally.

"A K-hole?" I ask. I picture a donut hole.

One of Simon's friends overhears and yells, "So that's what happened to the Special K you were supposed to leave me!"

I look from Simon to his friend and, though very little seems clear at this point, I'm able to make a crucial and horrifying connection.

"Special K?" I ask, and Simon and his friends all look like they're laughing but the volume of the universe seems to have been put on mute because I can't hear anything anymore. Even in this state, I know what Special K is—ketamine, a horse tranquilizer.

"But—" I start to try to tell Simon that he'd told me the line was a line of coke but then I can't remember if he said that or if that's just what I had assumed or hoped. Simon and his friends continue to talk, and I can't believe how a part of the world they seem, and how far away.

"Outside for air," I say and Simon nods. Part of me is offended that he doesn't offer to come with me, but mostly I'm just relieved. *I just need to sit down outside, have the wind blow on me, and feel better,* I tell myself as I weave through the crowd and outside. An enormous trash bin sits under a street lamp near the middle of the parking lot and I decide that it looks like the perfect place to sit and relax.

Part of me knows that I must be pretty out of it to be in such a disgusting place and not really care. The trash doesn't even seem to smell that terrible, which is weird because usually the stench from this back bin is noticeable from the street. I greedily suck in gulps of air, wondering why I don't feel any better. Then I lie down and close my eyes.

At some point, a Mexican guy, one of the valet parkers, starts trying to shake me awake. My eyes flutter open and I realize that a dirty brown jacket rests over me like a blanket.

"Hospital?" he asks, and I shake my head. It seems like a pretty ridiculous question to me, but when he starts pushing me up to a sitting position, I notice that I've thrown up all around me. Humiliated, I try to sit up, but my legs feel paralyzed.

"Two thirty A.M.," the guy says after muttering a whole bunch of other things I don't understand, and when I look past him, I see there are a few other Mexican guys gazing at me like I'm some kind of a circus freak. And suddenly I feel very clear, recalling that I did Simon's line at around ten, a lot of time has passed, and that's not good. I'm also clear on the fact that I'd very much like to go home but I know that moving right now is out of the question.

"I'm fine," I manage to say, as I lie back down again, this time in the direction away from my vomit. I decide to take a nap.

I've always heard about how people come to and have no idea where they are, but the minute I open my eyes—before I even look down at my depressing gown or glance at the sterile environment—I know that I'm in a hospital. Call it anti-amnesia: I had the misfortune of remembering with perfect clarity doing Simon's line, feeling paralyzed, learning that it was Special K, and taking that impromptu nap beside the Barney's Beanery parking lot Dumpster. I want to be surprised, and feel motivated to jump out of bed and demand that someone explain my whereabouts, but I just don't feel like bothering. Something about this absolutely shocking turn of events feels thoroughly unsurprising.

My overwhelming feeling is one of disappointment. Why, oh why, hadn't the mixture of coke and Ambien and alcohol and K conspired to kill me? Why hadn't I been one of the lucky ones who got taken away accidentally, who never had to live on in people's memories as a "suicide" but who was relieved of all her problems just as instantaneously as one? I know that these are incredibly depressing thoughts to be having and I want to cry over them, but I feel like that, too, probably wouldn't be worth the effort.

And then, just as suddenly as I'd felt alert, I become incredibly exhausted. I feel the way I would if I were watching a movie late at night and really wanted to see what was going to happen next but had to surrender to fatigue, all the while knowing that I was never going to find out how the movie ended.

*   *   *

Later that day, Mom and Dad show up with a man who seems to be
about Mom's height (five feet) and introduces himself as Dr. Ronald
Rand. By this time, not only am I fully conscious and moving around
the room, but I've also been briefed on the recent turn of events, and
they're neither pretty nor surprising. Essentially, after I passed out for
the final time by the Dumpsters, one of the valet parkers called the
paramedics and they came and brought me here to Cedars, where
I had a file, thanks to my Cedars gyno. When Mom got the your-
daughter-O.D.'d call, she got in touch with Dad and this height-
challenged shrink, and brought the two of them down from San
Francisco to help save me.

"Mom, can I talk to you alone, please?" I ask as soon as the three of
them turn up in my room. I feel overwhelmed by the triumvirate and a
little like I'm being ganged up on as I fall back into bed and pull the
covers around me. Mom looks more nervous than I've ever seen her
and she seems to be looking at me quizzically, like she's trying to rec-
oncile the concept she has of "daughter" with the one she has for "girl
who overdosed on drugs." She glances at Dad and Dr. Rand, and says,
"I think I'd like Ronald to stay."

So Dad leaves the room and I sit up in bed. Dr. Rand clears his
throat.

"Why don't I explain why I'm here," he says and I nod. "Well, my
work typically involves helping parents whose kids have joined certain religious groups, or cults."

"You're a deprogrammer?" I ask. This guy I met at a party once told
me that his parents sent him to one after he decided he didn't want to
be a Scientologist anymore.

"Technically, I'm a behavioral psychologist," says Dr. Ronald
Rand, "but I have been quite successful at reuniting children who
have been lost with their parents."

"But I didn't join a cult," I say. "I'd never join a cult. I just had a
bad night because I took too many drugs."

I can't look at Mom when I say the word "drugs," even though I know that she knows I do them. A few years ago, I met my mom and stepdad in Paris when they were doing a house trade with a Parisian family at Christmas for a month, and I managed to infiltrate the sleazy underbelly of Parisian party life rather easily. The coke in Paris was so pure that I regularly returned home from a night out just as my mom and stepdad were going out sightseeing for the day. But we sort of operated under the "don't ask, don't tell" policy.

Dr. Rand looks thrilled that he's been able to extract the word "drugs" from me. "Drugs!" he shrieks excitedly. "Yes, drugs!" He glances at my mom like he thinks she should be handing him a medal and then gazes at me. "I understand you like to do a toot now and then."

"A toot?" I ask. Who the hell was this Dr. Ronald Rand, and why on earth had Mom thought he might be the right person to talk to me about drugs? "Is that, like, a line?"

"A toot, a line, powder," he says, trying to appear casually hip.

"Look," I say, glancing down. "I like doing coke; I like it a lot." I hear Mom gasp, even though she'd told me years ago that our former handyman had given her coke once and she'd spent the entire night vacuuming every rug in the house. As soon as the confession is out of my mouth, though, I feel oddly relieved. "But still, what happened last night was a mistake. I thought I was doing coke, but it turned out to be something else."

Dr. Rand nods compassionately and for the first time since I set eyes on him, I sort of like him. He sits down on my hospital bed and gazes at me kindly. "Do you want to stop doing coke?" he asks.

I know what he's really asking me is if I want to get sober but he's just too much of a wuss to phrase it like that. A couple of the guys at my high school got sober when they were busted smoking pot at one of their soccer games, and I've known a few sober people over the years, but the truth is, I haven't ever understood how those folks worked. They probably go to, like, the theater all the time or sew group quilts or do something to replace going to parties and socializing, but I just can't see myself as Suzy Sober Girl.

"I can't imagine what I'd do for fun if I was sober," I say.

"My guess is that you'd find all kinds of new ways to have fun," Dr. Rand says. I look at Mom, who nods.

"But I don't want new ways. I like the old ways just fine," I say as I fall back into my pillows.

"Amelia," Dr. Rand says, finally sounding firm, "with all due respect, I don't think those 'old ways' are working for you anymore."

At first, I want to lash out and attack him, but instead I just lie there and think about what he's saying. I consider how horribly jittery I've been feeling since I started doing coke all the time, those suicidal feelings that plague me the day after I do it and the day after that— feelings that can only be dulled with more coke—and all the paranoia. I realize that I can't imagine my life with coke and I can't imagine it without. And I'm not going to kill myself, so what are my options? *Being sober would surely suck*, I decide, *but it might be better than dying.* Armed with that conclusion, I nod. Dr. Rand pats my mom, who now looks a little teary, on the back.

"We've picked out a local rehab for you," he says. "Why don't I bring your dad back in?"

"Whoa," I say, more alarmed by the mention of Dad than I am by the thought of rehab. "My dad just doesn't understand me," I say. "He scares me and he makes me feel uncomfortable and guilty and he's always criticizing and he makes me feel bad about money, and—"

"He also loves you very much," says Dr. Rand. "Did you ever think that he only says what he says and does what he does out of love and wanting you to have and be the best you can?"

I don't say anything.

"Do this," Dr. Rand says. "Picture a movie theater—one of those multiplexes with ten different movies playing at the same time. Now picture you and your dad, walking in the front door together. But you go into one theater and your dad goes into another. You leave at the same time and maybe your movie was terrible but your dad just loved the one he saw and you can't seem to understand how he felt that way because you thought he was in the same theater you were, watching the piece of doodoo you'd seen. Why don't you look at what you and your dad have experienced that way—like you were two people going through the same thing but watching completely different movies?"

Maybe my drug-addled brain is exhausted or I'm just feeling too weak to fight much longer, but something about Dr. Rand's ridiculous movie theater analogy works for me. It occurs to me that my dad isn't always trying to be awful but just doesn't know exactly how to handle me. I give Dr. Rand a half-smile.

"Your dad would like to pay for rehab," continues Dr. Rand. "And, after considering several options, he thinks the best place for you would be Pledges."

And that's where he gets me. Everyone knows that Pledges is the Four Seasons of rehabs and anyone who's even casually perused *Absolutely Fabulous* or any of the other weekly magazines is familiar with the fact that every celebrity with a well-publicized drug problem has gone there. I've seen pictures of its multiple pools, exercise rooms, and even horse stables. *It would probably be*, I think, *the ideal place to get a little pampering while they teach me how to stop wanting to do coke.*

Dad steps in the room, smiling, and I suddenly feel incredibly grateful for both him and Mom—the fact that they flew down here and still love me, despite what a fuck-up I am.

Mom, who's been silent for probably longer than she has in her entire life, asks, "Now, do you have anything you need taken care of? The cats—why don't I take them until you're back on your feet again?"

I think of my apartment and its piles of clothing and gray paint everywhere. I nod. "My place is a disaster."

Mom nods and says, "After this is all over, maybe you'll want to move back home?" This is always Mom's angle. I think she'd be thrilled if I still lived in my old bedroom. But for once, this doesn't bug me; I feel oddly grateful for the fact that she still wants me near her, even though I have no intention of moving back north.

Dad says, "I don't want you worrying about money for the time being—just concentrate on getting well."

And then Mom and Dad lean in to hug me. And, I kid you not, Dr. Ronald Rand throws one arm around Mom, one arm around Dad, and presses his face into our hug like we're all one big, happy family.

13

When we pull up at Pledges, I marvel over what a fantastic job the rehab has done of making it look casual and rustic. This place, with its threadbare living room, smoking patio littered with overflowing ashtrays, sad-looking "therapy" room, and broken basketball net, looks more like the camp I went to in Yosemite—plus about twenty years of wear and tear—than a rehab to the stars. And I decide I like the fact that they make an effort to downplay all the luxury—I'd hate if it was ostentatious, like a cruise ship, and I might feel intimidated if there were a bunch of movie stars with perfect bodies lounging by a pool.

A smiling forty-something guy bounces into the entry room and introduces himself as Tommy, adding that he's going to be my counselor. I wonder how such assignments are made. Does an efficient receptionist examine my facts and go, "Hmmm . . . magazine journalist, coke problem, serious smoker—this one's for Tommy"? But something about Tommy makes me feel immediately safe, so I decide to like him even though I already resent his cheerfulness.

"Have you been in before?" he asks me as I pick at a cuticle that is already bloodied from the abuse I've been giving it since checking out of the hospital.

"In?" I ask. Looking around, I ask, "In this room, you mean?"

Tommy bursts into a huge laugh. "Ah, I love newcomers," he says.

A few derelict types wander into the room: a Mexican guy wearing a T-shirt that reads, "Need your plumbing fixed?" and a nervous-seeming balding man who would look right at home sitting at a bus stop clutching a drink inside a brown paper bag.

"Joel, Stan, come meet Amelia," Tommy bellows. He pronounces the name "Joel" with an "H" so it sounds like Hoel.

Stan shuffles over while staring at the ground and Joel fixes me with a lascivious leer. Even though I'm fairly horrified by my soon-to-be rehab-mates, I know I'm going to have to make friends around here, so I smile and reach my hand out to Joel to shake. Stan is staring at the ground with his arms by his side, so I leave him alone.

"Welcome," Joel says, ignoring my hand and throwing his fleshy, sweaty arms around me, pulling me into him so that his B.O. is basically permanently embedded in my nostrils. I'm positive that Tommy is going to yank me away from this disgusting man and tell him to stop sexually harassing the women around here, but when I gaze out at Tommy's face from under Joel's armpit, he's smiling as if Joel and I are the cutest couple he's ever seen.

As I extricate myself from Joel's grasp, Tommy smiles at me. "Oh, Amelia," he says. "Soon enough, you're going to learn how to accept love."

I give Tommy the evil eye but he's obviously going blind or something because he continues to look at me with this huge grin. Mom is glancing around the place like she thinks someone might run up and snatch her purse—something that at this point actually seems like a somewhat reasonable fear.

"So, Tommy," she says in a super uncomfortable-sounding voice. "We have to be getting to the airport soon so we don't miss our flight."

"Yes, yes," Tommy says, looking from me to my mom. "She's in safe hands, don't you worry." He glances at his watch. "Group starts in about five minutes, so if you all want to say good-bye, I can take Amelia over there and she can unpack later."

Mom hugs me and Dad gets tears in his eyes, but I can't deal with their emotions right now because I have too many questions. Group what? Group isn't a noun, it describes a noun, and I want to lecture

Tommy about how he left off the second part of what I'm about to have to go do and how he should be more accurate when he's describing something that sounds absolutely terrifying, but Dad envelopes me in a hug before I have a chance to say a word.

"Bye Amelia," Mom says. "Please be good." I hug her and realize she's shaking. It dawns on me how disappointing it must be to have carried someone in your womb for nine months and put up with a whole slew of fights and hassles, only to drop her off at a torn-down-looking rehab with guys like Joel and Stan as playmates, and for a split second I think I'm going to collapse in shame-filled sobs. But I step away from her and stand up straight.

"I will be good, Mom," I say. "I promise."

Dad puts his arm around Mom and starts to lead her toward the front door. Then they turn back to wave, and I feel myself tearing up. Apparently, on my first day of kindergarten, when my mom tried to drop me off, I simply wouldn't let go of her hand. The teacher, Sue, eventually had to literally pry my hand away from Mom's and I cried inconsolably. Supposedly I was fine by later that day, but transitional moments have never been easy for me.

I wave at their retreating backs, and just as Mom turns around to blow me a kiss, Joel throws one of his bulking hands on my right shoulder.

"Don't you worry, Mr. and Mrs. Amelia!" he calls. "I'll keep her good!"

"Group" is apparently short for "group therapy," and this kind of group therapy involves each of us stating our first name followed by the word "alcoholic," just like in that ridiculously dull Faye Dunaway movie that always seems to be on the Independent Film Channel. Then Tommy calls on people to "share"—and sharing seems to mean talking about how much we miss "using." Using seems to refer to anything—drinking, shooting heroin, taking pain pills, whatever. I'm figuring all this stuff out, and feeling like I really may need to talk to the head of Pledges about this bizarre habit they seem to have of leaving off the second part of words—"It should be using *alcohol* or using *drugs*, not just the word 'using' without having it refer to anything," I can picture myself explaining—but the problem is that I'm feeling somewhat frozen into muteness. When I was younger, I was considered shy. I don't remember feeling shy as much as I remember being described as shy, and how much I hated it. I wanted to be gregarious and confident and outgoing even before I knew what those words meant. And when our family went on a cruise to Alaska when I was ten and I befriended a Southern girl named Amy, who everyone called "effervescent," I decided that was the personality I wanted to adopt. According to Mom, I changed literally overnight, and she suddenly had a loud extrovert for a daughter instead of the diffident girl who clutched her mother's hand in quaking fear. Occasionally, shy Amelia creeps back up—especially when I'm around new people—and I have to say, that's one of the reasons I liked drinking and drugs so much: they made me able to access my effervescent side at all times. Just as I'm thinking about this, and about how horribly traumatized I'm going to be if they make me "share" in this "group," Tommy turns to me.

"Guys, this is Amelia," he says, and suddenly, horrifyingly, they're all looking at me like I'm cocaine and they've been waiting for the dealer for hours. In addition to Stan and Joel, there are a couple of older men in brown sweaters, an overly tan blonde girl, an extremely gay black guy, and exactly one superhot specimen—brown hair, blue eyes, Abercrombie-type clothes—sitting in the corner. For his sake, I flash what I hope is a winning smile.

"Want to introduce yourself to the group, Amelia?" Tommy asks, even though that's what he just did.

"Oh, sure," I say, pretending that my heart isn't racing. "I'm thirty years old, and work, or at least until recently worked, at *Absolutely Fabulous* magazine." The gay-looking guy titters, but I ignore him as I gaze straight at Tommy. "Um, what else should I say?"

"Amelia, this is probably the one place in L.A. where we don't

care about how old you are and what you do," Tommy says. The gay
guy and Blondie laugh. "Just tell us about your disease."

I'm humiliated for having answered incorrectly and immediately
indignant. Clearly, these people—Joel and gay titterer and Blondie
and even hot guy in the corner—weren't holding down jobs, or if they
were, they obviously weren't very demanding or fabulous. And while
it's true that I'm not currently reporting to work anywhere either,
these people look like they hadn't been employed, like, ever. Where
the hell are the celebrities and high-level producers? That was the
group I needed to be in.

"Amelia," Tommy says, and I realize everyone's still looking at me.
"Your disease?"

Oh, yeah. My disease. When I read through the Pledges literature
Dr. Ronald Rand gave me at the hospital, I noticed that they made a
big thing about how I had a disease as real as cancer or Parkinson's but
my disease—alcoholism—was centered in the mind.

"See, that's the thing," I say, glancing around to catch different
people's eyes as a painfully obvious sympathy ploy. "I really have—
had—a problem with cocaine. I mean, I really love coke. When I
have it, I can't seem to stop using until it's all gone." I pause, waiting
for someone to congratulate me on my quick ability to use one of their
ridiculous vocab words in a sentence, not to mention my obvious
awareness of and honesty about my drug problem, but nobody says a
word.

"When it comes to alcohol, though, I can take it or leave it," I
continue. "It usually just gives me a headache or makes me feel achy. I
definitely don't have a problem with it." I give Tommy a decidedly
un-alcoholic smile.

"So, you don't drink at all?" Tommy asks with what I can swear is a
look of bemusement.

"Well, I drink," I say. "But just the regular amount. Or I would
more drink to come down a little if I was too wired from coke. But I
definitely don't have a drinking *problem*. I don't even like alcohol."

The blonde girl nods at me like she understands. Maybe she's in my situation, a person with a drug problem stuck in this room of people obsessed with calling themselves alcoholics.

"If that's the case," Tommy says, "I suggest you take some time—say, a year or two—off of drinking and see if you miss it."

My mouth threatens to fall open, but I try to appear blasé as I assess whether or not Tommy is joking. "A year or two?" I ask with a slight smile.

"Sure," he says, folding his arms. "If you can take a couple years off of drinking and not miss it, then I would say you're probably not an alcoholic." He smiles at me, and for the first time it occurs to me that Tommy may be an asshole dressed up like a nice guy. But I don't want to give these people any more ammunition against me than they already have.

"Actually," I say with a smile. "I was planning to stop with the coke—stop with drugs of all kinds, no problem—and cut down significantly on my drinking. In fact, I heard about a program . . . I think it's called a 'drinking cessation' program." I'd heard about this from someone who went there when his family was trying to get him to go to rehab. "Do you know about it?"

The entire room bursts into laughter and I feel myself blushing while also trying to pretend like I know what's funny. The guy had told me that it was a program you went to when you weren't an alcoholic but maybe drank too much or didn't trust yourself not to do drugs when you drank, and I was assuming that the people at Pledges would know all about joining. When everyone continues to laugh—Blondie, who I'd thought was on my side, included—I start to get pissed.

"What's so fucking funny?" I find myself snapping, alarming myself with the snideness of my tone.

Everyone stops laughing and Tommy glances at the hot guy in the corner. "Justin, you want to tell Amelia what's so funny?"

The hot guy, Justin, smiles and looks even cuter than he did when he was laughing. He catches my eye from across the room. "Amelia," he says, and I have an involuntary shudder at such a hot guy saying my

name and looking me in the eye, even under these depressing circumstances. "That program doesn't exist anymore."

Tommy looks at Justin and asks, "And why is that?"

"The woman who started it got wasted and killed a kid in her car
a few months ago," Justin says. "The program has since been dis-
banded."

"And that's funny?" I say, hoping to shame everyone in the room.

"No, it's not," Justin says. "What's funny is that when I got here, I
asked the exact same question."

"So did I," Blondie pipes up.

"Good for you," I say, not sure why they think any of this would be
amusing or interesting to me. "But my point is that while I've acted
addictively with drugs, I'm not an alcoholic." Everyone is silent and I
wonder if they've finally come around to actually understanding this
extremely simple point I'm trying to make.

"Would you be at least willing to consider the fact that alcoholics
and drug addicts are the same thing?" Tommy asks. He's looking at me
so kindly that I almost want to acquiesce even though I know he's
wrong.

"But they're not the same thing," I explain.

"I realize you feel that way," he says. "And that's why I'm asking if
you'd be willing to just *consider* the fact that they *might be.*"

I look around at all of them, noticing several people I hadn't even
seen before and an inordinate number of tattoos. Was one of the pre-
requisites for Pledges a certain amount of permanent ink on various
body appendages? Despite their general seediness and ridiculous optimism in the light of where they were currently seated, at this particular moment I find it strangely almost impossible to continue to hate all
of them. *And besides,* I think, *Tommy isn't asking for so much.*

"Fine," I say. "I'm willing to consider that." The group bursts into
applause, like I've just performed a vignette, and I stifle the urge to tell
them to stop clapping and get a life. Tommy stands up and walks over
to me, leaning down to give me a hug.

"Welcome to Pledges, Amelia," he says, pulling me close to him.

And for reasons thoroughly unclear to me, I burst into tears. Everyone in the room breaks into another round of applause.

Later that afternoon, I'm crying again. And I can't seem to stop. I'm in my room, looking around at my shabby surroundings, and sobbing. The gay guy, Peter, pokes his head in.

"You okay?" he asks. Why the hell do people ask that when the answer is so clearly *no*?

I shake my head and keep crying.

He makes a sympathetic face. "Why are you crying?" he asks, and I look up at him incredulously.

"Why am I crying?" I ask. "My question is, why aren't *you*? We're in fucking rehab."

Peter blinks and smiles like he's never experienced a sad emotion in his life. *He's probably thrilled to be here because he gets to room with other men*, I think. I feel thoroughly positive that Peter hasn't gone through a fraction of what I have and resent his put-together outfit and confused-looking head tilt more than I can even express.

"Please," I say to him, "just leave me alone."

He shuffles off and my tears eventually subside enough for me to go back to reading through the Pledges book that Tommy gave me after group. After a while, though, I mostly listen to the people out on the smoking patio. I'd hung around everyone after group and tried to feel comfortable while a girl talked about robbing people at ATMs to get money for heroin and a guy regaled the group with stories of popping "benzos" and other things I'd never heard of. A completely freaky-looking guy with about fifty pierces in his ear joked and laughed with the best of them. *I can't even fit into a group that clearly accepts everyone*, I thought as I watched Justin pat Multi-Pierced Guy on the back.

So I went to my room to try to start reading this book but when I cracked it open and saw all this stuff about how you stay sober by following steps that involve always looking for your part in whatever resentment you have, I thought, *What the fuck does that have to do with being sober?*

And that's when the tears started. Now that they've stopped and I can actually concentrate on this book again, I find myself far more interested in eavesdropping. *They all seem to be in complete denial over why they're here,* I decide, as I listen to them lighting cigarettes and cracking jokes. *They're not coworkers on an office break or college students blowing off steam. They're at the end of the line. It doesn't get any lower than rehab. What is wrong with these people that they're not more depressed by their circumstances?*

I don't want to start crying again—I'd actually planned to keep it together because I've been told that my roommate is going to be checking in any minute and I'm counting on her being some kind of a saving grace—so I just keep listening to them while trying to read the damn book. I've already decided that my roommate will be cute and normal and we'll smoke and eat candy and plan extravagantly creative good-bye parties for each other like people always do in movies about rehab.

I'm wavering between these my-roommate-will-save-me fantasies and thinking that checking in here was a horrific mistake as I listen to everyone laugh and read about how I'm going to have to go and apologize to everyone I've ever harmed. *I'm nothing like these annoyingly cheerful freaks,* I think, and decide I should probably call Mom and explain this to her. I'm thinking about this when Kimberly, the no-nonsense front desk lady, walks in to the dank, depressing room.

"Knock knock," she says, even though she's already inside. In drug rehab, this probably counts as a joke. "I'm here to go through your bags."

Joel had warned me about this. He'd told me that Kimberly would come and search my belongings for smuggled-in coke and pills. How desperate did people have to be, I wonder, to sneak drugs into rehab? Kimberly grabs my pink hobo purse from the floor and pulls my Black-Berry out.

"You won't be needing this," she smiled, as she tucks the Black-

Berry into her pocket. Even though I vaguely recall someone telling me this would happen, I can't help but feel horribly violated, and positive that Kimberly is getting some sadistic pleasure out of taking away my connection to the outside world. And then she continues to go through my bag until she lands on a bottle of Listerine.

"Oh, no way, Jose," she says while cradling it, sounding excited.

"You encourage bad breath?" I snap.

"Oh, that's funny," she says, not sounding remotely amused. "There's alcohol in there."

And then I snap. "Jesus Christ. I'm not going to drink Listerine for the fucking alcohol," I say.

Kimberly clearly doesn't feel it's necessary to respond, for she simply slides the bottle of mouthwash into her other pocket and looks at me the way one might a serial killer.

"You ready for your UA?" she asks.

I just look at her, not interested in explaining that I have no idea what she's asking me.

"Your test?" she says.

I continue to stare at her blankly.

"Urine analysis," she finally says, then adds, "You have to pee in a cup."

She turns and starts walking out of the room and I get up and follow her. It probably should have occurred to me, but of course I hadn't even considered the fact that they were going to be constantly testing me to see if I was taking drugs. While I can't imagine who the hell would take drugs while they're in rehab, after getting a look at Joel and some of the other residents, I'm beginning to gather an answer. I follow Kimberly to the front office, where she picks a clear plastic cup from inside her desk and hands it to me. At this point, I know what to do—I have been to the gyno, after all.

"Okay, be right back," I say and start toward the bathroom.

"Ha ha," Kimberly says, immediately on my tail. "As if." And that's when I realize this bitch is planning to come into the bathroom

with me. Jesus! What the hell does she think, that I'm high but stor-
ing some "good" pee in my side pocket that I plan to put in the cup if
she doesn't log my every move?

We go into the bathroom and as I pull down my pants, I think that
it's a good thing I don't have issues about being naked in front of people or I'd really be in trouble. I flip the toilet seat up and am about to
sit down when I realize that thousands of skanky, drug-addicted asses
have surely been here before me and, based on what I've gathered so
far about the Pledges hygiene policy, the remnants of those experiences surely still remain. In public toilets, I never have the patience to
bother with those toilet covers—I simply squat an inch or so above.
But am I going to be able to squat and pee in a cup with a humorless,
suspicious wench watching me?

I tell myself to ignore her, then just squat and hold the cup under
my stream, grateful that I'm not having performance anxiety. I fill
the cup, place it on the counter, finish peeing, and start washing my
hands. Kimberly stands there, gazing at my cup of pee.

"It's all yours," I say, gesturing toward the cup.

She walks over, picks it up, and gazes at it with wonder. "Amelia,"
she says, "you really ought to think about drinking more water."

"Why?" I ask as I think about how much I want to smack her.

"Healthy pee," she says, "should be almost clear." We both look at
mine, which is basically orange.

"Great," I say. "Thanks for the tip. Can I go now?"

She nods and sashays out of the room. As I follow her out, I wonder if she's going to write down the color of my pee in my file.

I yearn for my BlackBerry so that I can call someone. Of course, I
could wait in line for the pay phone that Rich—an eighteen-year-old
kid from Boulder, Colorado—has been dominating since I got here.
Asking twenty adults to share one pay phone is ridiculously inhu-
mane, but then again, so is silently accusing a nonalcoholic of packing
contraband mouthwash for a secret buzz or acting like she'll probably
cheat on a fricking pee test. Even if Rich, the Colorado kid, does ever

get off the phone, I know that I don't feel like talking to Mom or, in fact, anyone. I have no credibility anymore, so my announcing that these people are all psychotic wouldn't mean anything to anyone. It occurs to me for not the first time that I really don't have any friends. And for once, this thought doesn't make me cry. Maybe I'm just all out of tears at this point.

I'm sitting in the breakfast room the next morning, thoroughly exhausted, when Tommy greets me with a huge smile and says that sometime today I have to go see Dr. Thistle, the resident doctor at Pledges, for a checkup. The girl who was supposed to have been my roommate clearly came to her senses and decided to forgo rehab, so last night I slept alone in my creepy room. Of course, "sleep" is a pretty optimistic description of what I'd been doing. Staring at the ceiling, getting up occasionally to smoke and trying to read the Pledges book in order to bore me into slumber more accurately describes last night's nocturnal activities.

Here at breakfast, everyone's chattering but I can't think of anything to say until my third cup of coffee, when I ask the tan blonde, Robin, what she does for a living. She tells me that she'd been a model, once stripped down to her G-string on Howard Stern, and continues to go on sharing anecdotes about her life. I get the distinct sensation that she considers rehab another stop on her party tour—like, summer in the Hamptons, winter in Aspen, spring in Culver City—and I envy her relaxed attitude. Was there something wrong with me for thinking rehab was such a horrible place to be?

When we're done eating, Robin walks me over to Dr. Thistle's office and tells me she'll see me later in group. It's beginning to dawn on me that group happens constantly, like every moment we're not eating or sleeping or cleaning our dishes. So far, no one's mentioned a word about the pool or equine therapy.

Dr. Thistle—or "Doc" as everyone around Pledges calls him—

nods and takes notes as I tell him about all the coke I've done but when I explain my situation with Ambien, he starts shaking his head and looking disapproving.

"Up to five pills a night?" he asks, dumbfounded. This was a guy who listened to people come in and talk about shooting vats of drugs up their ass and doing eight balls in five-minute spans, if what people had been sharing during and after group was any indication, so I don't know why he had to be so judgmental about me taking a few sleeping pills.

"Look, I wasn't taking them for *fun*," I say. "I was taking them because I suffer from *insomnia*."

"I understand," he says. "And when did you stop taking them?"

"The other day," I say. "When I got out of the hospital, I decided to go cold turkey."

Doc shakes his head. "That wasn't smart. You should have told them how many you were taking when you were in the hospital so they could have detoxed you off of them with an IV. You could have had a seizure."

I don't think anything sets me off more than being told I've done something stupid—so I have to stifle an urge to start wringing Doc's neck. No one in the hospital asked me how much of anything I took and it certainly didn't cross my mind to offer it up. "Well, clearly I did not have a seizure, Doctor, so I guess we can conclude that I survived despite my stupidity," I say.

"It's going to be a while before you'll be able to sleep through the night," he says. This guy needs to be given a serious lecture about glass half-full versus glass half-empty logic, but I'm too desperate to get away from him to be the one to do it.

14

I'm trying to focus on reading the Pledges book when Tommy pokes his head in my room.

"Just wanted to see how you're adjusting," he says, cheerful as ever.

"Oh, great," I say. Even in this ridiculously downtrodden state, I seem to care about what my drug counselor thinks of me so I don't want him to know how scared and miserable I feel. I try to smile. "Everyone's really nice," I add, even though it's a bald-faced lie.

Tommy just looks at me. "Why don't you and I take a walk?" he asks.

A walk, like anything else right now, sounds absolutely unappealing, but what are my options? To sit here and think about how much I must have fucked up my life to be ensconced in this place with a bunch of losers?

"Can I smoke?" I find myself asking.

"Absolutely," he says, as he helps me to my feet. "In fact, I encourage you to."

I grab my Camel Lights and my lighter, slide on a pair of flipflops and follow Tommy outside as he picks up a pebble that was sitting on a picnic table covered with ashtrays and starts walking down the Pledges entryway toward the street.

"I'm going to say something and I don't want you to be offended by it," Tommy says as he tosses the pebble onto the ground and leads me onto a busy street lined with thrift stores and fast-food places. It's my first time seeing civilization since I checked in a few days ago, and it seems shocking that the real world has actually only been a few hundred feet away.

"Shoot," I say, lighting up what has to be my eighty-seventh cigarette of the day. I had to imagine that getting offended was probably going to be the nicest thing that would happen to me today, now that my life was shaping up to be a series of depressing incidents brightened only by Camel Lights and the occasional brownie. Besides, I like Tommy.

"You strike me as pretty much spiritually dead," Tommy says as he leads me across the street. He looks at me sadly while squinting his eyes, as if my face were the sun and he's not wearing sunglasses.

I'd expected him to tell me he thought I seemed really depressed or like I wasn't fitting in or that I'd clearly let myself go physically but this didn't seem particularly offensive. I wasn't, in fact, even sure what he meant.

"Spiritually dead?" I ask, exhaling smoke. "Well, I'm not religious. And," I add with a smile, "I'm not remotely offended."

For once, Tommy doesn't smile. He stops walking and steps in front of me so that we're standing face to face. "Spirituality doesn't always have to do with religion," he says.

I know what he's doing. I know that sober people are obsessed with everyone else believing in God—even though they called it a "higher power" so as not to put off people who weren't Catholic or whatever—and Tommy is going to try to do the God hard-sell on me.

"Absolutely," I say and hope that's the end of the conversation and we can just walk back to the rehab in peace.

"Going to the beach and staring at the ocean can be spiritual," he says, standing perfectly still. "Going to a pet store and getting on your hands and knees and playing with puppies can be spiritual. Going on a walk and smelling flowers can be spiritual."

For a straight guy, Tommy is pretty dramatic, and something about his heartfelt spirituality lecture makes me smile. I have to admit that sitting on a beach, playing with puppies, and smelling flowers sounds pretty damn nice. And I can't remember the last time I did any of those things.

Group that afternoon isn't all that different from group the day before, but this time the person who speaks gets to decide who talks next. I sit there picking my cuticles, feeling fairly safe that I'm doing a decent job of remaining mostly invisible. And I'm glad for it once the meeting gets going and I start hearing the bullshit coming out of people's mouths. A "pink cloud" is apparently a space you get in when you're sober and everything seems so good that you have to pinch yourself to make sure you're not dreaming, and roughly half the Pledges residents claim to be there. I can't for the life of me figure out why everyone is claiming something so ridiculous—it's not like they're being graded on their rehab behavior and performance. *They're probably all actors*, I think. *Like everyone else in L.A.*

Finally it's the hot guy's turn to speak. After introducing himself as "Justin, alcoholic," he says, "I have to be honest—I'm really not feeling all this pink cloud shit." He pushes his hair out of his eyes, and I basically fall in love with him on the spot, for both his cheekbones as much as the fact that he seems like the only honest one in the room. "I miss using with every pore in my body. I fucking hate being sober. It just feels so . . . unnatural for me."

"That's just your disease talking to you," Tommy says.

I expect Justin to snap that diseases don't talk, and that most people don't believe all this alcoholism-is-a-disease crap, anyway, but he actually nods.

"I know it is, and I know this feeling will pass because it did the other day, but I guess I'm just . . . pissed off that I'm an alcoholic, a drug addict, whatever. It just doesn't seem fair that my friends can party and not end up in here with all you crazies."

Even though I expect people to be offended, everyone nods and laughs and Robin even claps. *She's probably trying to sleep with him*, I reason. But I can't begin to explain what's going on with the rest of them. They *know* they're crazy and find it *funny*? People who know they're crazy should be seriously alarmed and not amused, I decide. Even Justin starts laughing, and I find myself incredibly confused by his behavior. He seems so cool, but maybe he's just as weird as everyone else. I mean, why is he looking so damn cheerful when he just shared about how pissed off he is?

Just as I'm deciding that Justin may not be worth my adoration, I hear him say my name. I'm simultaneously shocked, flattered, and horrified but try to remain cool.

"I'm Amelia, and I'm a drug addict," I start and pause for them all to say my name in unison like they're students in some sort of special ed class. My fear of speaking suddenly evaporates and I feel annoyed and angry and unable to be fake like the rest of them. "And, well, I think this fucking sucks, too. I don't understand why I'm here." To my horror, I start to cry and suddenly realize I can't stop. "It wasn't supposed to be like this," I say through wracking sobs. "I wasn't supposed to end up here. I'm from a good family. I should have known better." I end this dramatically, with a heaving sob, and the gay guy—Peter—pats my back as I cry. When I look up, I realize they're all just staring at me in silence.

"Amelia," Tommy says gently. "Pick someone else to share."

Tears continue to stream down my face as I point to Hawaiian Tropic.

"I'm Robin and I'm an alcoholic," she says. And then she turns to face me. "And Amelia, can I just thank you so much for your share? It was like the most honest, beautiful thing in the world. I so exactly felt that way when I came in here, so thanks so much for reminding me of why I'm so grateful to be here."

Part of me wants to remind Robin that she's been here like a week so thinking back to when she came in couldn't have been that much of a stretch, but at the same time I feel something sort of unleash in my heart, and for a split second I wonder if maybe I am in the right place. If this ditzy, fake-titted sometime bikini model felt like this a week ago and she's now clapping her hands at being called crazy, maybe there's a chance that I can learn from these people and not always be miserable.

Joel shares and then Tommy announces that it's time to wrap up group. He looks at me. "Before we end, I'd like to thank you, Amelia, for your honesty."

I'm starting to feel almost embarrassed by all this attention—something I'd never known was possible.

"This disease takes people from jail and people from Yale," Tommy continues and he looks me directly in the eye. "And it's not your fault. Do cancer patients beat themselves up for getting sick?" He's clearly on some kind of a roll because he then adds, "Remember, your disease takes on all kinds of forms, and telling you that you're a piece of shit because you're sitting in a folding chair in a rehab is just one of those."

I smile at Tommy. Maybe there's something to this disease thing. Or maybe just hearing that people from Yale end up in rehab, too, makes me feel better.

We end the group by holding hands and saying the serenity prayer, which I'd only heard before I came here at the beginning of a Sinead O'Connor song. I have to admit I find it far more comforting than any of the prayers I used to have to say at temple. But it also has the added advantage of not being in Hebrew.

As I reach down to pick up my cigarettes, Robin walks over to me and gives me a hug.

"Thank you so much," she says as she holds me.

"Thank *you*," I say back to her and mean it, surprising myself for not immediately trying to disentangle.

"I love you," she says, and I don't even flinch. In just a few days, I've noticed that people in rehab announce their love for each other more often than honeymooners. "Thanks for passing the Equal," someone might say at a coffee table, "I love you." Or, "Your share was awesome—I love you." But this was the first time anyone here has said it to me.

And then the most shocking thing of all happens.

"I love you, too," I say, and even though I only say it because I feel like I have to, as soon as it's out of my mouth I realize that I feel better than I have in months.

15

I'm not sure when rehab starts to seem like the most normal place in the world because it seems to happen without my being remotely aware of it. One minute I'm horrified by my roommate—a black middle-aged woman from Vegas who shouts in her sleep and leaves after three days, when she decides that she can still smoke crack "casually"—and the next I'm helping to set the table for dinner and not even remotely repulsed while listening to Joel talk about how he hasn't had sex in three months. The days and nights at Pledges are so spectacularly consistent—every meal, group, and outing happens at the exact same time each day—and after a few days, I realize what a relief it is to have someone telling me where to go and what to do. I even find myself using their ridiculous vocabulary words myself—this, too, seems to have seeped into my system completely subconsciously—and feeling, for the first time since I can remember, happy. Even the revelation that there are two Pledges facilities—one in Malibu, with the horse stables and movie stars, and this one, which is one-sixteenth of the price and thus lovingly referred to as "Ghetto Pledges" by its residents—seems kind of hilarious.

Okay, I'll admit that having a beautiful specimen like Justin around helps. After group the day that I shared about hating everyone and everything, he asked me if I wanted to go on a walk. We walked and smoked and bonded about absolutely everything. He's from the Palisades and went to USC but, details aside, we've been living nearly parallel existences. Before he'd gotten into using coke, Justin had been a screenwriter and producer and was dying to get back in the business. We took turns telling each other that our respective businesses would surely want us back once we were clean and sober. And before I knew it, Justin was my best rehab friend. I always made sure to keep my obsessive crush on him on the down-low—Tommy had warned us extensively about what happens when people substitute their drug of choice for sex and had all but begged us to ignore our sex drive for the month we were in treatment. I was shocked to discover that, despite the way I've been living the past two decades or so, I'm something of a rule follower.

One day when Justin and I are wrangling everyone for group, Tommy leads a newbie down the driveway toward the basketball court. Unlike the previous new people, however, who all seemed to walk in with their heads hanging low and their clothes drooping off their skinny frames, this one wore stiletto heels, spandex pants, and a leopard-print tight tank—sartorial decisions that seemed all the more shocking because she's pushing her mid-forties. With a jolt, I realize the leopard-printed spandex wonder is Vera, my go-to dealer before I found Alex.

"Vera!" I shriek as I rush over to give her a hug. She gazes at me quizzically and a little freaked out. Tommy looks from me to her.

"Oh, you know each other?" Tommy asks excitedly. The man gets excited about anything that he thinks might help someone stay sober.

"Yes, I—" I'm about to launch into the whole story about how I met Vera at a party in the Hills, where she gave me free coke all night—but she winks knowingly at me and I shut up. I've been here for a few weeks so I know that we can confess our most horrific sins in rehab and never get in trouble—I'd literally listened to Peter, the gay titterer who turned out to be really cool, talk about having male prostitutes shoot heroin up his ass in bathhouses—but Vera clearly didn't know that yet.

"Yes, we know each other from temple," Vera says, reasonably convincingly. Tommy looks absolutely delighted and just a bit confused, seeing as I'd explained to him that I hadn't seen the inside of a religious establishment in over a decade.

"People from temple," I say, feeling a little bit better about the lie because surely if I did go to temple in L.A., someone there could have referred me to Vera. Rehab hammers home this idea that we have to be "rigorously honest" and "we're as sick as our secrets," so lately I've been extremely uncomfortable with anything even close to a lie.

Despite Vera's external confidence, deafeningly loud outfit, and overall smooth demeanor, I can see in her eyes that she's basically terrified. They make a big deal at Pledges about "getting out of yourself" and "being of service to other people" and while at first I thought that was a scam to get us to do all the dishes and clean toilets and stuff so that they didn't have to hire actual housekeepers, I've been surprised to discover that doing things for other people actually feels good. If I'm cleaning or helping out someone who just got here and is as freaked out as I was when I came in, I'm not thinking about the fact that I'd become a cocaine addict who ended up in rehab at thirty. And somehow, when I went back to thinking about that later, it didn't seem so depressing anymore.

"We still have a few minutes left before group," I say to Tommy. "Why don't Vera and I take a walk and I'll give her the lay of the land?"

Tommy nods and smiles and Vera looks relieved as I take one of her spandexed arms and lead her in the direction of where Tommy took me the day we discussed my spirituality. Before Pledges, I'd never say something like "lay of the land"—not only was it a cliché, but it also sounded incredibly lame—yet something about being here had helped me not be so hard on myself.

"Look, this place is great, it's just a little overwhelming at first," I say to Vera as I light two cigarettes and hand one to her. "I think I was in shock my first few days. The only thing that gave me any comfort at all was that Tommy would say things to me like, 'When you first come here, it's so different from anything you've done before, it's like walking on the moon.' That helped me realize that it was normal to feel completely confused and overwhelmed."

Vera smokes the cigarette furiously and gazes out at the Venice Boulevard traffic. "That's cool and everything, but I'm really just here to stay out of jail."

"Oh, you got busted?" I ask and Vera nods. Two other dealers here, both guys, had been busted and were trying to get the judge to reduce their sentences by completing thirty-day treatment programs. But both of them had come to really like staying sober. It was cute to see bad guys melt and become good.

"Look, if you don't mind, can you not tell everyone you used to buy from me?" Vera asks.

"They're not going to care," I say. "It's a really nonjudgmental place."

"I'm just really trying to keep everything on the down-low," she says and I smile because I've learned that reasoning with an alcoholic or addict—all of whom seem to be a bit paranoid, self-obsessed, and insecure, myself included—can be futile.

"No problem," I say. For just a split second, I fondly recall the pink Post-It notes that she used to wrap her grams in.

"I don't know if I should be here," she suddenly says, her eyes darting from the rehab to the street, as if she's weighing the possibility of literally running off. A guy named Jack did it the other day—checked in and then, in the middle of introducing himself to the other residents, ran away and took off in his truck—and I've learned that we can't stop people from leaving if they want to. Tommy says that rehab isn't for the people who need it but the people who want it—a bit of wisdom I opt not to share with Vera at this particular juncture.

"Why don't you stick around for a day and see how you like it?" I ask. "Then, if you still think it doesn't feel like the right place, you can do something about it tomorrow."

Vera nods and I pat myself on the back for taking the logic I'd heard Tommy use on Peter when Peter was swearing he'd die if he didn't go out and get a hit of crystal meth right then.

I throw my arm around Vera and start leading her back to the Pledges gate, marveling at the fact that I'm clutching a spandexed former drug dealer, grinning like a maniac.

Later that night, we residents get invited to a mini auditorium around the back of the Pledges property, where the alumni—people who got sober here—come by for meetings. The alumni meetings happen around here pretty much 24-7 and once you "graduate," you're encouraged to go to as many as you want. Being able to mix with all of them once a week sort of feels like getting invited to the adults' table after an entire childhood of sitting only with the other kids.

According to Tommy, finding a sponsor and going through the steps outlined in the Pledges book is a fairly rigorous process that involves making lists of people we resent and apologizing to them. The alumni agree to show us how to do this so they can "be of service" and get out of their own problems, and the idea is that one day we become sponsors ourselves. I'm supposed to be looking for "someone who has what I want" but since the one thing I really want now is sobriety and all the alumni seem to have that, I'm not exactly sure what criteria I'm supposed to be using.

"I like the look of Mustache," Justin whispers to me as people shuffle in for group. We're in full-on sponsor shopping mode and he's tilting his head in the direction of a good-looking, lean guy with an ironic handlebar mustache. Mustache looks like he's a little on the depressed side, but I smile at Justin enthusiastically.

"Just promise me you won't let his facial hair philosophies influence you," I whisper and Justin shakes his head and crosses his heart. Although Justin could shave the hair on his head into a mustache shape and still look hot, his permanent five o'clock shadow is too much of a gift to the female race to be messed with.

A pixieish girl with short brown hair sits down next to Mustache and I immediately decide that she's going to be my sponsor. And then I'm just as quickly stricken with the fear that she's not going to be available or is going to say no because she doesn't like the look of me or because Vera and Robin and all the other girls are going to also ask her and she's going to be overwhelmed. But I also know that's unlikely. Although Tommy has hammered home how important it is that we all get sponsors, most of the people here don't seem to be in that much of a hurry.

I watch Pixie Girl throughout the meeting. She doesn't share but she smiles a lot, and when the meeting is over I rush up to her and ask her to be my sponsor. She nods and smiles. "By the way," she says, as she gives me a hug, "my name is Rachel, drug of choice heroin. And I have five and a half years."

"And I'm Amelia," I say, shaking her hand even though we've just hugged. "Cocaine fiend. Twenty-one days." This kind of introduction is standard around rehab. Since almost no one comes in just for alcohol abuse anymore—we only have Stan, the guy I met on my first day—identifying yourself by your drug of choice and how long you're sober can help clarify a lot. You can kind of tell what drugs people do sometimes—the meth people are jittery and blink a lot, the cokeheads tend to have the kind of manic energy that makes them seem like they're still on it, and the junkies tend to be mellow and live in Silverlake or Los Feliz—but we all mix well together, even if our drugs didn't.

"Well, Miss Amelia, cocaine fiend," she says. "Do you believe that drugs and alcohol have made your life unmanageable?"

"I know they did," I reply. I partially hate myself for sounding like such a sycophant, but also love how good it feels to not always be so defiant.

"We're going to get along just fine," she says, and she smiles as she walks away.

16

The day I'm getting out, I decide to check the messages on my machine. Everyone else has been calling their voicemail somewhat obsessively, but I've been doing a decent job of acting like I didn't actually exist before I came to Pledges. We talk a lot about how we're being reborn here in Culver City, but I've taken that even further by deciding that everything that happened before wasn't really my life. Even though I've gone over everything in group and in post-group smoke-athons, when I talk about the girl who did coke all day at work or Special K with strangers and passed out besides Dumpsters, I feel like I'm actually talking about someone else—a troubled girl I once knew, but not me. Here in rehab, I've been learning that I'm not much like who I thought I was—I'm more nervous and thoughtful than I am bitchy and fabulous—and I'm starting to see that I'm also reliable and considerate, and do actually care about other people. Thinking about my behavior with Stephanie and Brian and everyone else makes me shudder, but Tommy and Rachel keep telling me not to regret the past, and that I can deal with all of that when I'm ready.

But on my last day, I know that acclimation back into my life will feel less overwhelming if I deal with my messages, or even the fact that there might not be any messages, ahead of time. So even though the receiver for the pay phone feels like it weighs about a hundred pounds, I force myself to dial the numbers. I'd gotten so accustomed to that cold-sounding computerized woman's voice informing me that I had no new messages that I'm shocked when I hear her announce that I have twenty-three. Christ, I don't think I've had twenty-three people I know call me in the past year. The first one's about a sample sale I missed, the second is a wrong number, but my heart starts racing on number three.

"Amelia, it's Stephanie," I hear, and I prepare for a verbal assault. But she continues, "I heard about what happened with *Absolutely Fabulous*, and . . . God, this is stupid. I'm an asshole for e-mailing you that ice princess note. Will you call me? Also, someone is spreading these crazy rumors about you going to rehab!" She punctuates that with an enormous laugh. "Please call and let me know you're okay. Are you up north with your family?"

I push "2" to save the message and wonder what the hell I'm going to say to her. She said the word "rehab" like someone would say "mime school" or "prison"—like it was basically inconceivable. I remember feeling the same way before I got here.

The rest of the messages are from random acquaintances, some who'd heard that I'd been fired, some just checking in. It seemed shocking to realize that I actually do have people who care about me when I've spent so much time alone, convinced that the whole world hated me. I guess this is the "alcoholic mind" Tommy's always talking about. In one of the first groups I went to, someone had shared about how alcoholics and addicts see things as black or white—either everything's terrible or it's wonderful, we're in love or we're in hate—and that accepting that life is full of gray areas, of days and people that are just okay, is challenging because we can't get high off that, or create martyrlike drama around it. I suddenly understand that share completely, as well as the ones I'd heard about how our minds are out to convince us of things that aren't true in order to make us feel bad. Tommy likes to call this "the beast," and Justin is always saying, "Your mind is a dangerous place—don't go in there alone!" Standing there and listening to the messages from my former life with the ears of my new life, all the small comments and shares I've heard over the past four weeks start piling up and making even more sense than when I first heard them.

When I finish listening to the messages on my home voicemail, I check my BlackBerry, which Kimberly unceremoniously returned to me this morning. And that's when I almost pass out.

"Amelia, darling, this is Tim Bromley—I trust you remember me," says a voice I could never forget.

I can't believe this is actually happening. Tommy talked a lot about how our dreams would all come true if we stayed sober, but he'd also given a lot of lip service to the fact that we should try not to get into serious relationships during our first year of sobriety. I feel certain that an exception could be made for a perfect British man I'd been pining for, but I try to stay calm as I listen to the rest of his message.

"Well, I wasn't going to leave this on an answering machine but, you see, I heard what happened with you at *Absolutely Fabulous*."

My heart sinks as quickly as it lifted before when I realize he's just calling to console me over getting fired. For a second, I hate him—there's nothing more horrifying than being pitied.

He continues, "And I say their loss can be my gain. You live a wild life and tell fabulous stories about it. Come write a column documenting your exciting, crazy adventures for *Chat*. I can surely pay you better than whatever you were getting to do those naff celebrity stories. And, well, I hope you don't think I'm incredibly pompous for telling you this but, well, the job would surely launch you into the cultural stratosphere and possibly make you a household name. Call me when you get this, can you? Oh, and by the way, I already have the perfect name for the column." He pauses, possibly for dramatic effect, even though the moment has plenty of drama already. "Party Girl. What do you think? I say that it's straightforward and intriguing, just like you."

I'm bouncing off the walls ebullient when I walk into my last group. The weather has been so stunning that everyone, Tommy included, is wearing shorts, and I feel hopeful, excited, and like my life has entered some sunny, problem-free zone. I'm dying to share my good news about Tim's message, but Tommy starts off group talking super earnestly—the way he always does when someone's leaving.

"Let me just say that although I'm proud of you, Amelia, your work in sobriety has really just started," he says, making it a point to look me in the eye. "Remember, we're like people who have lost their legs—we never grow them back."

I start resenting Tommy, thinking that this is hardly the best way to congratulate me for having survived—and for the most part flourished in—thirty days of not particularly glamorous rehab. Even though I've heard him do this number on Justin and Robin and everyone else on their last day, it never sounded as stern as it does now.

"The statistics for sobriety are incredibly discouraging," he continues. "Most of us don't make it. Today, with thirty days of intensive program under your belt, that may seem impossible to imagine. But out there in the world, when you start getting your life together, you may let other things come before your program. You may find yourself getting the career you've always wanted or the guy of your dreams, and forget that these things are possible only because you're sober."

"Actually, I—" I start but Tommy holds up his finger and continues.

"I can't tell you how many people say they get it when they leave," Tommy says. "And then they're back here again—next year or even next month. Alcoholism is a cunning, baffling disease, and that's what makes it so dangerous."

Even though I'm still resenting Tommy for making my last group such a downer, I think I get why he's doing it. The whole time we've been here, we've been hearing about people relapsing or "slipping," which seems to be another word for relapsing that doesn't sound half as bad. But Tommy has also promised us that if we go to a meeting every day, are rigorously honest, do the steps with our sponsors, and try to be of service to people every day, we will stay sober. And although I'm completely committed to all that, I can already tell that people like Vera and Robin, who have been talking about setting up a company together, where they'll promote certain nights at various

Hollywood clubs, are less so. Rachel has been reinforcing this idea that I have to keep sobriety my "primary purpose" if I want to "keep what I have" and I've said that I can. I'm constantly telling her that she doesn't have to worry about me because I never even really liked drinking and the mere thought of coke sounds disgusting at this point.

When Tommy finishes talking, I share about Tim's message and how excited I am to be embarking on this new phase in my life. When group ends, I go over to Tommy to savor my news even more.

"That's nice, Amelia," he says, as if I've just informed him that I emptied an ashtray filled with cigarette butts.

"I'm not sure you understand, Tommy," I say. "In my field, getting offered a column at one of the world's biggest and best magazines is considered a very big deal." I know I'm being slightly condescending, which seems especially inappropriate given that Tommy has almost single-handedly saved my life, but I want him to swoop me into a hug and congratulate me.

Instead he asks, "You say it's a column where you'll be documenting your 'crazy adventures'?" I nod and he continues, "Well, seeing as your primary purpose is now to stay sober and be of service, I don't imagine you're going to be having all that many 'crazy adventures.'"

Amazing as it seems, this hadn't actually occurred to me. And just as I'm about to freak out over the fact that I have to give up the best possible job I could imagine before I've even had a chance to accept it, I realize that I have a rich history to draw on.

"Tommy, the stuff I got up to pre-sobriety could fill ten thousand columns," I say, and he finally smiles.

"You don't need to tell me," he says, finally laughing. "I've been listening to you for the past thirty days!"

We hug, and then I go around the room hugging everyone else good-bye. When Robin and Peter left, they sobbed, but I've never been a big last-day-of-camp-or-school crier. Still, when Vera wobbles up to me in her spandex and heels, crying that she's going to miss me, I get a little misty-eyed. *World*, I think, *here I come.*

17

"Would you like to have your lawyer look over the contract?" Tim asks me, as he leans back in his Aeron chair and puts his Converse-encased feet on his desk. We're sitting in Tim's penthouse corner office on Sunset, which is understated and elegant, and filled with books on media and politics, most of them presumably written by Tim's good friends, and the fact that he is wearing an adorable striped Armani suit with Converse sneakers is doing nothing to dampen his overall cuteness. Still, now that he's minutes away from becoming my boss, something in me has switched off—I'm not massively crushed out on him anymore.

I'm flattered that Tim thinks I'm savvy and important enough to even have a lawyer but seeing as I don't even have a dentist—and I already know that I'd happily sign on the dotted line no matter what the contract says—I simply shake my head and motion for him to hand me a pen.

The publisher, John Davis, comes in. "Can I be among the first to congratulate *Chat*'s first and only 'Party Girl'?" he asks, as he gives me a hug.

"John, I can't thank you guys enough for this opportunity," I say. Tim had told me that while hiring me had been his idea, John had backed him up immediately.

"No need to thank me," John says. "I hope I'm going to be the one thanking you when you become world famous."

Even though this entire situation should make me feel an unbelievable amount of pressure, I am, for some reason, completely calm. It could be that I'm sober thirty-five days—something I never imagined I'd be able to do—but I actually seem to have complete faith in my ability to pull off this column. The fact that they're going to be paying me $2,500 a month to write essentially off the top of my head—no reporting, no transcribing—feels like a blessing, but a blessing that I deserve.

John starts talking about how the timing is perfect for me to become a sensation through this and how I'll wipe Candace Bushnell, Helen Fielding, and *The Devil Wears Prada* chick off the map while I weigh whether or not I should tell them that I'm sober and thus can't imagine getting up to very many crazy adventures in this new life of mine. Since I've been out of rehab, all I've done is play with my cats, meet Justin and Rachel for coffee and cigarettes, and go to meetings back at Pledges, but Tim has made it abundantly clear that he's fine with me dipping into my past for material. "So long as it's true, I don't care whether it happened last night or last year," were, in fact, his exact words.

After I sign my contract and tell Tim that I'll be turning in copy to him by the end of the week, I feel undeniably like Carrie Bradshaw in *Sex and the City*—minus the Manolo's, adorable apartment, and three sex-crazed best friends, not to mention the Cosmopolitans.

"So, there's something I think I need to tell you," Justin says over double-shot lattes and Camel Lights. We're sitting at Starbucks later that day, and each of us is preparing to meet presobriety friends for the first time since being out.

I'm going to be meeting Stephanie, and Justin is planning to have dinner with his old roommate Jason, so we're doing what Rachel calls "book-ending"—that is, getting together before something challenging, and then planning to talk afterward. I feel strangely calm about seeing Stephanie again but Justin is completely freaking out about seeing Jason.

He talked about Jason a lot in rehab—usually about how much Jason hated it when he used and about how they seemed to always fight—and even though Justin was still at a Sober Living house right near Pledges, he was planning to talk to Jason about the possibility of moving back in with him today.

"You *think* you need to tell me—what does that mean?" I ask, dipping a finger in my latte to do a temperature test. "Ouch," I say, licking the hot liquid off my finger.

"It means . . ." Justin looks more uncomfortable than I've ever seen him. "It means I *know* I need to tell you something."

"What is it?" I'm immediately in a panic, positive that he's going to confess that he's been sneaking out of Sober Living to smoke crystal meth. "Did you go out?"

"Dear God, take that back," Justin says, shaking his head.

"Then what is it?" I ask. "Whatever it is, it can't be that bad. Remember what Tommy used to say: 'There are no big deals'?"

Justin nods and looks down. "Jason wasn't just my roommate," he says, and before he utters another word, I know exactly what his big confession is going to be, and something inside of me isn't all that surprised.

I should have known. Whenever Justin talked about people he dated, he'd say "this person" and never "he" or "she." And of course it was kind of weird for a thirty-five-year-old to have a roommate, let alone one he was always brawling with. Even though when we first met, I fantasized that our friendship would one day morph into true love, something in me had basically abandoned that concept long ago, and I think that something was a sixth sense that he wasn't exactly oriented that way.

"I know," I say.

"You do?" he asks, looking immensely relieved. "How?"

I smile. "Honey, I live in West Hollywood and grew up outside San Francisco. As far as I'm concerned, we heteros are the minority."

Justin laughs. "I know, it does sometimes seem that way," he says. "And I'm not ashamed of it. Or maybe I am. I don't know. Jason thinks I am. But I think it's just that I have a kind of deep voice and don't wear supertight clothes and so people just assume I'm straight." He shakes his head. "Straight people will say, 'Wow, you look so straight,' like that's a compliment."

"I get it," I say. "When people find out I'm Jewish, they say, 'You're Jewish? But you're pretty!' I'm never sure if I'm supposed to thank them or tell them to fuck off."

Justin laughs again. "Well, I'm glad I could tell you this," he says softly, once he's stopped.

I grin at him. "Me, too."

He takes a sip of his latte and licks foam off his upper lip. "And, I want you to know that if I were ever going to be with a woman, it would be you."

"And if I were ever going to be with a gay man, I want you to know that it would be you."

"Shut up!" he exclaims, tossing a napkin at me. "I'm being serious."

"So am I," I say, tossing the napkin back.

"Seriously deranged," he says and then we both start laughing like we've just inhaled entire tanks of nitrous oxide. The phrase "high on life" floats through my mind and I want to share it with Justin, but I'm laughing too hard to get the words out.

Stephanie and I meet at the bottom of Runyon Canyon. She's the one who had suggested hiking, and while the old me would have tried to convince her to do anything else, I'm realizing that there are so many things in L.A.—and the world—that I haven't experienced or even been aware of because trying them has always seemed more daunting than just, say, meeting for drinks.

I'm not exactly sure what's going to happen here—if Stephanie wants to talk about my making out with Gus or just proceed as if nothing happened—but I feel clear about the fact that I want to apologize either way. With some sobriety under my belt, I see how truly out of control my behavior was. It really didn't start and end with making out with Gus the night of the party, either; I'm starting to see how much I've always felt entitled to whatever I've thought I wanted and how few boundaries I've had with friends. But I'm also learning not to beat myself up for that. Rachel is always reminding me that alcoholics and addicts are naturally self-centered people, and that I haven't been bad but "sick." And now I'm trying to get well.

"Hey there," Stephanie says, giving me an awkward hug when I walk up to her at the Gardner entrance. "You look good."

"You do, too," I say, and mean it. I'd never really noticed how pretty she was before.

We start walking in sync, and I notice that our legs are literally taking strides that are the exact same size. It reminds me of how women who spend a lot of time together get on the same menstrual cycle—supposedly, foul as it is, because their bodies subconsciously smell each other, and then adjust—and it seems surprising that after so much time apart and so many changes, Stephanie and I should be in the same groove in any way at all.

"Stephanie, I want to apologize to you for being an asshole," I suddenly say.

"Please, Amelia. I'm the one who wrote you that foul note. Why don't we just forget everything that happened and move on?"

I stop walking. "In a second. But first let me just say that I'm sorry for always making everything about me—what *I* want to do, where *I* want to go, who *I* want to talk to when we're there. Kissing Gus that night was the ultimate selfish act, and I'm so sorry."

Stephanie looks pleasantly surprised. "I miss you," she says, starting to head up the path again, with me just a step behind. "It was hard not to call you. And then, when I heard about what happened at work, and you going to rehab and everything, I literally couldn't stop myself from calling."

"I miss you, too, Steph," I say. We stop walking and I throw my arms around her. "I'm really sorry for the way I've acted," I say, feeling tears sting my eyes.

She surrenders into my hug. "Me, too. Can we be friends again?" I nod, and I know she can feel my nod because my head is cradled against her neck. After a few seconds, we disentangle and I ask her about Jane and Molly.

"Molly's good but Jane is thoroughly immersed in the whole coke scene," Stephanie says, shaking her head. "We've completely lost touch."

"That's sad," I say and mean it, genuinely hoping Jane finds a place like Pledges and knowing that if she's like every other addict I've met, my calling and telling her about it would probably only piss her off.

Stephanie and I continue up Runyon and even though I did this walk once before, I was seriously hungover at the time and didn't notice that you can see almost all of Los Angeles from the top.

"God, this is stunning," I say.

Stephanie nods, but looks distracted. Then she blurts out, "By the way, I've cut back a lot on drinking myself."

I nod—I'd kind of expected her to say something about her own drinking habits, assuming I'd be judging them now. "The way I look at it, I'm the one who lost the privilege to do that stuff—not anyone else," I say. "So please don't think I'm going to be some antidrinking Nazi."

I've thought a lot about this because when I first got to rehab, I couldn't stop declaring every person I thought about a complete and utter alcoholic. But I've come to learn that alcoholism and addiction is a self-diagnosed disease and that it doesn't have much to do with how much someone drinks. An alcoholic personality is one where the person is massively self-involved and always wants to be the center of attention but still has low self-esteem—"the piece of shit in the center of the universe." An alcoholic is someone whose life is unmanageable as a result of drinking and using. And for however much Stephanie and I used to party together, I'm the one with that personality, not her.

I learned at Pledges that there's a big difference between alcoholics and heavy drinkers.

We continue to walk and then Stephanie stops suddenly. "Oh, I almost forgot to tell you—I got promoted to managing editor."

"Oh my God, that's amazing." I'm so accustomed to taking other people's success as a personal affront, like they've received something I should have had—no matter whether I was qualified for it or even wanted it myself—that it feels foreign to be genuinely happy for her. "Congratulations."

"It's crazy—the less I care, the more they reward me. I'm the very definition of failing up."

It occurs to me then that Stephanie maybe isn't as unambitious as she pretends to be, and that perhaps she acts self-deprecating around me because she knows I compare myself to everyone and will thus feel bad. "That's ridiculous," I say. "You're about twenty times smarter than anyone you come into contact with, so you don't even have to *try* to succeed. That's why you're always getting promoted."

Stephanie smiles but looks at me somewhat quizzically. "Okay, who are you and what have you done with Amelia?" she asks and we both laugh.

"Hey, congratulations," I hear as I walk back to my folding chair. It's a few hours after my walk with Stephanie and I've just taken a sixty days sober chip at Pledges. "That's quite an accomplishment." As other people take their chips, I glance at the person talking and realize I'm staring into the face of Damian McHugh, the boy-next-door sitcom star with a drinking problem that's gotten more ink than his career. He'd been going through his very public battle with the bottle— throwing up in bars and licking the faces of reporters—while I'd been an inpatient at Pledges and though we'd all jokingly talked about "saving a seat" for him there, I hadn't expected him to simply show up one day to shake my hand for getting a chip.

"I'm Damian," he says, holding out his hand.

I'm about to say "I know" before remembering how uncool that is. "I'm Amelia." I smile and shake but he doesn't let go of my hand. "Nice to meet you," I add, taking my hand away.

Just then, the meeting starts breaking up and people begin their rush outside in order to get as much nicotine as possible into their systems as soon as humanly possible.

"Want to go smoke?" he asks. I nod and follow him outside as I marvel at how surreal my life has become—writing about celebrities going to rehab one month and smoking with them the next. Damian walks past the clusters of people smoking right outside the meeting doors and toward the basketball hoop, lighting a cigarette and holding the lighter out for me.

"You know how when some people get sober, they start glowing and shit?" he says suddenly. "You really seem to have that."

"Thanks," I respond, taken aback. *Is this a special sober pick-up line?* I wonder, deciding that if it's not, it should be. It seems like the polite thing would be to tell him that he's glowing, too, but it would be an outright lie and outright lies aren't escaping from my lips with ease anymore. "So did you just finish up the thirty-day program?" I ask.

He nods. "Yeah, at the Malibu Pledges. But I like the meetings better here." He stares at his cigarette as if it, and not me, asked him the question.

"And?" I ask. "How did you like it?"

He blows smoke rings. "About as much as I figure I'd like open-heart surgery," he says.

I can't help but laugh. It's actually an appropriate analogy if you thought about it, but I got the feeling Damian hadn't. "Really? That much?" I ask.

"If I needed the open-heart surgery in order to survive," he adds, grimacing.

"I see," I conclude. "Miserable but necessary."

"Something like that," he says, eyeing me as he tosses his cigarette butt on the ground and smashes it out with his Nike Airmax–encased foot. "You?"

"Actually," I say, "I loved it. I feel like I've been given a whole new life." I know I sound like a walking cliché when I say things like this but I don't know how else to explain how different everything has become.

"Really?" Damian asks, looking at me skeptically. He gestures his head toward the meeting room. "Don't you feel a little like all of this is . . . I don't know . . . sort of cultlike? Like they're trying to brainwash us or something?"

I shrug. Of course, I'd heard people say this kind of thing before—to the point where I pretty much had a standard response. "I guess," I say, "but my brain really needed some washing." I smile to try to alleviate how annoying my response must sound to him but at the same time realize that talking to this guy who's paid, like, $10,000 for every second he's on camera is about as stimulating as examining an ant farm—and having the ants crawl up your arm.

He smiles and takes a step closer to me. "Say the word and we could be naked and in my pool in ten minutes," he says.

Stunned, I feel positive I must have misheard him. "What?" I ask.

"Say the word and we could be in my pool in a heartbeat," he repeats, editing out the nude part, and I realize that Damian has, indeed, asked me—a girl he met under five minutes ago whose name I feel certain he hasn't retained—to leave an alumni meeting on a sunny afternoon and go home with him, assuming that his celebrity—and, I guess, the fact that he has a pool—would be enough of a selling point.

"Thanks," I say, "but I'm going to have to pass."

"No one has to know," he says. "I mean, don't you want to just get out of here and away from all these people?" He lights another cigarette.

I look up and see Tommy walking over with Vera trailing behind. Then I glance back at Damian. "You know, I really don't." I gesture toward one of the all-female smoking groups. "But I'm sure you could find someone who would."

Damian nods. "Cool," he says, not looking even the slightest bit perturbed by my denial. I smile and start to walk away. "Hey, congratulations on your sixty days," he adds as he waves. *Is this really how things work?* I wonder as I watch him walk up to the girls smoking. When I glance back and see a blonde girl with a scarf on her head nodding at him and smiling, I have to conclude that it is. Even in Culver City, we're still in Hollywood.

18

I'm sitting at the Starbucks smack in the middle of the gayest part of West Hollywood staring at a blank screen and sipping the remains of my grande latte when Adam walks by. He doesn't see me, just marches right by and goes to wait in line, and my first instinct is to duck and hide. I can't really believe I've joined the ranks of people who sit in coffee shops with laptops—easily as established a Hollywood cliché as the casting couch—but when I had sat down to write my first column at home this morning, I panicked. I had spent so many nights in the same, cat hair–filled, stuffy apartment completely high on coke, and the four walls seemed like they were going to descend upon me as I stared at my computer screen. And then a thought came to me, as clear as if I were a cartoon character and it was printed in a thought bubble printed over my head:

I could call Alex.

Even though I'd deleted his number from my BlackBerry, I still knew it by heart. Would I ever forget it? And that's when I started to panic. We'd talked a lot in rehab about how the obsession to use gets removed at a certain point and after a few days in Pledges that had basically happened to me. But there in my apartment, with a new lease on life and a fantastic dream job to do, the thought of doing cocaine popped into my head like it was the most natural thing in the world.

And that's when I realized I had to get out. Grabbing my laptop and cigarettes, I drove over here, and even though I know it's good that I'm out of my place, I can't help but feel like one of those iBook-toting poseurs I always judged so harshly.

But then I remind myself of what Rachel always tells me, which is that what other people think of me is "none of my business" and that what they're really thinking probably isn't as bad as whatever it is I imagine they're thinking, anyway. So when Adam walks by again and I know I could blend right into the marked-down coffee mugs if I don't say anything, I call his name.

He turns around and looks surprised. "Amelia," he says. He says it softly.

I haven't seen him since he left my apartment the night we made out, and for a split second, I feel myself about to surrender to a shame spiral. But there's a thought I'm having about Adam that is thoroughly distracting me from how ashamed I feel.

Roughly translated, the thought is that he's adorable.

How come I never really noticed his olive skin and square jaw before? And why did I fail to note that he has the exact body type I've always been drawn to—tall, boyishly lean, and not overly muscular? I don't have much time to ask myself these questions before words just start tumbling out of my mouth.

"Look, I'd really like to apologize for the last time we saw each other—the night of Steve's party," I start to stammer. "I was a mess and—"

Adam smiles and holds up a hand as a gesture for me to stop. "Don't worry. Come on, we all have nights like that." He suddenly gestures toward the empty seat in front of him. "Can I join you? Would I be interrupting?"

"Not at all," I say, sliding the seat over to him. "I'd love it."

Adam looks at me as he sits and our eyes stay on each other long past when they should. "My God, you look amazing," he says. "I don't think I've ever seen you look so good." His green eyes peer into mine, and then he takes a breath. "What bothered me about the night we hooked up wasn't the fact that you were high," he says. "Or, I should say, what bothered me more than the fact that you were high was hearing after the fact that you'd also hooked up with Gus." His eyes stay on me the entire time he talks.

"I know, but that didn't mean anything," I say.

His eyes flicker over me and he looks the slightest bit cruel. "You and Gus or you and me? After a while, isn't it hard to tell the difference between which ones mean something and which ones don't?"

"No, it's not," I say. I hadn't planned to tell him about being sober, and feel wholly unprepared for some kind of "this is me now" speech but I can't seem to stop myself. "I have to tell you something."

"No, hear me out," he says. "I really liked you, and that hurt me."

"But I get it—"

"It's just that . . . I don't know, Amelia. You're such a cool girl, but I don't know. . . . You're wild. And while I love that—it's part of what attracted me to you from the beginning—being around you that night made me realize, I guess, that I'm not."

There's a pause, and I realize he's done. "Can I talk now?" I ask.

He nods. "Yeah. Sorry about that rant."

"It's okay," I say, subconsciously putting my hand on top of his before realizing what I'm doing and snatching it back. "It's just that I'm now a reformed wild woman. I'm sober." I glance down and then force myself to look him in the eye. "And, well, I'm not at the part of my recovery where I start apologizing to everyone yet, but can I just say that I'm sorry for the hurtful and silly things I did?"

He nods, looking extremely surprised.

"The fact is, I had a great time with you that night, and it wasn't about the coke," I continue. "The coke was actually the only thing *wrong* with that entire experience." He's about to say something but I keep talking. "And maybe it's because I'm sober now or maybe I would have seen it anyway but what happened with you *did* mean something to me." I find myself unable to look him in the eye when I say that.

He smiles. "So you're sober?" He's looking either stunned or confused, and since at least half of L.A. is sober, he surely couldn't be confused. "You mean, you don't drink or anything?"

I nod and then shake my head. "Yes—I mean, no I don't."

"You don't even smoke pot?"

I smile. I've pretty much always hated pot. It would just make me more paranoid than usual that nobody could understand anything I was saying. Right when I was first getting into buying coke, it occurred to me that regularly buying pot would be far less expensive than getting coke so, in an effort to get myself hooked on a more economical drug, I bought an ounce and smoked it for three days straight. And that's when I proved to myself once and for all that I hated it.

"No, not even pot," is all I say.

"My God, that's amazing," he says. "Congratulations."

"Thanks," I say. "It feels great."

Adam still seems to be in shock. "But I mean you . . ." He shakes his head, as if trying to clear up space in his brain for this information. "You were the ultimate party girl."

Smiling, I opt not to tell him about my new column. I'm enjoying this interaction far too much to allow it to turn into a conversation about work. "Well, now I'm the ultimate ex–party girl," I say.

He smiles as he looks at me with mock seriousness. "Do you think the bar at Jones will survive without your business?"

After we both laugh, I ask, "So what about you? How's Norm's?"

He grins. "Still standing, I assume. But not really my concern anymore."

"You quit?"

He nods. "I got a series."

"Are you serious? Which one?" It never really crossed my mind that Adam would become a really successful actor; most of the aspiring actors I know seem to get, if anything, a small role in an indie that no one sees outside of Sundance, or like a one-line part on *Without a Trace*.

"*The Agency*."

My mouth goes slightly agape: *The Agency* is Darren Star's new dramedy about the lives of four young male real estate agents. "Are you serious?"

He nods. "It's crazy, I know. I'm the only unknown."

"Congratulations," I say, leaning over to hug him. "That's incredible."

"Incredibly convenient, too," he says as we disentangle, "seeing as I was getting so sick of Norm's that I was on the verge of pouring soup on the next person who ordered it."

I laugh but in my head I'm thinking, *It figures. Just as soon as I'm sane enough to realize how adorable Adam is, he gets on a series and will now have women fighting over him like he's the last pair of Hudson jeans at a sample sale.*

Adam's cell phone rings and he doesn't answer it but glances at the time and seems to realize he has to be somewhere. "Damn, I have to go," he says, looking like he doesn't want to, "but it's really fantastic to see you."

I feel myself panicking. I could have had the moment we were having go on, like, forever, and yet it's ending. I want to do something but I'm not sure what. *He said he "really liked" me,* I think as I sit there trying to look casual. *Why did he use the past tense? When exactly do you stop "really liking" someone?*

Then he says, "I have to go to New York for publicity stuff for a month or so, but can we go out when I'm back?"

I can't help but smile. "Definitely," I say, wondering if I should try to pin him down to a specific date. I had a roommate once who always said it was good to nail guys down to a time and place if you really liked them. *Girls are allowed to be aggressive now,* she'd say. *This isn't the fifties.* But she also terrified most every man she came into contact with and stayed in on weekend nights so she could read the dictionary. "Have a great trip," I finally say.

"I will," he says, then leans down to give me a kiss on the cheek and adds, "I'll talk to you soon." As I watch him walk away, I wish that I had a time machine that could make it be "a month or so" already. Just then, Adam turns around and walks back to me. "How much do you know about puppies?" he asks.

I think about the dogs we had when I was growing up and then about Tiger. "Some," I say weakly.

"Well, I got one—a golden retriever—and while she's basically the cutest thing I've ever seen in my life, I don't know entirely how to handle her. I've only had her a week and she's already chewed through almost my entire sneaker collection. And she runs in circles around my apartment, like she's just inhaled helium or something."

I laugh. "Inhaled helium?" I ask.

"Weird imagery for a dog, I realize," he says. "Point is, right now she's sitting in my apartment, potentially tearing the entire thing to shreds, and I could definitely use a wise woman's help in taming him."

I stand up. "Should we take two cars or one?" I ask.

"One," he says, smiling. "You're fun to drive."

"If it hadn't been for cocaine, I probably would have been a practicing, miserable alcoholic my whole life," I say, as Adam drives us on the 10. I see a smile creep onto his face as he switches lanes, and I playfully punch him. "Glad you're so amused by my sad tale of addiction and recovery."

His tentative smile breaks into a mammoth grin. "I'm not amused. Just happy."

I smile and ask, "And what are you so happy about?"

He gestures from me back to him. "This. You. The way you talk. All of it. If I could bottle your voice, pheromones, and words, I'd be a rich man."

I laugh. I'm about to give him a hard time for being such a cheeseball, but instead I just grin. I reach over and grab his right hand, placing it under my left leg, and it feels like the most natural gesture in the world. "I feel lucky right now," I say. Adam smiles as he exits the freeway, and then he bursts out laughing.

"Let me guess: just laughing out of the joy of this moment?" I ask.

"Sort of," he laughs. "That, and the memory of you sleep-singing the last time you were in my car."

Now I start cracking up. "Christ, why didn't you drive me to the nearest insane asylum?" I ask, cringing at the memory.

"Don't think I didn't want to," he says, smiling. "But then I knew I'd never have a chance with you." Still chuckling, he pulls up in front of a garage in Venice. "Now prepare yourself for a creature so cute, she even gives you a run for your money." Adam stops the car, jumps out, and rushes to open the door for me. "My lady," he says, giving me a mock bow.

"Sir," I say, mock bowing back, opting not to confess what a horrific surrogate Mom I was to Tiger. "Please bring me to my arch nemesis, the other woman vying for your love." As soon as the word "love" is out of my mouth, I want to hurl. The primary way to terrify a man—probably right behind sleep-singing in his car—is to tell him you love him. I hadn't, of course, but the word is potent enough on its own.

But Adam doesn't seem remotely ruffled. "Don't you worry, now," he says, leading me down a path to his apartment. "There's enough love in my heart for both of you." As he opens the door and an adorable, tiny golden retriever comes bounding over to him and immediately starts humping his leg, I tell myself not to make too much over the fact that he said the L-word back. And I don't really have time, seeing as the image of this tiny dog thrusting back and forth on his shin like her very life depends on it is so hilarious that I immediately lose it.

"I thought you said she was a girl!" I gasp, between laughs.

"She is!" he shrieks, cracking up himself. "Doris, stop!" he yells at the dog, who seems to take that as a cue to hump Adam's leg all the more furiously. Adam looks at me. "Is that totally weird—a female dog being this sex-crazed? Is Doris some kind of a mutant, gender-bent pervert—possibly a preop transsexual?"

"Doris?" I ask, actually trying to get myself to stop laughing. "What kind of a dog name is that?"

"It's not," he says, gesturing for me to pull Doris the dog off him, which I do. Falling back onto the floor, Adam sighs. "It's my favorite grandmother's name," he says. I look at him, not sure if he's kidding, and let Doris go. Instead of rushing back over to Adam, she digs under his couch, where she seems to have stashed a roll of toilet paper. "Oh, God," he says, watching Doris grab the toilet paper in her mouth and start tearing it apart. "She loves to TP the place," he says, smiling, gesturing for me to come sit next to him. "She's worse than a drunk teenager on Halloween." I sit on the ground, next to where he's lying down, and he pulls himself up and faces me. I see Doris kick the toilet paper across the room and lunge at it, then skid with it in the other direction.

"We should probably take that away from her," I say. "I predict nothing good can come from this."

Adam moves closer to me. I can suddenly hear my heart beating in my chest as he moves less than a foot away, staring at me and not breaking eye contact. "Screw the dog," he says. "I'm sorry but she's just going to have to share me with you." He leans in and, before I can wonder if he's going to kiss me and if it's going to feel as amazing as it did the last time, our lips are touching and pressing together and opening and meshing as perfectly as two things not belonging to the same person could.

After being with Adam—two hours of the best kissing of my life, followed by him telling me he had to pack because he was taking the red-eye that night, both of us saying we couldn't wait to talk and see each other soon—I feel so much better that I realize I'm perfectly capable of writing at home without succumbing to any urges to call Alex. Now that I'm filled up with joyful thoughts about Adam, the idea of coke is actually back to sounding completely disgusting again. So I go home, ignore all the thoughts I'm having about how I don't know the first thing about writing a column, and just type.

I decide to write about Mark's wedding, and start by titling the piece "Here Come the Groomsmen." And then it just flows.

It's not every day that a wedding takes place in the house where you grew up. And it's certainly not every day that a wedding takes place in the house where you grew up, and you end the evening in bed with two of the groomsmen. Then again, everyday experiences have never really been my thing.

I keep going from there, describing the competitiveness of my ménage partners in the sauna, the triangular dance we did all night, and finally the bedroom antics, adding, as almost an afterthought, the cousin-of-the-bride incident earlier in the evening. I decide to leave nothing out, except for the alcohol. It's obvious that Tim thinks of my partying as the frosting to my fabulous life, not understanding that without the drugs and alcohol, all of these so-called exciting things would never have happened. And since Tim wants this column to be funny and sexy, and there's nothing funny or sexy about drug addiction, rehab, and sobriety, I opt not to mention the succession of Amstel Lights we were drinking or the bottle of champagne I'd had at dinner. If people wanted to believe I could be this wild without any chemicals in my system, they were welcome to.

When I finish the column and print it up, I try to read it the way a stranger would. And, I have to say, I'm impressed: it's amusing, self-deprecating, and somewhat titillating. Then I start to second-guess myself, deciding that since I wasn't pulling my hair out over it, it couldn't be good. *How could I possibly be making the equivalent of a month's salary at* Absolutely Fabulous, I think, *to write something funny off the top of my head?* And then I hear Rachel's voice telling me that sometimes things are easy. People in recovery call it the "easier, softer way," and as I think about that, I realize how so much of what Rachel and Tommy and Justin and everyone else has told me just flows naturally through my brain now.

Before I can talk myself out of it, I e-mail the piece to Tim and try not to obsess over what his reaction is going to be. So then I switch over to my other newfound obsession, Adam. I decide to Google him and discover that there's all this information out there about this "unknown Norm's waiter" who just landed a major part on the hottest new TV show. I'm getting fully into fantasy mode now, imagining the two of us on the red carpet at a premiere and having picnics at the top of Runyon when I realize what I'm doing. One of the reasons it's not a good idea to get into a relationship in your first year, Tommy always said, is that alcoholics and addicts can do anything alcoholically. Books, movies, Pop-Tarts, Cosabella thong-buying, dating—whatever it is, if you can lose yourself in an obsession with it, we will.

So I force myself to step away from the computer and set about cleaning my apartment, which always seems coated in a thin or thick layer of cat fur, and the activity feels good. I don't recall actually enjoying the act of cleaning before. I know I've liked it when things have been clean, but having fun while Dust Bustering and scrubbing is altogether new to me. I start blasting Eminem and singing along as I clean the living room floor and the music is so loud that I almost don't hear the phone ring. But I see the red light on my cordless flashing so I turn down Eminem and answer.

"Hello," I say, as I plop down on the couch.

"Amelia, darling," says Tim, "John and I were just sitting here discussing how we have to do big, glamorous, sexy shots of you to accompany each of your columns. We were thinking of using Jean-Paul Blanc unless you have a photographer you prefer."

I try to slow my heart, which seems to be racing like Lance Armstrong in his last mile. Jean-Paul Blanc does all the *Vanity Fair* cover shoots and his photos are constantly being exhibited.

"Pictures of me by him—really?" I manage. "Are you sure?"

"Of course I'm sure," he laughs. "In fact, it turns out that he has a hole in his schedule—meaning, if you're game and approve Jean-Paul, we could get you shot this week."

I don't know what to say, and don't want to ask him again if he's sure. "So does that mean you like what I turned in?"

"Like it?" he brays. "*Like* it? Darling, it's ace. You and 'Party Girl' are going to take us to the next level. I have no doubts now—not that I did before, mind you. But after reading your copy, which is lively and sexy and at times laugh-out-loud funny, we're all terribly excited."

My heart continues to do its dance and I don't say anything because I don't think I know the words that are supposed to accompany
the ecstatic feeling flowing through me. In a strange way, this moment
reminds me of sitting in Robert's office being fired. *This can't be happening*, my inner voice seems to be saying, *but it is.*

19

"*Tres belle,*" Jean-Paul coos as his camera snaps away. Three assistants flank him, holding various and sundry lights and pieces of equipment, and a hairdresser, makeup artist, and clothing stylist stand to the side—ready to rush in should they see something on me that doesn't look exactly perfect.

While this shoot—which is taking place in the penthouse of the Chateau Marmont, which I happen to know rents for $10,000 a day— is far more exciting and surreal than anything I've ever experienced, I'm doing a decent job of acting like I'm used to having everything re-volve around me, and assistants fetching me Evian, apples, or really whatever else I might desire. I'm afraid that if I let on how shocked I am by the sheer amount of money clearly being spent on my shoot, I'll reveal just how small-time I am.

The stylist, a well-known one whom I'd actually interviewed over the phone several times while I was working at *Absolutely Fabulous*, had greeted me when I got here with racks of everything from Armani gowns and Gucci blouses to Chloe suits and Marc Jacobs jeans.

"Tim said he wanted us to shoot the photos for your next several columns," the stylist informed me. "Since we don't know what's going to be in the columns yet, he said we should choose a bunch of differ-ent looks: casual, dressy, sexy, demure, whatever we could think of."

I nod and decide not to remind her that we've spoken before. *It was,* I think, *a lifetime ago.*

She has me try on beautiful skirts, dresses, shirts and jeans—even lingerie from La Perla—and while I usually obsess over my protruding stomach, she seems to know exactly what's going to hide the tummy and play up my assets and I end up feeling like all I've ever needed in order to feel constantly beautiful was a stylist.

Jean-Paul came over to introduce himself when we were first going through the clothes, and I immediately found him sexy, even though the stylist has already warned me that he's a "dog," "pig," and every other animal you can imagine. Figures I'd like him.

"Ah, you are truly exquisite," he said with a strong French accent and devilish smile. "The photos will take themselves." He continued to watch me as the stylist pinned the gown I was wearing so that it hoisted my cleavage up.

And then, once I've been made up and gelled and sprayed and shellacked until I look like the supermodel version of myself, Jean-Paul starts snapping. The entirety of my knowledge about modeling has been culled from *America's Next Top Model*, but one thing I'm positive of is that I love having my picture taken. Apparently, I cried nonstop for my first three months of life, until a professional photographer showed up to shoot me and I suddenly gave him the biggest, most toothless grin a person who's only been alive for ninety days possibly could. As I switch my poses around, Jean-Paul mumbles words like *magnifique*, *belle*, and *tres belle*.

In between shots, Jean-Paul and I smoke while his assistants set up the lights for the next set of pictures, and a stand-in takes the place where I'll be. Then, when I'm done with my cigarette, the stylist comes and gets me to change. Rather than allowing all of this treatment to bring out my inner diva, I'm the very picture of kindness, asking everyone else how they're doing. I swear, if I was treated like this all the time, I'd be a pleasure to be around 24-7.

We're getting ready to do our last set for the day—I'm in an insanely flattering purple, pink, and black-striped Missoni gown and tottering around in high-heeled purple Jimmy Choo's—when Tim and John show up.

"You look stunning," Tim says, as he leans in to kiss each of my cheeks. John trails behind him and gives me an awkward salute. Then Tim turns to Jean-Paul. "Have you done the champagne-drinking shot yet?"

I sort of inadvertently flinch at the word "champagne" as Jean-Paul hits his head. "*Mon Dieu*, I almost forgot," he says.

Jean-Paul says something to two of his lackeys and they leave the room, then come back holding these plastic contraptions that they piece together to make an enormous, six-foot-tall champagne Plexiglas. Tim shows Jean-Paul how he'd like me to sit in it as John lets in a room service waiter delivering bottles of Dom Perignon. And even though I may well be in the middle of the single most validating day of my life so far, I grow concerned enough by what's happening to wander over to Tim and ask him if I can speak to him for a moment.

"Of course, go ahead," he says, continuing to stand there next to Jean-Paul and his minions. Couldn't he see that what I wanted to say was private?

Completely uncomfortable, I force myself to ask, "Is it absolutely imperative that we do this champagne thing?"

Tim looks slightly flummoxed. "Oh, do you not like it?" For the first time since we've met, I get a glimpse of the fact that Tim may not be perfect. He looks, in fact, slightly irritated by my intrusion.

"Well, I just was wondering, do I have to be holding champagne in the shot?"

Tim, now making no effort to hide his annoyance, sighs. "Amelia. You're the Party Girl. We have to convince readers of that not only through your column, but also visually—through pictures." He's suddenly talking to me like I'm seven and don't understand what the word "visually" means.

I nod. Ridiculously, I feel tears start to well up, but I close my eyes for a second and force them to go away. It seems like it should be simple enough to explain my situation to Tim, but I just can't seem to. *Tell him you're sober*, my head says. And then I think, *Hell, no. He'll start asking questions and figure out that you're really not this wild-and-crazy girl anymore.* Instead, I try channeling the confident, egoless diva-in-the-making that I'd been acting like all day.

"Is there going to be a problem?" Tim asks, quite sternly, just as John wanders over to see what's going on.

I take a breath and push all my negative thoughts to the back of my brain. "No. Not at all."

Jean-Paul asks, "So you are ready, *ma cherie?*" I nod, allow two of the assistants to hoist me into the mammoth champagne glass, get as comfortable as I can in an enormous piece of plastic, and accept the bottle and glass of champagne that the set designer hands me. Tim and John move to the back of the room while Jean-Paul starts clicking and muttering his French compliments.

But the magic seems to be gone. Before, I'd been feeling natural and happy and pretty just by smiling or laughing or gazing into the camera and thinking of funny or intense moments. But now, lounging in this life-size champagne glass, I feel forced. I keep thinking, *This is what a girl who's playing the part of a "Party Girl" should look like.*

Jean-Paul apparently doesn't notice because he keeps shooting and cooing at me and calling me *belle* and *tres belle*. I try not to concentrate on the fact that my lips and nose are less than a foot from a glass of champagne.

When I got into rehab, I was perfectly willing to admit that I had a problem with coke and sleeping pills, but I still never really bought into this whole idea of being "alcoholic." I'd told Tommy on one of my first days at Pledges that I was willing to consider the fact that alcoholism and drug addiction might be the same thing, but I still wasn't convinced. In fact, in those meetings, when people introduced themselves by saying their name and the word "alcoholic," I clung steadfastly to what I truly knew about myself, so I replaced the word "alcoholic" with the word "addict." I wasn't the only one. A guy who used to be in Twisted Sister, who'd done the Pledges program the month before me and I'd heard share in the alumni meetings, was also clinging hard to the word "addict."

And sitting in the champagne glass, with the scent of Dom Perignon wafting up my nostrils, I become more convinced than ever that my problem never has been with alcohol. The glass is so close that I could easily tip the flute into my mouth and sip—a slew of assistants would surely spring to attention at the opportunity to re- fill it—but I really have no desire. All these wonderful things in my life—this new gig, my friendship with Justin, the reconnection with Stephanie and potential romance with Adam, not to mention the overall sense of peace that seems to have replaced all those self- absorbed feelings of misery that I'd come to accept as normal—are, I feel, completely related to my having gotten sober. And I'm not inter- ested in screwing any of that up, even if it means having to go along with this notion of being an "alcoholic" without actually believing it.

I seem to be shooting okay pictures during the entire time I'm zoning out and thinking of the proximity of the glass to my lips, be- cause Jean-Paul is looking genuinely thrilled and Tim and John are smiling as they whisper to each other and point at me. And I think, *Screw what the people at Pledges are going to think if they see this picture of me that's essentially an ode to champagne. I'm wearing a Missoni gown in the Chateau Marmont's penthouse suite being fawned over by a pho- tographer who's a household name. Why the hell should I care what any- one thinks?*

20

I'm dreaming about signing autographs—and in the dream, my hand-writing doesn't look the way it does in real life but like it did when I was little and just learning how to write cursive letters—when the phone wakes me up.

I usually sleep through the phone, but I'm being devil-dialed—that is, someone is calling my home phone, and when I don't answer, they're calling my cell phone, and when I don't answer, they're calling my home phone again. Eventually, I reach over and garble a hello.

"Oh, thank God you're there." It's Tim, sounding more ex-cited than I've ever heard him. "What's your schedule like? Can you make it?"

"Make what?" I try to move my cat off me so I can sit up.

"Haven't you gotten any of the messages from me or Nadine?"

"Who's Nadine?"

"The publicist we hired to promote you."

"Publicist?"

"Sweetheart, get yourself out of bed and to your computer. Nadine has proven herself to be worth every penny: according to *Page Six*, *Gawker*, Perez Hilton, and Liz Smith, you're a sensation."

"Me?!"

"We slipped advance issues to the gossips, not sure how they would react. And each of them went bloody crazy for your column."

"My column's *out*?" I hadn't seen the photos of the shoot, let alone the actual magazine.

"Oh, dear. We didn't send you a copy? Well, I'll have one messengered over right away. In the meantime, the *Today* show wants to do a segment on you ASAP and if you won't be too knackered, we'd love to put you on the red-eye tonight—in fact, I'd come along but I have a damn dinner with the Ford people here. Regardless, *The View* wanted you, too, but Nadine thinks it makes more sense to wait and put you on there once a few more columns have come out."

For some reason, my heart isn't going a mile a minute and I don't feel like I'm out of my body observing a girl named Amelia Stone receiving this absurdly good news. I guess I'm getting better at handling surreality. But glancing around my paint-splattered bedroom, I'm highly aware of the ridiculous dichotomy between my world and the one I'm hearing about on the phone.

Tim continues to talk excitedly, about how I'll probably want to join AFTRA so I can get paid for my TV appearances, about how we might want to try to sell a book of my columns now even though only one of them has been written, and about how we should set me up with a film and TV agent in order to try to sell the rights, and yet all I seem to be focusing on is the fact that I'm going to be in New York, where Adam is. *Focus*, I tell myself, *on being fabulous*.

By the time I shower, brush my teeth, and feed the cats, three copies of *Chat* have arrived at my front door in an enormous brown envelope. I bring them upstairs and place one in my lap. The magazine is spectacular, from its stunning cover shot of Jude Law through its table of contents—which lists an essay on literary salons by Dave Eggers, a humor piece by Augusten Burroughs, and an interview with Jude Law, done by Jay McInerney. *How on Earth did I get included in this group?* I wonder as I flip to my column.

And there I am, Missoni-encased and lying in the enormous plastic champagne glass, legs extended, wearing an enormous, toothy grin. *Is that really me?* I wonder as I examine the photo. It looks like a far more flawless and ecstatic version of me—me if I'd been born into a different family, era, and life. There's no evidence of the discomfort I was feeling when the picture was taken.

The copy, too, looks and reads much better than it did when it was just a Microsoft Word document on my computer. Maybe it's just seeing it in *Chat*'s elegant font? I notice with surprise that Tim made almost no changes to my text.

Then I log onto the gossip websites and read about this "stunning" "sexpot" whose debut in *Chat* "hints at what is surely to be a lengthy and notable career," according to Liz Smith. "Forget Carrie Bradshaw and Candace Bushnell," raves Perez Hilton. "Amelia Stone writes about what sex today is really like. Mr. Big? Try Mr. Bigs." *Page Six* praises the column and wonders if Stone will delve into her lengthy love relationship with sexy singer-songwriter Kane (now married to an actress) in future columns. *I always knew I was underappreciated*, I think as I imagine Brian and the entire *Absolutely Fabulous* staff gathered around his computer reading these items.

My phone rings, and even though I haven't had a chance to even listen to the morning's messages yet, I answer it. "Amelia, how are you?" a voice booms. "This is Richard Johnson from the *New York Post*. Do you have a minute?"

I try, probably unsuccessfully, to keep the excitement out of my voice. "Richard, it's great to hear from you," I say. Remembering what Tim had instructed me, I add, "Would you mind if I referred you to my publicist?" I expect Richard to laugh, or at least act snippy, but instead he says, "Not at all." I suddenly feel like I'm acting out a scene from one of those movies you'd watch and go, *Hah—like all this would ever happen to someone.*

21

"Oh, you're adorable!" a brunette in a wraparound Diane Von Furstenberg dress shrieks as I make my way through JFK toward a driver carrying a sign with my name on it. Even though I managed to sleep a few hours on the flight, the red-eye has left me exhausted enough to not hear her very well or even imagine she's speaking to me. She looks like the kind of person who would typically give me the once-up-once-down fashion disapproval look, but her voice is so much kinder and softer than it looks like it would be that I'm completely thrown off and for a second I think that she's a random, well-dressed lunatic. "It's great to finally meet you in person," she says, pumping my hand with enthusiasm, then adds, "I'm Nadine, your publicist. I hope you don't mind my intruding on what would have been a peaceful ride into the city, but I wanted to be able to talk to you before you go on *Today*."

I smile and shake her hand, and she grabs it so that she can pull me along as we follow the driver out to his car. It seems like such a girlish move for someone who looks so sophisticated, but I'm too busy trying to keep up with her *Chipmunks*-speed style of speaking that I barely have time to ponder it.

"Tim had told me you wouldn't need any media coaching, but I just wanted to go over a couple of things," she says as we get in the car. It lurches forward and she pulls out a notebook scrawled with lists and filled with Post-It notes of more lists. "Now, I've been pitching you as the embodiment of the modern-day, sexually evolved, intelligent woman. A Marilyn Monroe for the twenty-first century, but not so out of it or self-destructive. Carrie Fisher with sex appeal. The woman who really lives *Sex and the City*. Capische? She has a sex drive and she's not afraid of it. If she goes to a wedding and can't decide between two groomsmen, she takes them both to bed. Am I right?"

I nod, finding myself so caught up in the notion of this perfectly evolved and confident-sounding creature that I forget we're even talking about me. *I'm not sexually evolved*, I think. *The main word I associate with my own sexuality is "confusion."* In the column I'd just tried to have a sense of humor about what I'd done. But as Nadine talks, I find myself a bit won over. I liked the idea of being a sexually evolved woman. It makes me sound so much more together than I actually feel.

"But you're not slutty," Nadine continues, making a face. "You're not Jenna Jameson—who, by the way, I represented and actually found to be quite sweet. You're classy, with both a brain and self-knowledge. You're the ideal modern-day woman."

I nod. How could I do anything else?

"For the *Today* show, I want you to just be you. Always keeping in mind, of course, that you are representing *Chat* and all that *Chat* stands for. You're witty but not silly, aware but still carefree, serious and yet spontaneous. In essence, you're wild but you also know exactly what you're doing. Make sense?"

I nod.

Nadine continues, "After this, I think our best plan of attack is to sit quiet?" She suddenly starts turning her voice up at the end of sentences so that they're questions, and I get the sense she's doing it so that I feel more included. "Let everyone see who you are, and make them want to find out more, but don't let them have it yet? Until, of course, you have a few columns out, when we put you on *The View*? And oh my God you look a little overwhelmed? Am I overwhelming you?"

I hadn't realized any anxiety I was feeling was actually apparent on my face but something about Nadine's master plan is starting to make me feel dizzy.

"I'm fine," I say, "just a little tired."

"Oh, no!" Now it's her turn to look alarmed. She looks like the kind of person who might typically gaze at me with some sort of disapproval, and I immediately know that my gray James Perse sundress isn't appropriate. "We'll need to stop by the Marc Jacobs showroom to pick up something a bit brighter. You look adorable, of course, but we need something a little more TV friendly? You won't be able to check into the Royalton until after the *Today* show, but you can rest then, before we have dinner with *Chat* editors tonight at Schillers? And then it would be nice if we could put in an appearance at Butter afterward? Just so we could get something in one of the gossip columns tomorrow about how you came into town and managed to be everywhere all at once?"

I nod, suddenly feeling the effect of the double-shot espresso I had on the flight and realizing I'm excited. "Everything sounds great." I smile. "Bring on the Marc Jacobs showroom."

Nadine seems to exhale for the first time, and smiles back at me. "Are you sure you're okay with going there? I know you might be feeling rushed so I could call ahead and let them know that you're not going to wear Marc today unless we're guaranteed that no one else is in the showroom?"

Remember in *Pretty Woman* when Richard Gere is giving Julia Roberts strawberries and champagne and she reminds him that she's a sure thing and he doesn't need to woo her? I want to say some version of this to Nadine, to explain to her that everything that's happening is already beyond my wildest dreams and she doesn't need to worry. But I feel fairly certain that stress is so built into her DNA that whatever I say won't calm her down.

"That's sweet but I don't think it will be necessary," I say, as Nadine's cell phone starts bleeping. She gives me a manic grin and a thumbs-up as she answers the phone.

As Nadine starts chatting into her phone, I sit back and look out the window, willing myself to be as cavalier about everything as Nadine seems to expect me to be.

"Do you think the modern-day woman should be able to sleep with whomever she wants to?" Meredith Viera asks me.

"Well, I guess that depends on how often she wants to," I say, smiling. "I don't think anyone should look at sex like it's an all-you-can eat buffet." Meredith and Matt crack up.

I'm shockingly calm and composed on TV. I'd sort of assumed that I'd be filled with the same neuroses that used to plague me before I did anything where a lot of people would be watching me but I can only imagine that being at Pledges—where I'd grown accustomed to regularly sharing my most personal details with a group of strangers—has eviscerated any nervousness I used to feel about being the center of attention. With the camera on, I feel witty, attractive, and charming—qualities that I only occasionally feel I possess in real life. I think of my first three colicky months of life and the toothless grin I gave the photographer who came to photograph me. *Turn on the lights and watch me shine*, I think, as I answer one of Matt's questions.

While I field a question Meredith asks me—if I've heard from either guy since the column came out (*That would be no*, I'd said, which was met with extensive laughter)—I marvel at how easy this TV thing is. It feels like being at a party where the entire focus is on me, and everyone else is just dying to laugh and be entertained by what I'm saying.

"Let's just say that I wouldn't mind if either of them disappeared into the ether," I add, and again, I'm rewarded with the sound of laughter. How come my friends and family have never been so appreciative of my sense of humor?

Even though it feels like we just started, before I know it, Meredith turns to the camera and says, "If you know what's good for you, get yourself down to the newsstand, grab *Chat*, and check out Amelia

Stone's Party Girl column. If anyone represents the modern-day woman we all want to be, it's her."

And then it's over. I shake each of their hands, feeling as close to high as I have since getting sober, and make my way to the green room where Nadine is waiting.

"Honey, you were brilliant!" she shrieks. "Who knew you were so funny?"

Even though her question is clearly rhetorical, I feel somewhat compelled to fill the silence that follows. Silence between two people tends to terrify me, sending me into a full-blown panic that the other person is in the process of discovering how uninteresting I actually am. But I'm so buzzed from the TV shoot—feeling like serotonin is suddenly dashing through my veins with stormlike speed—that I decide it doesn't matter. And then Nadine says something that makes me feel even more confident that I probably don't have to do much else for people to think I'm interesting now.

"There's virtually nothing you can do to stop yourself from becoming huge now."

For the next few hours, my BlackBerry rings nonstop—apparently everyone and their mother watches the *Today* show because as soon as I clear out the congratulatory messages that have gathered, the voicemail fills up again. I'm getting ready for dinner and am just about to toss the damn device out the window of my hotel room when it rings again.

"Hello?" I sort of say and sort of shriek.

"Amelia? Is this a bad time?" When I realize whose voice it is, I want to dance a jig across the room.

"Adam!" It's the first time I've heard from him since the day we spent together and I don't make any effort to hide how happy I am to hear from him. "How are you?"

I expect him to launch into the same speech everyone else has been giving me about how funny and natural I was on TV, but he doesn't. "Good," he says. "Just been in back-to-back interviews for the show. The only problem is that I'm completely distracted."

"Distracted? Why?" I smile as I lie down on my king-size bed.

"Honestly? Because I can't stop thinking about you."

Hooray, I think. I wish for superhuman powers that could allow me to break through the phone and touch him.

"Me?" I ask, dying to hear more.

"Yes, you. Spending time with you the other day just sort of sparked something obsessive in me, I guess."

I allow the pleasure of hearing these words bathe me in happiness for a second. Then I say, "I'm thinking about you a lot, too." Fuck the "rules" and playing hard to get. "And guess what, Adam? I'm in New York."

"What? Are you serious? For how long?"

"Just till tomorrow."

"This sucks," he says. "They have me on this insane interview schedule the rest of the day and night."

I glance at the clock and realize I only have forty-five minutes to get uptown to meet the *Chat* editors for dinner. "And I have to go to dinner and this club and—"

"Wait, have you even told me why you're here?" he asks. "Oh, shit. They're motioning for me to go back into the room. Why don't we just stick with our plan to see each other in L.A.? I'll call you in a week or two when I'm back."

After we hang up, I marvel over the fact that this phone call has made me feel about a thousand times better than the entire collection of enthusiasm on my voicemail. I'm sitting on my bed thinking about that while I rock back and forth and grin like some special ed student when I hear Nadine knocking on my door and telling me she has the car downstairs to take us to dinner.

At dinner, where a few of the editors split a bottle of wine and the rest of us drink sparkling water, I listen to basically every single one of them call me a genius, and act like this is something I'm actually used to or feel I deserve. Afterward, we go to Butter, where a steady stream of well-wishers come up and congratulate me on my column or tell me how funny I was on the *Today* show. A Nicole Miller publicist hands me her card and tells me she'd like to send me some outfits that she hopes I'll consider wearing "out on the town." A *Playboy* senior editor asks me if I'd be willing to write something for him and then hits on me when I explain that my *Chat* contract is exclusive. An actor who's on *CSI* drunkenly confesses his love for me and tries sticking his hand down my pants. Eventually, I return to the Royalton to sleep, and before I know it, I'm back on a plane home.

Just after the plane boards, I get a call from Mom, who's a bit underwhelmed by the process of explaining to people how she feels about her daughter writing about a ménage à trois experience at a wedding she hosted. The details I'd given Mom about the column had been deliberately sparse, both because I hadn't known quite how to broach the content topic and because I thought my chances were decent that Mom would be too submerged in her poetry world to be more than even tangentially aware of her daughter's "highly fictionalized" column. But appearing on the *Today* show was clearly like taking a banner and waving it in front of her face.

"I just don't understand why you can't write about something that's meaningful to you now," she says.

"Mom, no one in the world at large wants to read about the adventures of a girl who goes to meetings at Pledges and hangs out with her gay best friend."

"Nonsense—you just think that because you haven't tried to write it yet."

"Jesus," I find myself screeching, causing a model I just saw on the cover of *Elle* who's sliding into a seat a few feet away from me to glance over with some concern. I lower my voice. "Why can't you just be happy for me?"

"Oh, I am happy for you, honey," she says, sounding anything but.

I've never met someone less able to hide how she truly feels than my mother—or maybe it's that I've never been quite so skilled at interpreting someone's subtext. "And Dad is, too."

The mere concept of my dad reading my column is horrifying and a thought I'm planning to repress as soon as humanly possible, but luckily, I won't have to hear about this from him since Mom is the family's unofficial gossip columnist and spokesperson when it comes to dramatic events.

"Look, Mom, they're asking me to turn my phone off," I say, even though passengers are still coming onto the plane and all anyone has done to me since I've gotten on board is smile ear to ear. I hang up and think about calling Adam, but it feels like it's too soon. I could phone Stephanie, but I already talked to her a few times yesterday. Justin has been hanging out with his old boyfriend again and has been increasingly distant, and Rachel will remind me that humility is especially important when the outside world is validating me. For the first time since I've been sober, I don't feel like being grateful. I was the one cracking up Meredith and Matt. I was the one being fawned over wherever I went. I'm publishing's latest sensation. With a slew of saved messages from well-wishers on my voicemail, why the hell can't I think of anyone to gloat about that to?

22

"Here we go," Tim says as the Town Car pulls up outside the Roosevelt Hotel. "You're on."

We've just had dinner at Mr. Chow's and are on our way into Brent Bolthouse's night at the Roosevelt, where Paris and Jessica Simpson are regulars and the paparazzi wait outside knowing that they can make their week's worth of money on this one night. It's all part of Tim and Nadine's plan to have me "out there" more, and while part of me loves the attention, this other part of me is exhausted by it. *It's a full-time job keeping up the persona of Party Girl*, I think as the driver opens the door and helps me out.

As we approach the throng of people gathered outside, the doorman, Andrew, lifts the velvet rope to let us through. "Hey, Amelia," he says, as I walk past, Tim and John on my heels. I spent years introducing myself to Andrew and he never gave me the time of day. Having people know me now is, while wonderful, also surprisingly unnerving. It makes me feel like I'm constantly under observation. But I smile at him and smooth down my cleavage-revealing Marc Jacobs silk dress.

As we walk toward the bar, I wonder if Adam is going to be here. It's been over two weeks since we talked in New York, and I'm shocked he hasn't called but I know there has to be a good reason. I keep seeing promos for his show and torturing myself with the idea that he's fallen for the main girl on it—a former Miss Teen USA in her acting debut—and forgotten all about me. And even though I know that I could call him, I can't seem to bring myself to. *A connec-tion, by its very definition, can't be one-sided,* I keep thinking. *Of course he's going to call.*

When we get to the bar, Tim asks me what I'd like. It's our first time out together and I've been preparing for this question for many days. Rachel has said that I don't need to tell anyone why I'm not drinking if I don't want to and that if somebody really wants an an-swer, I can always just say that I'm on antibiotics. *Just tell him you're sober now,* my mind says, as I scan the bottles lined up in front of me. *What's he going to do, take the column away?*

Instead I ask for a cranberry and soda and he just nods and orders that, along with vodka tonics for himself and John. I've been noticing lately that a lot of people just don't seem to think about alcohol all that much, and Tim could be one of them. *He probably thinks I'm just wild twenty-four hours a day, drunk or sober,* I think, and I can't decide if that's something I should be horrified by or relieved.

"So what have you gotten up to lately?" Tim asks as we settle into a booth. John looks up from his drink expectantly, and I suddenly feel enormous pressure to be all that they think I am. *Think of something,* my mind says, *quick.* I go over the past few days: Monday night I went to a meeting at Pledges to meet Justin but he didn't show, Tuesday I played with my cats, obsessed over Adam, and read the Pledges book. Wednesday? I can't remember what I did on Wednesday and I get mo-mentarily excited, thinking that I'll surely have an exciting story to share with them when I remember that I'd randomly flipped to this show on Animal Planet about polar bears and had become instantly riveted. I start to panic, thinking I'm surely going to disappoint them, when I remember the night I went to Guy's with Chad Milan and left with Rick Wilson. *It's not like I'm making it up,* I think. *I'm just fudging the dates a tiny bit.*

"Well," I say, "I went out with a CAA agent the other night."

Tim nods politely but looks a little disappointed.

"And left with this random, out-of-work actor I had a crush on when I was sixteen years old."

"No!" Tim shrieks disbelievingly, suddenly wearing a huge smile. He glances at John and adds, "You naughty girl."

"Well, I was looking for a way to get out of having to kiss the agent guy goodnight," I say, shrugging, like I think a modern, sexually evolved woman would. *Channel Angelina Jolie pre-her humanitarianism,* I say to myself as I continue to tell John and Tim about making out with Rick in the car, leaving the message for Chad and then being busted by him at the gym the next day.

"This is why she's so good," Tim says to John as he sips his drink. "She sees what she wants and goes after it, while the rest of us get mucked up in always trying to do the right thing." I nod and smile, thinking, *I am a total fraud. I can't stop thinking about Adam and don't do a damn thing about it, but I sit here and act like I'm some kind of warrior woman.* I will Tim and John to stop talking about me, and then marvel at the fact that I'm even thinking such a thing.

Suddenly, the music gets turned up louder. Tim and John continue to talk but because they're sitting next to each other and I'm across the table, I can't really hear them anymore so I pretend to look like I'm completely wrapped up in the scene around me, while inside I'm thinking about how I'd much rather be in a bubble bath.

Just then, the waitress stops at the table and deposits a tequila shot in front of me, motioning her head toward the bar where Jeremy Barrenbaum, a producer with a Sony deal, stands and smiles at me as he holds up his own tequila shot. I smile at him and look down at the shot.

"From a fan?" Tim asks, as he leans over and I nod. I glance down at the lime and salt the waitress is depositing on the table and when I look up, Jeremy Barrenbaum is standing right in front of me.

"Party Girl, would you do me the honor?" he asks, slurring his words slightly and holding out his shot. When I don't respond, he says, "Okay, fine—if you insist on doing body shots with me, I'll acquiesce."

Years ago, I'd had a crush on Jeremy. Someone had pointed him out to me at one of the first Hollywood parties I went to, mentioning that he had produced these two movies I'd liked and had dated this actress on *Melrose Place*. I'd thought he was cute, but knew for a fact that if he were a plumber and not a successful producer, I wouldn't necessarily think so. Later that night, someone introduced me to him and he spent the whole time we were talking glancing around, giving me the distinct feeling that he was simply killing time until someone more important or famous came along. Eventually, he excused himself to go talk to Rachel Hunter. After that, when we saw each other, we would do the sort of Hollywood head nod, that I-know-we've-met-but-maybe-one-or-both-of-us-don't-remember-the-other's-name, and when someone started to introduce us at a premiere last year, I explained that we already knew each other while he held out his hand expectantly, looking like he'd never laid eyes on me before. I'd wondered at the time if he just walked around doing that Hollywood head nod to everyone or if he was pretending not to know me as some kind of a power move. Was being introduced over and over and only occasionally acknowledging it a distinctly Hollywood tradition or did this happen in other cities?

"Here's to the best little wedding guest out there," he says, clicking his shot glass against mine. I watch him pick up my salt and pour it on his hand, lick it, take the shot and then reach down for a lime wedge and bite into it. The smell of tequila is so strong I feel like I've practically ingested it myself. "What's your problem?" he asks, gesturing to my still-full shot glass.

I glance at Tim and John, who are watching us with interest, and introduce everyone, after which there's an awkward pause. "Got sick on tequila in high school, and haven't been able to touch it since," I finally say, smiling. At least the first part was true. "How about I do a shot of something else?"

"Sure thing," Jeremy says. "I'll do another one with you." He motions the waitress over and she stands there expectantly.

"Hmmm," I say, wondering how the hell I'm going to get out of this. Then, buying time, I say to the waitress: "You know, for some reason I can't decide. Can I follow you to the bar so I can assess my options?" She shrugs and starts walking so I gesture to Jeremy, Tim, and John that I'll be right back before following her. And once we get to the bar, I remember how I'd drink from my parents' vodka and gin bottles in high school and fill them back up again with water. Why wouldn't the reverse of that work now? So I say to the waitress, "I know this sounds crazy, but can you give me two shot glasses and fill one with vodka and one with water?"

She glances at me for a second, then nods. I swear, nothing is too bizarre for L.A. waitresses. She's probably thrilled I'm not asking about the caloric intake of Absolut versus Ketel One. "Can I charge him for two shots?" she asks. I nod, and she hands me the vodka and water shots.

Oddly empowered by my water trick, I start to feel the "Party Girl" persona come over me the same way it did when I went on TV. Confidence and a sort of brazenness flood through me as I make my way back to Jeremy, swaying my body back and forth to the Jay Z song that's now blasting through the speakers. I reach the table, where Jeremy, Tim, and John are now chatting animatedly, and hand Jeremy his shot.

"Here's to running into each other," I say, in an attempt to figure out if he realizes I'm the same girl he's been introduced to before, or even if he cares.

"And to our continued relationship," Jeremy grins, clinking his glass with mine. He downs his shot as I chug my shot of water, crinkling my nose as if it were vodka. I swear I should win a fucking Oscar for this.

"God, I love Ketel One," Jeremy says, then takes out his cell phone and adds abruptly, "We should go out this week. What are your digits?"

I give him my number, wondering why it's him and not Adam wanting to go out with me this week. *Be excited*, I tell myself. *Tim and John are watching. And this would have been an entirely thrilling prospect at one point.*

Just then, a Kanye West song comes on and these two girls wearing bright tube tops and roughly inch-long jean skirts jump up on the bar to dance.

"Hey, Party Girl, you should be the one up there!" Jeremy shrieks exuberantly. Tim smiles and John nods. I shake my head and think, *I'm too old and way too sober for this shit,* just as Jeremy starts chanting, "Party Girl" over and over. Tim and John join in the chant, and the next thing I know, Jeremy is grabbing me by my waist and trying to hoist me over his shoulder onto the bar. When I notice his friends, two agent types, walking in our direction, I realize that it's too late to turn back now.

So I accept a bartender's hand as he helps me to my feet on the bar and feel all eighty or so people in the club staring at me. Trying to act like this is perfectly normal, I turn toward the two prepubescent-looking tube top girls and start dancing. I'm a good dancer—I don't flail my arms around spastically, nor do I just stand there and step back and forth self-consciously—but it can take me a few minutes to find my groove. Alcohol used to help with that. But now I have no alcohol and no crowd to surround me, just two girls whose ages together probably don't add up to mine. I suddenly remember once trying to join a hopscotch game when I was little and being shut out.

Please acknowledge me, I think as I try to project calm confidence while I face the girls and dance. *And please don't let Adam be here.* One of the tube top girls looks at me and grins.

"Look, it's the real-life Carrie Bradshaw!" she says, as she juts her body back and forth in what looks like a succession of hip-hop dance class moves.

"Cool!" her friend says, less impressed or perhaps completely indifferent—I can't tell which and don't really care. I'm just grateful that the first girl moves past her friend to start dancing with me.

"Woo hoo!" Jeremy yells from down below, and I notice Tim moving in his seat and John clapping. It all starts to seem kind of amusing, and I find myself swiveling my hips into Tube Top as she swivels hers back into mine. Someone turns the music up even louder as Tube Top moves in closer to me. The next thing I know, we're full-on dirty dancing. And she must be the one in the Patrick Swayze role because she starts moving forward into me and I have no choice but to move back as we sort of grind our hips into one another.

And, while I still don't think I have a lesbian bone in my body, Truth or Dare kiss be damned, something about dancing on the bar at the Roosevelt with a Paris Hilton wannabe feels oddly exciting. It's less about being turned on and more about letting myself go. I surrender to the music, and manage to almost forget where I am. *This is why I liked doing drugs*, I think, as Tube Top and I swivel and gyrate. *They gave me a break from this busy head of mine*. The self-consciousness that usually seems like an intrinsic part of my DNA evaporates completely as I keep dancing, suddenly dripping in sweat.

A flashbulb goes off, a few more girls jump up on the bar, and when I look around the club, I notice that most of the people are now dancing—even, shockingly, Tim and John. The attention seems to be totally off me and Tube Top, who's now dancing with her original friend again. Jeremy walks up to the bar, snapping his fingers from side to side, looking like he's concentrating really hard on the finger snap.

"That Ketel One really went to your head, didn't it?" he yells up to me.

I look at him as I keep dancing and smile. "It sure did!" I yell back.

23

"I can't imagine doing all of that sober," Stephanie says, as she takes the cup of coffee I offer her. She's stopped by to bring me a copy of the *New York Post*, which happens to contain a picture of me and Tube Top (the daughter of some famous photographer and his supermodel wife, as it turns out) dancing on the bar—along with a story about our secret affair. "Stone, who goes by the moniker 'Party Girl,' after the highly publicized column she writes for *Chat*, has been seeing the nineteen-year-old Crossroads grad for some time," Stephanie reads. " 'Amelia may claim to be straight,' says a close friend of the comely columnist, 'but it's all a front. She's as gay as can be.' "

Stephanie tosses the paper onto my Shabby Chic coffee table and takes a generous gulp of coffee. "I love it," she says. "You know you've made it when the gay rumors start."

I pick up the paper and slide it into a folder that contains the other press I've received. "Come on, you know you haven't really made it until people start saying you're a Scientologist."

Stephanie laughs and puts her coffee down. "It's just hard for me to picture you dirty dancing with a scantily clad prepubescent when you're stone cold sober. I mean, how do you do it—just pretend you're drunk?"

I think about how I used to drink and do drugs to escape how I felt, even though it never really worked—if anything, partying only exacerbated my loneliness or discomfort. At Pledges they say that it's important to create a life so comfortable that you don't need to escape, and I guess that's what's happening to me—the sort of self-conscious, occasionally shy daytime personality I've always had is mixing with my wild-while-intoxicated nighttime persona. *I don't need what other people need to help them let loose anymore*, I think, deciding that such a skill is so rare that it should almost be considered a superpower.

Out loud I say, "I don't know. Maybe I was experiencing a kind of 'natural high'?"

I make a quote mark gesture around the phrase because it's just the sort of expression Stephanie and I would have mocked not too long ago, but I secretly love the idea of it. *I can get natural highs while other people need chemical ones*, I think before I remember that Tommy used to say if you feel better than people, all that means is that at some point you're going to feel worse than them. But then I think, *Tommy doesn't know everything. If he did, why would he spend his days working at an almost completely dilapidated rehab in West L.A.?*

"Amelia Stone on a natural high." Steph laughs. "Who could have ever predicted it?" She smiles and sips her coffee.

I light a smoke, careful to blow it out the window, and think about how grateful I am that she feels comfortable talking to me about my sobriety. Other people who've heard about me going to rehab have been so awkward that it's unnerving. "We should meet for a drink," this publicist said to me at a premiere last week. And then, as if my sobriety had rendered the word "drink" sinful, she added nervously, "I mean, a water or soda?"

"I'm just worried that Tim's going to find out," I say, grabbing a bag of Trader Joe's Sweet, Savory & Tart Trek Mix from the kitchen and scooping a handful into my mouth.

Stephanie motions for the bag, which I hand her, as she leans back on the couch. "Please—it doesn't matter. If you look the part and hand in great copy, why should he give a rat's ass if you're sober as can be or on 12 hits of E?"

"Good point," I say.

"Maybe I'll sell *Page Six* that story," Stephanie says as she brushes peanuts that have fallen onto her lap into her hand and tosses them

into the garbage can. " 'Amelia Stone Not Really a Party Girl!' " We
both laugh. My phone starts ringing, so I walk over to it and see Tim's
cell phone number on my caller ID.

"Tim," I say, deciding not to pick up. "I'm sure he just wants to
know when I'm sending him copy."

"When's the column due?"

"Tomorrow." I peel a bit of my right thumb cuticle off.

"Jesus! Why do you always wait until the last minute? You're insane."

I shrug. I noticed when I did the first column that something in me
really got off on the adrenaline that started flowing through me when
my deadline was imminent. I almost feel like I'm setting myself up for
some impossible sprint and my fear of not making it to the finish line
motivates me all the more. Or maybe I'm just a martyr. But I suddenly
feel incredibly stressed, like the first column was a fluke and everyone
has gotten overly excited about me when I really can't deliver.
Stephanie must see the look of panic that crosses my face because she
walks over to the couch as she picks up her bag. The idea of a line of
cocaine floats through my mind and that terrifies me, but I don't say
anything. I'm sure it's perfectly normal.

"You'll be fine, Party Girl," she says as she walks toward the door.
"And if you're not, look at it this way: you can always start writing a
Sober Girl column."

"Ha ha."

As soon as Stephanie leaves, I turn on the computer, open a new
Word document, and stare at it, thinking, *Okay, here's where the
writer's block happens*. I've never actually had writer's block, but people
are always talking about it, so I figure that it's only a matter of time
for me.

Then the phone rings and I jump at it eagerly without even glancing at caller ID, grateful for the procrastination tool.

"Amelia?" It's a young girl's voice.

"Yes."

"It's Charlotte. We met the other night? We, um, danced?"

Oh my God. Tube Top. I'd just sort of assumed she would disappear into the ether.

"Hey, Charlotte. What can I do for you?" At first I think, *Christ, is she going to ask me out on a date?* Then: *That would make a really great column.*

"I hope it's okay that I'm calling you. You were listed, so I figured you wouldn't mind." I make a mental note to get myself unlisted. "It's just . . . well, I really love your column. When I read it, I thought, 'Oh my God, this woman is describing my life,' except, to be honest, my world is a bit crazier."

"Hmmm," I say, still not remotely clear on where she's trying to go with this.

"And, well, I was just curious how you got started? I ask because I want more than anything to be a writer. I actually wrote my first novel when I was twelve. And I've been doing poetry since eighth grade, and journaling for as long as I can remember."

I think it's around the time that she uses the word "journaling" that I start completely tuning her out. *She sure is a pushy little thing,* I think as she regales me with stories about editing the school newspaper and literary magazine.

"Look," I say, cutting her off before she starts reciting poems written to, like, her dead grandmother. "I can't help you get a writing job. The best thing I can tell you is go to college, then go get a job at a magazine. That's what I did."

Tube Top—Charlotte—laughs. "Oh, I'm not trying to get a job yet. I'm only eighteen. I just wanted to know if you'd read some of my work and . . . I don't know . . . tell me if you think I have promise."

I don't know if it's the shock of hearing "I'm only eighteen," or my resentment over the fact that this chick manages to boogie her perfect body on top of bars and still be motivated enough to have written multiple novels before puberty. But her whole I'm-more-motivated-than-anyone-else shtick is really rubbing me the wrong way.

Of course I don't say that. "Why don't I give you my e-mail address and you can send me some of your stuff?" I say, figuring I can always delete it and then duck her calls if she ever bugs me again.

"Oh, that would be so great!" she yelps. I listen to her tell me how cool and great I am and how she wants to be just like me when she "grows up" until I can't take it any longer.

"Charlotte, I really have to go—I have a column to write," I say and hang up the phone before she can say anything else that makes me feel ancient, and then go back to staring at my computer and picking at my cuticles.

I stand up, sit down again, then stand up to go get the bag of Trader Joe's Sweet, Savory & Tart Trek Mix, then plop down again at my desk. Tim and John responded so well to my story about going to Guy's with Chad Milan and leaving with Rick Wilson that I figure that's a good topic. And once I come up with a title, "The Obligatory Good-Night Kiss," I just start typing.

If a guy shells out for your tiramisu, you'd better accept the fact that he's going to expect some tongue. I realize that nine out of ten men surveyed wouldn't admit this (and the tenth would only if he thought that confessing as much would get him some tongue) but I'm here to tell you that we women make an intrinsic promise every time we allow the check to be pulled to the other side of the table. Still, going to a bar afterward and leaving with someone else because you "can't find" your dinner date will probably create more problems than it will solve.

For a second I worry about Chad Milan reading the column, but then I realize that the only person the incident really reflects negatively on is me. *You're a genius when it comes to self-deprecation*, one of the *Chat* senior editors had said at dinner in New York. *Besides*, I tell myself as I continue to type, *this material is too good not to use.* I light a cigarette and think about the possibility of running into Chad at the gym and being confronted by him again. And then I think, *I'll switch to Equinox. It's supposed to be a much nicer gym anyway.*

24

When I walk in the door after a pre-Emmys party, the phone is ringing but I decide to hang a metaphorical "Do Not Disturb" sign and not answer. I feel the need to chain-smoke while unpacking the three shopping bags I've filled with thongs, conditioner, skirts I won't ever wear, and cleansers that promise to deliver "face lift–like results."

The fact that I've just been to a freebie Emmys event and have nothing to do with the Emmys—in fact, I couldn't even begin to guess who's been nominated—hardly seems relevant. I was invited by a publicist who sounded so thrilled I'd accepted her invitation that it was immediately obvious she thought getting me there would somehow generate coverage in *Chat*. *Oh, well*, I'd decided. I'd heard about these award show events where all the nominees and presenters are invited to some mansion to get all this free shit in exchange for allowing photographers to catch them clutching the newly acquired products, and figured there wouldn't be any harm in attending.

Inhaling deeply on my cigarette, it occurs to me that I may have been wrong. From the minute I'd been allowed into this English Tudor mansion that was rumored to rent for $20,000 a day and walked from booth to booth, I'd felt this childish greed well up in me. My eyes darted around in a feverish panic—I wanted to be at the Keds shoe booth and the MAC makeup table and the Toys "R" Us mini castle all at the same time, even though I don't like Keds, rarely wear makeup, and certainly don't need any toys. Every person stopping me from getting everything all at once—which is to say, every person there—

seemed an irritant. Yet no one booth seemed to whet my appetite. *The best stuff is over to the right*, I'd think. Or, *ohhh, Nailtiques nail polish— now that's what I should be getting.* I felt like a contestant on a game show I used to watch when I was little, where the winners could take home everything they could pile into a shopping cart in the allotted time. It used to bring up simultaneous feelings of panic and excitement that I could barely stand. But actually being one of the participants inspired a far more powerful emotion: greed.

And I didn't much like the sycophantic aspect of my personality the event seemed to bring out. *I absolutely adore sarongs*, I'd found myself saying to this woman giving out inexplicably tacky tie-dyed sarongs. Or *I've been looking for sunglasses just like this* I said to the guy giving out Ray-Bans I'd never wear. Most everyone was almost painfully nice—way too nice, considering the fact that I was taking things they typically sell and not giving them anything in return— and it seemed impossible to believe in that environment that something like poverty or a famine in Africa or even George Bush existed. Conversations seemed to revolve around plastic surgery and Emmy after-parties and the new line of Juicy now at Lisa Kline. And where were the Emmy nominees, anyway? The crowd seemed to be comprised of tabloid reporters, publicists picking things out "for their clients," and other seemingly soulless moochers. And I couldn't deny the fact that I was one of them.

Now that I'm home and have all the contents out of their bags and divided into small piles, I have this strong desire to give everything away. Not to the homeless or anything crazy, just to friends. *I don't deserve all this stuff*, I say to myself as I mash a cigarette out, *but I don't know why.*

Then I start resenting the event for making me depressed. I'd been feeling so good since getting sober—like I'd exited my life and wandered into someone else's—that I guess I'd begun to assume that malaise was simply a feeling from my old life that I no longer had to be bothered with. But in my heart, I know it's not the event that has me down; it's the fact that it's been over a month since Adam and I talked in New York and he still hasn't called.

My phone rings and, as soon as I check caller ID and determine that it's not Adam, I return to the couch and my pack of cigarettes. *I shouldn't be isolating*, I think as I eventually pick up my phone to listen to the messages. They'd warned us about isolating in rehab, telling us that if we felt like being alone, we should do "contrary action" and get out. But I really just don't feel like it.

There's a message from Tim saying that he loves the new column, a couple of hang-ups, Stephanie asking if I want to go to a screening with her, and Rachel wanting to know why I hadn't checked in with her for a few days. *How the hell can he claim to be thinking about me obsessively and then not call?* I wonder.

I turn on my computer to start going through e-mails I still have to respond to and somehow land on the one Charlotte (aka Tube Top) sent with all her writing attached. I open up the first document, thinking that reading her attempts to sound like a writer should make me feel better about myself.

And then something altogether shocking happens: I'm thoroughly transfixed. Her first attachment is an essay she wrote about meeting a nude photographer, asking him to take pictures of her and then almost backing out of the portraits until he gives her painkillers that subdue her enough to help her lose her self-consciousness. The piece so perfectly captures the conflict I've felt about being proud of my body while simultaneously ashamed of that pride. It's funny and honest and so unlike anything I'd ever imagine an eighteen-year-old—let alone an eighteen-year-old that looks like her—writing that I'm in complete shock. *Screw her*, I think, wishing I hadn't read her e-mail in the first place.

My phone rings and it makes me half jump out of my skin. It's a private number but I will myself to do "contrary action" and answer.

"Hel-lo." I sound a bit singsongy and, I notice, almost shockingly normal.

"Party Girl?" I immediately recognize the voice but pretend I don't. "Yes?"

"Jeremy Barrenbaum. What are you doing there? Why aren't we out tearing the town up?"

I feel immediately self-conscious about having been caught at home with no plans on a Thursday evening. "Oh, I'm on my way out," I say, glancing at the clock: 7:30 P.M. Sounds reasonable.

"Cool, where to? Maybe I'll join you."

Momentary panic, and then: "Just to a friend's. Private party, sorry."

"That's cool," he says. "How about tomorrow? Nobu in Malibu?"

I've never liked fish so I certainly don't eat raw fish, which has long made me a complete anomaly in Los Angeles. But, most of all, I don't like the idea of being out with Jeremy Barrenbaum and having to continue to perpetuate this notion that I'm wild when I'm not. What am I going to do, have the waitress crack open a bottle of Martinelli's apple cider and pretend it's champagne?

I take a breath. "You know, Jeremy, I should have told you something the other night."

"Oh, I read that *Page Six* thing about how you're not into guys. I don't buy it for a second."

I stifle the urge to hang up on him. "Oh, I'm straight. But I am actually seeing someone. A guy."

A slight pause and then: "Look, I don't care. I'm seeing someone, too."

Oh my God, no wonder he has so many movie credits, I think. *What a pushy bastard.* "Yeah, well, I only want to be with the person I'm seeing," I say. I picture Adam and for a second believe he and I really are dating.

"Oh, okay." He doesn't sound put out in the slightest. "Want to take my number? Things may not work out with this guy."

"Sure," I say, knowing I'm being spineless. He recites a few numbers—home, office, cell, and a place in Palm Springs—and I pretend to be writing them down while I lie on my back not moving. Then I say, "I'll talk to you soon." I immediately know I shouldn't have said that because I don't want to but it just automatically comes out of my mouth when I'm trying to get off the phone. He says goodbye and I sit there holding the phone for only what seems like a second when it rings again. A 212 number on caller ID. I figure it might be a *Chat* editor trying to close my column so I answer.

"Hello." I'm not as singsongy but my voice still sounds misleadingly cheery.

"Sweetie, it's Nadine. What on earth are you doing home?"

Oh, God. Nadine seems to be under the mistaken impression that I spend every waking minute going to A-list parties, and to be fair to her, I haven't done anything to correct that impression. "Just stopping home for a minute," I manage. "I had to change my purse."

"Oh, of course." I'd known that excuse would work; people like Nadine changed their purses a lot, while I tend to carry the same one for months or years at a time. "Where are you off to?"

"Just a friend's private party." By now, I was definitely beginning to believe myself. "A movie producer." I plan to give her Jeremy Barrenbaum's name if she presses further.

"Oh, fabulous! And I'm calling with even more fabulous news! Ryan Duran's people called. Apparently, he read your column and wants to go out with you."

Now I've heard of this kind of thing happening. Supposedly, Tom Cruise saw Nicole Kidman's first movie, *Dead Calm*, then called her agent and set up a date. But it still shocks me to hear that it's possible to look at life like it's a Pottery Barn catalog or Pink Dot menu, and order people—even if you happened to be world-famous and adorable.

Ryan Duran, a well-respected movie star who had first become well known as a teenager in the '80s and somehow managed to avoid the inevitable backlash that should have followed his initial success, has a fairly well publicized reputation as both a troubled soul and a ladies' man—which means, of course, that I've had a crush on him for as long as I can remember. I'd actually just read a piece on him in *Premiere* where he'd talked about how all he wanted to do was run with his dog on the beach near Zuma, and I'd fantasized about being the one waiting at the Malibu house for him to come home to after said run. All I can manage to say is, "What?"

" 'He thinks she's hot,' his manager said. 'Can he call her?' I told him I thought so, but I'd have to check with you."

I feel a bizarre internal tug-of-war—I don't really care but this latent adolescent part of me is beyond thrilled. "What am I supposed to say?"

"Say yes! It could be fabulous publicity for the column!"

I'm slightly surprised by Nadine's response, even though I probably shouldn't be. What did I think, she was suddenly going to transform into a spiritual giant and talk to me about something besides publicity?

"In that case," I say, fantasizing that news of my date with Ryan will get out and Adam will be fantastically jealous, "pass my number along."

"Hooray! I'm so glad you said that—because, actually, I already did."

"Nadine!"

"He actually should be calling any minute."

"But you called to ask if it was okay with me."

"I pretty much assumed you were going to say yes. I mean, who says no to Ryan Duran?"

Just then, my call waiting bleeps in. Private number. "Oh, Nadine. That's my other line."

"It's probably him!"

I can't imagine Ryan Duran making the effort to do something like call a person when surely everything is always delivered to him before he can even realize he wants it. I'm about to tell Nadine not to worry, that I'll just call whoever it is back, but she shrieks, "You're answering it!" and hangs up the phone.

I click down and clear my throat. "Hello?"

"Amelia?" I immediately know it's him. His voice seems more familiar to me than my mother's, or even the AOL Moviefone guy's. Of course, I'm not remotely willing to let this on. "Yes?"

"It's Duran. How are you?" I'm simultaneously repelled and charmed by his last-name-only introduction—turned off by the potential cheesiness of someone doing that to a person they've never met while also touched by the bizarre sense of intimacy our interaction already has.

"I'm well. And you?"

"It's all good. Except for one thing. I'm sitting here on my deck, having watched an insanely beautiful sunset. And I'm wondering why I'm doing it alone."

Was this really how he introduced himself to people? Was he not even going to bother with the whole *Hey, I know this is a bit out of left field but I was reading your column and I thought, why not ask my manager to try to get in touch with her?* If you were a household name, were you simply allowed to skip over the small talk the rest of us believe is absolutely imperative?

All I say is, "Is that so?"

"Mmmm hmmm," he says, and I can picture him on the other side of the phone, sitting on an expansive deck talking on a cordless phone, wearing the close-lipped smile I've witnessed in at least half a dozen of his movies. "What are you doing?"

"On my way to a friend's house for a party." I've said it so much that at this point, it may as well be true.

"What do you say you blow that off, drive over to the beach, and hang out with me? I've got my kid tonight."

Ah yes, I'd forgotten. Ryan had been briefly married to a Spanish aspiring actress/singer in the mid-'90s and he sometimes talked about his kid in interviews. Even though all I'd wanted for the night was to go into a TIVO coma and everyone knows that you don't go over to a guy's house the first time he calls, I feel hopeful that hanging out with Ryan could potentially take my mind off Adam.

"I can be there in half an hour" is all I say.

*   *   *

"Come on in," Ryan says as he opens the door to reveal a minimalist, cavernous white loft. Looking every bit the way he does in movies, he gives my lips a quick peck and gestures for me to follow him into his kitchen. "Can I get you a drink?" He picks up a glass, shakes it so that the ice cubes in it rattle, and then takes a generous sip.

"Water?" I ask, feeling nervous and hating myself for it.

"Pellegrino okay?" He says this as he opens the fridge.

"That's great." Ryan produces a small bottle of Pellegrino, pulling the corkscrew top off by wedging it under a wooden table and pushing the bottom of the bottle down. It's such a casually masculine move that I find myself unnervingly turned on by it. He hands me the bottle and I take a sip.

"What do you feel like doing? Want to take a walk on the beach?" He asks me this like I come over here all the time and determining our nightly plans is simply part of our ritual. Just then, a small dark-haired boy comes barreling into the room and throws himself around Ryan's legs.

"Hey, you. What's up?" Ryan says, tousling the kid's hair. "Want to come walk with Daddy and his friend on the beach?"

The child gazes at me with wide eyes. "I'm Diego," he announces.

"I'm—"

"Amelia," Ryan finishes and I'm both impressed by Ryan's ability to remember and say my name and horrified by how easily impressed I am.

"Hi, Amelia." Diego scatters out from under his dad's arm and runs up to me. "Are you going to be spending the night?"

Total silence, and then I force a laugh. Ryan's the one who should probably be embarrassed by the direction this conversation has taken, so why am I the one blushing? When it becomes clear that I don't have an answer, Ryan smiles. "Chill out, kid," he says affectionately. "Where's Sam?"

Diego yells, "Sa-am!" and a towheaded kid comes scampering into the room. "Are we going out for pizza?" he asks Ryan.

Ryan doesn't introduce me and I decide that it's not worth getting offended over not officially meeting a prepubescent. Ryan glances at me and then at the two kids.

"No, we're going to play ball on the beach," he says and, even though I'm still stricken with the memory of all those notes I forced my mom to write so that I could get out of P.E. on "Dodgeball Day," I try to smile. "Right, Amelia?"

Maybe it's that Ryan's face is about as familiar to me as my own. Maybe it's that he's undeniably sexy. Or maybe I just hoped that a game of ball (football? baseball? who knew?) would calm my nerves ever so slightly. Running around on the beach with a couple of kids could maybe help me forget the fact that I was standing in the home of someone I'd had posters of my entire adolescence or that the guy I was obsessed with—who happened to live mere blocks away—was clearly blowing me off.

"We sure are," I say, kicking off the platform heels that I'd so carefully selected for this excursion. "Who's coming?"

"Here you go!" I shriek, tossing an enormous beach ball toward Sam. He catches it, which makes me feel enormously validated, and tosses it back. Next to us, Ryan and Diego kick a soccer ball back and forth.

"Bet you can't catch it if I throw it really high!" I yell and toss the ball up what I imagine is going to be hundreds of feet in the air only to have it fly about a foot up before flopping to the ground. Sam good-naturedly runs toward me to retrieve it.

"That was lame!" he yells as he scoops the ball up and makes his way back to where he was standing before.

Does Sam know that I'm faking interest in this impromptu beach ball game? Does he understand that I'm self-consciously watching myself try to act cavalier playing nonsensical ball games on the beach with Ryan Duran and two eight-year-olds? Or does Ryan have so many different women over that the sight of a slightly uncomfortable, overly enthusiastic young woman doesn't even seem like a fact worth noting?

As Sam tosses the ball back in my direction, he doesn't seem remotely aware of any of the thoughts racing through my brain. He seems intent, actually, on having the ball reach me, and I'm oddly touched by his fervor and the way he's acting like all of this is all so normal. Inside I'm thinking, *It's probably not good to be excited about getting validation from an eight-year-old*, but on the outside I think I'm doing a fairly decent job of acting like an all-around beach and sports enthusiast.

Then Diego kicks the soccer ball to Sam, and Ryan walks over to me and grabs my hand. "I'm just trying to tire these guys out so they'll crash," he says, and his face cracks into one of his famous, beautiful smiles. "You're an angel for helping me out here."

"Are you kidding? I love it," I say, worrying that my voice sounds fake, even though, at the moment, I feel like I'm telling the truth. He falls down onto the sand, pulls a crumpled pack of Marlboro Reds from his jacket pocket, and starts searching for matches. And even though I don't have a clue what the hell I'm supposed to be doing or saying, I smile and think, *Ryan Duran called me an angel*, pretending that Adam was somehow walking by and heard it.

"Red or white?" Ryan asks as he glances at the wine menu and then looks up at me. We're in a casual Italian restaurant down the street from his loft, after having finished the beach ball games and left the kids watching *The Lord of the Rings* at home with a babysitter.

"Neither—I don't drink," I say without even pausing to feel self-conscious about it. I'm not sure if that's because I sense that Ryan doesn't seem judgmental or because he seems really only focused on himself and probably wouldn't care.

"That's cool," he says, sliding his napkin onto his lap. "I used to be sober, you know."

Since getting out of Pledges, I've run into some people who have casually explained to me that they're not sober anymore and while none of them have had heroin needles dangling from their arms, I've tended to treat the whole concept of "formerly sober" somewhat skeptically. *Nobody ends up here by accident*, people at Pledges say, meaning, like the Hair Club for Men, if you thought you needed sobriety at one point, chances are you still do. *But maybe there are exceptions*, I think as I unfold my napkin and put it on my lap. You never hear about the people who leave and have perfectly wonderful lives where they're able to drink and do drugs casually. We only learn about the ones who go out, screw it up royally, and come back after having lost everything—or, of course, the people who overdose.

"It just really didn't work for me," Ryan is saying. "The whole sponsor thing. Like I really need some asshole telling me what to do? You know?" He focuses his bright green eyes on me, clearly seeking validation of some kind.

"Some sponsors are assholes," I say, feeling a bit guilty for deriding the program instead of telling him he sounds like he's trying to justify not being sober anymore. "But some are great. Just like with anything, I guess."

I'd hoped my statement would show how open-minded, nonjudgmental, positive, and yet realistic I was but once it's out of my mouth, I realize it sounds pretty inane—a fact I'm even more convinced of when it becomes clear that Ryan isn't going to say anything in response. I can hear *Just like with anything, I guess* echoing in my brain and I cringe.

Glancing at Ryan, I see he's examining the menu with serious intent. I gaze at mine, too, but can't seem to rustle up the same level of concentration. Eating when I'm around a guy who makes me nervous has always been slightly difficult, so I can only assume that getting any food down during this interaction will be out of the question. I used to think being nervous around a guy was good—it meant I really liked someone. But I'd felt the opposite hanging out with Adam that day. I'd felt, cheesy as it sounds, like I'd come home. *Chicken—I'll just have whatever the first chicken dish is*, I think as I try to brainstorm possible topics to bring up with Ryan.

Now, it's always been my firm belief that when two people are eating together, it is the equal responsibility of both parties to contribute to the conversation. Of course, it usually happens naturally—one person says something or asks a question, the other responds, and conversation starts to just unfold—but it's always annoyed me when I feel like the communication responsibility rests solely on me. *Why the hell doesn't this long silence make you feel uncomfortable?* I've wanted to shriek across the table before. *Don't you at least feel slightly compelled to try to change it?*

The waiter comes over. I order chicken marsala, Ryan asks for tortellini and a glass of the house Chianti. I wonder if I should judge him for drinking or be offended that he didn't not drink because of me, and Ryan sits in what looks to be completely enjoyable silence. I already know that Ryan's dad was a character actor, his parents divorced when he was young, he dated Maria Bello throughout his twenties and didn't go to college, so all the *what-did-you-want-to-be-when-you-grew up*, *what-do-your-parents-do*, *what-did-you-major-in* types of questions—standard first date fare—would be silly and redundant.

Forcing a conversation about what's going on in the world would feel just that—forced—and I'm not interested enough in food to start discussing the menu. I am, for one of the first times I can remember, at a complete and utter conversational loss.

And then I feel just the slightest glimmer of hope in him. He could ask me the typical first date questions, or about my column, or about why I decided to get sober. Flooded with sudden optimism, I smile at him. He smiles back and I assume he's going to ask me something, but instead he takes his index finger and taps the table, then his other index finger and does the same thing. And, before I know it, he's doing some kind of impromptu drum solo on the table of Café Italiano, clearly grooving to some wild beat inside his head.

*   *   *

"Mmmm, you smell so good," Ryan says as he breathes in my ear. He's just finished kissing me, expertly, and we're looking into each other's eyes. I'm much more comfortable now than I was at dinner when, in between Ryan's drum solos, we made allegedly casual conversation about the restaurant, the weather, and the waiter. Of course, there was nothing casual about my end of the conversation—each sentence I tossed out was attached to a prayer that he would respond in a way that would allow me to answer back—but at some point I realized that he didn't seem to be expecting a lot of scintillating talk, and I relaxed as much as someone who's in the process of gnawing a cuticle into a bloody stub can be. *Maybe some people just always eat in semi silence*, I started to think. I've often speculated that the conversations I have are a thousand times more bizarre or boring or superficial or whatever else my mood tells me they are than the ones everyone else is having. But dinner certainly convinced me that stressing about it wasn't going to help anything.

After dinner, we'd walked the few blocks back to his loft, during which he grabbed my hand to point out a shooting star and I couldn't help but see us as a stranger, or a camera, might. Were we secretly being snapped by paparazzi hiding behind sand dunes? Again, I picture Adam walking by right now, seeing us, and kicking himself with regret.

Right at his front door, Ryan had turned his face toward mine and started kissing me. And that's when the chains that had seemingly been wrapped around my tight shoulders released. I felt comfortable as we kissed, even more so when he told me how good I smell. Maybe he really will be able to replace Adam in my mind.

"Let's check on the little ones," he says after we make out for a few minutes, so we go into the media room where we'd left them riveted by *The Lord of the Rings*, and they're both sound asleep while Elijah Wood pontificates on screen. "Sit," he says, smiling and pointing to the couch, as he pulls cash out of his pocket and hands it to the babysitter. I find myself aroused by the cool simplicity of his demand. For such a domineering person, I certainly do like to be ordered around sometimes.

So I sit on the couch as Ryan picks up Diego with one hand and Sam with the other to carry them upstairs and I'm simultaneously turned on by both his strength and his fathering skills. Within seconds, he's back and kissing me even more passionately than before.

And then we're just lost in the kissing, and I finally feel like I have some control. Sober people have warned me about sober sex and how disorienting it is, but I feel a million times more comfortable making out with Ryan than I did making conversation with him. I compare it to kissing Adam that day and have to admit that this falls short. *I just think that because I've known Adam longer*, I tell myself, annoyed that I'm kissing a household name and thinking about a guy who won't even deign to call me.

I'm concentrating on doing a good job, reasoning that all men seem to like the same things when it comes to kissing: slow, tender, quick pecks at first, followed by openmouthed exploration with the tongue trailing on the upper gum, followed by neck nibbling and ear breathing, with soft moans thrown in for good measure.

Ryan is kissing me back so well that in my light-headedness, I wonder if the reason he's been so successful in his career is that he's made out with all of the casting directors. As we kiss and breathe and nibble, all memories of the awkward dinner dissolve. Now *I could talk to him*, I think as I trail my tongue on his upper lip and he softly moans. *But I'm just not willing to stop kissing him long enough to prove it.*

Pretty soon, Ryan and I are lying down on the couch and he's on top of me so that I can feel his full erection through his jeans. He starts moving his hips up and down ever so slightly and, even though one of my least favorite expressions, "dry fucking," floats through my mind, I don't stop him. But when he starts unbuttoning my Joie cords, I take his hand and move it away.

"I just don't feel comfortable going there right now," I whisper and he nods, but a few seconds later, he goes for the buttons again. When fingers enter my nether region, all rational thought—as well as any ability to say no to anything else—seems to escape me, and I know that having sex with Ryan Duran right now is simply out of the question. I may have run right over here the minute he asked, and be grinding up against him despite the fact that he hasn't given me any indication that he's actually interested in anything about me, but I know I'm going to follow the no-fucking-on-the-first-date rule because I'm not willing to screw this up yet. *Cosmo* says that you can give it up after three dates, but I'm harboring some notion that Ryan can be the one who will take my mind off Adam, and I know I'm going to have to strategize if I want to reel him in. *I should probably make him wait three months*, I think, as I breathe in his ear and feel his body shudder. Then his hand is on my cord buttons again, so I move it away and look him in the eye to shake my head.

"Are you sure?" he asks.

"Yes. I want to wait. It doesn't feel as good when you don't know a person well."

He furrows his brow as if he's confused and it occurs to me that this may very well be the first time Ryan Duran has even heard of the concept of not jumping right into bed. "You mean, maybe go out again and fool around a little more that time?" he asks, and I nod. "God, that sounds nice," he says, looking suddenly completely relaxed and I wonder why I allowed myself to be so intimidated by him earlier. He kisses me again, and then says, "Want to spend the night? We wouldn't have to do anything—we could just spoon."

I shake my head and Ryan pouts somewhat adorably. "Are you sure?" he asks. "It would be so sweet—the kiddies are up in my bed."

I sit up suddenly, too surprised to worry about how I'm probably killing the moment. "The kids are in your bed?" I ask.

"Sure." He smiles and reaches for a Marlboro Red, which he lights with a Zippo. "That's where Diego likes to sleep."

"And you want me to sleep there with all you guys?"

He nods and smiles and inhales on his cigarette and I can't decide if I'm a secret straitlaced conservative or if asking a girl you just met to spend the night in the same bed with your son and his friend is normal. I gesture for him to let me take a drag off his cigarette and decide that the sooner I leave, the less time I have to discover other potentially disturbing things about my adolescent obsession.

"I should go," I say when we finish the smoke. He nods, kisses me on the nose, pulls himself up off the couch, and takes my hand to lead me out through the kitchen.

"Thanks for a great night," I say as he walks me to the door. What am I supposed to say—*Thanks for drumming throughout dinner and inviting me to your Michael Jackson-esque slumber party?*

25

"I need to talk to you," Justin whispers in my ear as he walks behind me in the middle of a Pledges meeting.

"There you are!" I yell, getting dirty looks from a few people standing around me.

For the past three days, I've been throwing myself into a manic schedule of round-the-clock shopping and working out to distract myself from the fact that Adam still hasn't called, and peppering Stephanie and Justin with constant *he's-going-to-call-right?* messages, none of which Justin has returned. It occurred to me after the third unreturned message that I essentially haven't seen or talked to him in the past month and a half. "Where the hell have you been?" I ask him.

An emaciated man with a shaved head and tattoos covering every bit of visible skin glowers, and so Justin grabs my hand and starts to lead me out the front door of the meeting. As we pass people, I feel the weight of their stares on me. It's strange because before the column and all the hype, I'd have sworn up and down that I could never receive too much attention. But I hadn't been prepared for what comes with it. I feel like I hear whispering now wherever I go and I'm not sure if it's real or coke has left me permanently paranoid. I'll walk by two girls and swear that I hear one of them mention "Party Girl" or the word column or something, and then I'll feel them dissect everything about me. Are they criticizing what I'm wearing, deciding that I should be more put-together? Are they accusing me of not really being sober, speculating that a girl who goes by the moniker of Party Girl and lounges in champagne-soaked magazine shots couldn't possibly be clean? Pledges has taught me that what people think of me is none of my business, but I guess I wasn't really prepared to have to remind myself of that so many times a day.

"Ick," I say to Justin, as we make it outside and I light two cigarettes.

"What?" he asks as I hand him one of the smokes.

"The way people look at me now is annoying," I say, wishing that he noticed this without my having to point it out to him.

"Oh, Amelia," he says, flicking his cigarette ash to the ground. "Most people are just thinking about themselves. I think you're too in your head and just being a typical self-absorbed addict."

For some reason, I want to take my lit cigarette and mash it into his face—or at least onto his hand, where it wouldn't cause as notable a scar. While the whole world seems to have jumped up to speed and is treating me like I'm worthy of being celebrated, Justin has barely seemed to notice. And suddenly I hate him for this. I've always really liked friends agreeing with what I'm saying, and if they disagree or don't seem to want to indulge in the conversation, I feel like they've broken some unspoken contract we have about always backing each other up. In recovery, people get away with this so much—by saying things like "I'm not going to cosign your bullshit" or accusing someone of being too "in their head" or self-absorbed—and I suddenly feel myself as much annoyed with the Pledges world as I am with Justin.

"Whatever," I say, not even looking at Justin. "They're probably just jealous." I pause, and then, "Did you get my messages? Do you understand that I've basically been heartbroken?"

Justin takes a drag off his cigarette and nods as he exhales. "Look, I've got to tell you something," he says after a beat.

"Shoot." He's still bugging me but I'm willing to let it go—something that wouldn't have even been a remote possibility before the program.

He tosses his cigarette to the ground and smashes it out. "I'm not really sober," he says.

"What?" I feel suddenly dropped into a moment of surreality. *He's lying*, I think. *He's sober a week longer than me and I almost have six months.* "That doesn't even make sense," I say, feeling myself start to panic. "How is that possible?"

"Well, I smoked pot last week, had a couple beers a few nights ago, and the night before last, stayed up all night with this guy I met at Marix, doing blow until sunrise." He says all this completely casually, like he's explaining the errands he ran at lunchtime yesterday. Where the hell are his emotions?

"Why would you do that?" I ask, and even though I can hear my accusatory tone and know it's not the right one to have, I can't seem to stop it.

"Why? Fuck if I know. Maybe because I'm an addict."

"How did it happen?" I ask.

"Well," Justin looks down, sadly. "I moved back in with Jason and everything was amazing at first. Turns out I must have been the one instigating all the fights before because with all my new rehab knowledge, we were suddenly one of those sickeningly perfect couples planning picnics at the Hollywood Bowl, going antiquing on the weekends and all that."

"And then . . . ?" Something has kicked in, some almost maternal instinct that makes it seem like the only thing in the world that matters is making sure Justin is okay. I put my hand on his shoulder and squeeze.

"Nothing monumental—Jesus, I wish it had been," he says. "We just started hanging out with other couples, going to Dragstrip, house parties, dinners, whatever. And they all drank—wine with dinner, beer at house parties, nothing big . . . I mean, none of them drank alcoholically."

I nod. I'd noticed the same thing when I went out to dinner with some publicists—one of them ordered a glass of wine and nursed that same glass the entire night, and the other had a gin and tonic. A single gin and tonic. And I'd sat there, silently marveling over what would make someone want to drink just one drink when all one ever did to me was make me achy, tired, and coke-hungry. Tommy would tell us that when a normal person drinks and starts to feel a little buzzed, he'll see a figurative red light and know that it's his cue to stop drinking. When an alcoholic or addict gets to that same place, however, all he sees is a green light.

"And then last week it occurred to me that smoking pot wouldn't really be such a bad thing—that it didn't really count," Justin says. "I didn't tell my sponsor or anyone and nothing bad happened when I did it. So then I had a couple of drinks with Jason. He doesn't know shit about recovery—just what I tell him, really—and when I explained that drinking would be cool as long as I only had a few, he basically bought it. Cut to a couple nights later—me coked out of my gourd at this total stranger's house."

"Was it horrible?" I ask, and my whole body clenches in anticipation of his answer. I picture Justin, teeth grinding, paranoid as hell, getting creeped out by this weird guy and tearfully calling his sponsor.

Instead he says, "I wish I could say it was, but it was fun as hell. I don't know why people say that a head full of recovery and a body full of chemicals is a bad combination, because I felt amazing. It was nice to just get out of my head for once, you know?"

That's when I feel horribly betrayed. *Why is he acting like this?* I wonder. *Why isn't he horrified and crying, begging everyone in here to understand, the way other people who slip do?* Even when I remind myself that this could be Justin's "disease" talking, I resent him for casually embracing a way of thinking that's different from the one we've shared since we met. And I feel something else: jealous. *I* want to be able to get out of my head, to have coke rush up my nose and through my veins, and not feel guilty about it. But then I remind myself that that's *my* disease, and that I know for a fact that even allowing my thoughts to go here is wrong.

So I say what I know I'm supposed to. "You should call your sponsor," I tell him gently, "and raise your hand in meetings." When you relapse and have to start counting your time all over again, you have to raise your hand in meetings and reintroduce yourself to the group as a "newcomer."

He nods. "I know," he says. "I just don't feel ready yet."

We sit there in silence and I glance back in the meeting. "I'm just really sort of weirded out by this," I finally say.

"I know," he says, and looks uncomfortable. Then he catches my eye and says, "I love you, Amelia. And I could really use your support right now."

It's the first time Justin has ever said this to me, so I'm surprised. In rehab and recovery, "I love you," roughly translated, seems to mean, "Hey, we're both sober" or "You're cool," but since I've been out of there, I haven't been comfortable saying it. Even though I grew up in a family where we said those three words constantly, it always felt obligatory—like it was the way you had to end a conversation, whether it was true or not. So I seem to be much slower than everyone else at tossing the phrase out. My neurosis kicks in, and I go, *Wait, do I really love that person? I don't even know them well enough to say* and then I start to feel disingenuous.

I want to feel perfectly comfortable saying it back but I don't.

"I love you, too, Justin," I finally say, but the sentence sounds and feels awkward and we both just stand there uncomfortably as people start filtering out of the meeting and lighting their cigarettes.

26

It's a Sunday night, arguably the most depressing time of the week, when I realize that Adam is never going to call. It's been months since we talked and he's obviously either completely psychotic, a pathological liar, or both. But since I have a column due tomorrow, I'm desperately trying to take all the anxiety and burgeoning depression I feel over being rejected by Adam and convert it into work obsession. I'd heard people in meetings talk about "trading one addiction for another," so as soon as a thought about Adam pops up, I force myself to write about the Truth or Dare night, which seems oddly appropriate. Before I know it, I've written the beginning.

The bar for wild behavior had already been raised higher than it should have. Yet somewhere between making out with a girl and having the nether region of a guy I'd just met shoved in my face repeatedly, I realized that it was too late to turn back now.

I finish the column, describing my impromptu striptease and the horror I felt when I realized someone was watching it, ending with a line about how much Truth or Dare had changed since I was a kid.

As soon as I finish the piece, I realize that what I need to do to feel better is call Adam and find out what the hell happened. *There's probably a really good explanation for why he hasn't called,* I think. Maybe he lost my number or has been so crazed with his show premiering that he literally hasn't had a free moment to get in touch but would be absolutely thrilled to hear my voice.

As I contemplate this while staring at the TV screen half watching *The Surreal Life* castmates throw plates at each other, a commercial comes on and I suddenly see Adam, in a three-piece suit and talking on a cell phone as he walks down the street, looking so good that I can't believe I ever doubted his attractiveness. *"The Agency,"* that guy who seems to narrate every single commercial in the world blathers, "promises to be the hottest show of the season, says *TV Guide*."

I'm so convinced that seeing his commercial is a sign I should call him that I pick up the phone almost subconsciously and am horribly disappointed when I get his voicemail. This isn't what I'd imagined happening when I allowed myself to fantasize about calling him but I improvise, leaving a message that I diligently try to make sound both sweet and mellow. And then I wait.

And then, realizing I'm on the verge of driving myself mad, I call Stephanie and ask if she wants to go on a walk.

27

"He didn't call me back," I say into the phone as I take a bite out of my thumb's cuticle. It's five days of intense cuticle picking later.

"Asshole," Stephanie says, sighing.

"Who the hell doesn't return a call after five days and three hours?"

"Well, you want the truth? You. Me. All of us, at one time or another."

"But that's only when we don't want to actually talk to the person!" I wail.

Stephanie lets that sink in for a bit, and then says, "I know it hurts." In the last five conversations we've had about this, she's been the perfect sport, trotting out and analyzing every last possible reason—maybe Adam is intimidated by me now, or was just completely immature like Gus (who she'd stopped hanging out with months ago) or was worried he'd end up fodder for a future column or was temporarily fucking his costar and she deleted all his messages because she was psychotically possessive. I don't blame Steph for feeling exhausted by the process of coming up with more excuses for him, but accepting that he simply doesn't want to talk to me causes me to hang up and curl into a small ball of messy tears and torn cuticles.

I'm not entirely sure why I'm taking this Adam rejection so hard. Of course, I have some ideas. In rehab, I've learned about how dangerous it can be for alcoholics and addicts to have expectations because we tend to not be able to handle the disappointment of having them not met, but that realization isn't doing anything to get me out of my doldrums. The day I spent with Adam was the first time in my life I felt like I knew what people meant when they talked about finding the one. But they usually got years, or at least months or weeks, with the person. Why the hell did my discovery have to be so ephemeral?

Once the crying turns to sniffling, I realize that I'm in the midst of a full-blown depression. *Depression is something you're bound to experience*, Tommy would say, and it would stun me how casually he'd mention the word "depression"—like he was talking about having the flu and not something completely overwhelming and debilitating that made life seem unlivable. *It, too, will pass*, he'd always add, sounding like someone who couldn't ever possibly have lived through a depression.

After three solid days of not showering, cleaning, eating, answering the phone or really doing anything beyond dumping cat food into dishes and coating my pajamas in cigarette smoke, I decide it's time to check voicemail. My mom, Stephanie, the *CSI* actor who'd tried to put his hands down my pants in New York, Tim, Stephanie again, and what seems like about a thousand hang-ups. Even though I already knew that none of the messages would be from Adam, it doesn't stop me from crying when I get to the last one and it's not him. When I hear who it is, however, I cry even harder.

"Amelia," says a voice that's at once both immediately familiar and hard to place. "What can I say? You're the cat's meow. The toast of the town. The bee's knees." Who do I know who would use those expressions?

And then it hits me.

"I guess part of me is glad to see that you actually remembered what happened between us," Chris says, his voice cracking slightly, "but, what did you think—that I wouldn't see it? Or did you just not care?" I sit there, frozen, as he does exactly what I hope he won't and starts reading from my column. "*It was only after an impromptu reunion several weeks after the fact that I realized I'd gotten the basic elements of the ménage altogether wrong: most girls had them with their hottest female friend and, say, a Red Hot Chili Pepper. I'd had mine with a couple of guys who'd probably have an easier time working their way around the Starship Galaxy than they would a woman's body.*" Chris clears his throat. "Maybe I wouldn't care if you hadn't treated me like a leper ever since," he says. "But Jesus, think of someone besides yourself for once."

That throws me into yet another crying jag—though, much like someone covered in tattoos might have a difficult time identifying how many there actually were, I decide I needn't bother calling them crying jags anymore but just consider the entire day one long, extended singular crying jag. Afterward, I set about smoking myself into oblivion. I contemplate calling Stephanie to ask her if it's possible that I'm the worst person in existence but settle instead for falling asleep on the couch when I'm too exhausted to cry anymore.

Sometime later—it could be twenty minutes, it could be two hours—I wake up to the sound of someone banging on my front door. I stumble to it, groggy to the point that I almost feel hungover. Stephanie stands there, a bag of Trader Joe's Sweet, Savory & Tart Trek Mix in her hand, and a plump Mexican woman behind her.

"Don't say a word," she says, gesturing for the woman to go inside. "I told Rosa I had an emergency for her." Handing me the bag of trail mix she adds, "I wanted to bring you something healthy to eat but knew I'd have to start you on something you wouldn't reject outright."

"Thank you," I croak gratefully, as she opens my living room window and starts dumping overflowing ashtrays.

"You're welcome," she says. "Now, will you please let Rosa clean your apartment and stop Plath-ing it over this guy?"

28

"Here you go," Stephanie says, reaching through a throng of wannabe starlets to hand me a Diet Coke. I accept it gratefully and motion my head toward the side of the room, where I then go stand.

It's been almost a week since she showed up with Rosa and basically single-handedly delivered me back to the world at large and I have to admit that I'm feeling significantly better. Of course, I'm still miserable over being blown off by Adam, but Stephanie has convinced me to treat it like a nagging toothache or headache—horrible, in other words, but something I can live with. The launch party for a new Condé Nast magazine, Stephanie convinced me, was just what I needed. But standing here, waiting for her to retrieve her drink from the bar, I remember that depression, like a grating Britney Spears song stuck in your head, has a way of coming back even when it seems like it's gone away forever.

Parties like this used to fuel me—I always had that feeling that something exciting could happen—but being sober didn't so much highlight how fun drinking was as much as it made me realize how intensely boring parties like this are. *We're all talking and no one is saying anything,* I think as I tell a publicist who used to snub me when I worked at *Absolutely Fabulous* that it's good to see her, too, and accept her "You go, girl" congratulations for the column. When I was drinking, if I had a boring night, I'd blame myself—for not being fabulous enough or not talking to the right people. But now I can see that I didn't drink to make *myself* more interesting; it was to convince myself that other people were.

Stephanie joins me, sipping from her icy Amstel Light, and we watch a slew of club kids filter in, so perfectly outfitted in their Vans and True Religion jeans and tattoos that they may as well have come from Central Casting.

"You okay?" Stephanie asks, and I nod. She'd asked me the first time we went out together once I was sober if I'd prefer if she didn't drink, and I told her that she shouldn't feel like she had to deprive herself because of me. Tommy used to say that anyone out with a sober person shouldn't drink, and if they did, they may well have a drinking problem themselves. But Tommy worked in a rehab and didn't really understand the world of plus-ones and doormen who had articles written about them in magazines and open bars and gift bags. *Drinking is as normal as putting on shoes to most people at parties like this*, I think. *Besides, it's not my job to go around diagnosing people as alcoholic when it's a self-diagnosed disease.*

And then, just when Stephanie and I see Nicole Richie and Lindsay Lohan pitch their skeletal frames against each other on the dance floor, a thought occurs to me, a thought infinitely more depressing than any others I've been having during this recent bout of depression: *Wherever I go, there I am.* It floats through my head as I stare at the anorexic starlets, until I feel Stephanie poking me in the shoulder.

"Holy shit!" she exclaims. "Three o'clock. With a bimbo."

Stephanie's not known for her histrionics so I instantly know what her exclamation means and who she's talking about, but I'm nevertheless not remotely prepared for the physical stab I feel in my chest when I look toward the entrance and see Adam walking toward us with a thin blonde who isn't his Miss Teen USA costar but is nevertheless scantily clad and inarguably attractive—albeit in a siliconed, Playmate-esque way.

And now that he's less than twenty feet away, and growing closer by the millisecond, he seems less real to me than he has while I've been obsessing over him the past few weeks. It's almost shocking to remember he's an actual person and not simply a construct of my mind.

"Remember—you're cool," Stephanie says, under her breath. "And cool girls do not make scenes."

I nod and then force myself to laugh like she's just said the most hilarious thing I've ever heard in my life and that, in fact, I've been doing nothing but laugh uproariously since Adam and I last talked. He's now just a few feet away so I glance at him and act surprised, like I've completely forgotten he exists until this very moment.

"Hey, Adam," I say, as casually as I can. I don't lean in for the requisite-in-L.A.-hug-greeting but smile so broadly that it doesn't seem like I'm being passive-aggressive—just that I'm maybe too busy being happy to hug him.

"Amelia," he says, looking me in the eye in a way that gives me the good kind of chills. "Stephanie."

"Hi," I say softly. He gives Stephanie a kiss on the cheek and then leans toward me. I hold my breath as his lips brush my cheek. Amazingly, horrifyingly, all the resentment I have for him seems to evaporate instantaneously.

"A-dam," the blonde whines, nodding her head toward the bar. "I want to get a drink."

"Oh, sorry, um . . ." He just stands there, looking at me. Our eyes are locked on each other but he breaks our gaze by glancing at the blonde distractedly.

"Lizzie," she huffs. He continues to look at me while Lizzie literally stamps her foot and points toward the bar.

Stephanie, God bless her, looks at Lizzie and says, "What does everyone want? Lizzie and I will make a bar run." Without even waiting for a response, Stephanie grabs one of the girl's probably siliconed arms and starts pulling her away.

"Diet Coke!" I yell after her, gratitude and anxiety rushing through my veins simultaneously.

"Make that two!" Adam adds.

And now that I have Adam in front of me, I don't know what to say. *Why the fuck didn't you call me back?* occurs to me. *Why don't you like me?* also floats through my mind.

Instead I say, "You look good."

He smiles, and I notice dimples that had somehow escaped my notice before. Christ. Did he have to get better looking by the millisecond? Wasn't this bad enough already?

"I'm sorry I didn't call you," he says.

I want to play it cool, but can't seem to. "Yeah, what happened?" I ask, feeling sure-to-be-embarrassing tears springing to my eyes.

"What happened?" he repeats, looking hesitant.

"Yeah, what happened?" I suddenly feel enraged. "You wanted to but first you had to raid the Playboy Mansion for one of Hef's cast-offs?"

This last part comes out of me before I even realize it. I've always seemed to lack the filter that stops thoughts from turning into phrases and it can be incredibly inconvenient when I happen to be intensely jealous.

His eyes flare. "Jesus, Amelia. You're one to talk."

"What the hell is that supposed to mean?"

"It means that I run into you and you tell me how much you've changed, how pure and innocent your life is today, how that wild girl is just a part of your past."

"It's true."

He doesn't even seem to hear me, just keeps talking. "So I'm all excited, thinking this girl I've always thought would be perfect if she just wasn't so out of control has actually tamed herself."

I try to talk but he cuts me off.

"But then it turns out that the very day I'm telling you how excited I am about you, you're all over TV, selling yourself as this sexy, wild woman who fucks groomsmen at weddings."

I have the strong feeling that if this were a movie, now would be when I'd slap him. But I don't actually feel offended—just misunderstood. "I didn't fuck them," I say.

"Next thing I know, you're dangling from massive champagne glasses in magazines," Adam continues, ignoring me. "And dancing on bar tables with, like, bisexual teenage nymphos. And here I am, the sucker who actually believed you were telling me the truth."

"Adam, I was telling you the truth. The wedding was a long time ago—before I got sober. And the photo shoot, and dancing in the bar—all that is me just trying to play the 'Party Girl' part."

He looks confused. "So you clean up your life and tell me you're thrilled about it, meanwhile you're trying to convince the world at large that you're still wild and what's more, being wild is the most glamorous thing imaginable?"

"When you put it like that, it does sound a little crazy," I admit. "But it's just a column. It's what I write. It's not *me*."

He looks angrier than he has the entire conversation. "So I'm supposed to believe that you would attach your name to something, go on TV shows and get in gossip columns publicizing something that's 'not you'?"

And now I'm pissed and sick of being judged by him. "Christ, Adam. It was an opportunity. I took it. No, I'm not the girl I write about in the column anymore, but I've lived that life, and no one's ever made a big deal about anything I've ever done before. So if people want to give me money and make me famous for writing something that comes very naturally to me, what's so wrong with taking them up on it?"

He seems to consider this, and takes a breath. "I don't know. Nothing, I guess. It just seems like—"

Just then, I feel a large, sweaty hand clasp my shoulder. And, next thing I know, Jeremy Barrenbaum—an extremely drunk, exceedingly sweaty Jeremy Barrenbaum—is embracing me from behind.

"Party Girl!" he shrieks, forcing large, fleshy lips directly onto mine. I pull away but he keeps a damp, possessive arm around me.

"Jeremy, this is Adam," I say, giving Adam a "please help me" look, which he either doesn't see or completely ignores. Jeremy notices Adam standing there, and holds out one hand while the other stays firmly clasped to my shoulder. "How are you, man? Jeremy Barrenbaum."

Adam shakes one of Jeremy's hands as he eyes the other one, which is in the process of snaking its way from my shoulder to my waist. "Adam Tencer," he says, somewhat coldly. Hearing the tightness in Adam's voice, I actually feel physical pain. Is he telling the truth? Am I really "this girl he always thought would be perfect"? And who the hell is the wannabe Playmate girl?

"Um, Jeremy. Adam and I were actually in the middle of a conversation," I say, removing his hand from my waist.

"Hey, no problem," he says, but he has "bad drunk" written all over his face and doesn't move. He surveys the room, spies a waitress carrying a tray of Jell-O shots, and motions her over. Grabbing two cups off her tray, he leers at me. "What do you say, Party Girl? Want to do shots and get crazy like last time?"

"No!" I snap. This is all going so horrifically wrong. I turn to Adam to explain things, thinking he may even laugh about how I tricked people into thinking I was doing shots, but the look on his face tells me not to bother.

"Excuse me," he says to Jeremy, not even looking at me. "I'll leave you two to your shots." He glances at me as he starts to walk away, and I start following him.

"Adam! Stop! I need to explain." I grab his arm and he turns around to face me.

"No you don't, Amelia. Seriously. I don't know what game you're playing here but I really don't want any part of it." He shakes me off and keeps walking.

Tears sting my eyes as I start to follow him but I suddenly realize that there's no point. As I watch him make his way over to Stephanie and Lizzie near the bar, I feel Jeremy enter my personal space yet again. Adam whispers something to Lizzie while Stephanie gives me a questioning look. I shrug as Jeremy envelops me in a hug.

"Forget about that tool," Jeremy says, and for some reason this seems incredibly soothing. "He probably thinks he's hot shit because he's on some sure-to-be-canceled series about real estate agents."

I feel suddenly grateful for Jeremy's presence, so I turn around and smile at him. He takes my hand.

"Seriously," he says. "I don't know what you have going on with that guy but he sure doesn't seem to treat you right."

I nod as a tear falls down my face. "You're right."

Jeremy reaches over and wipes the tear away and the act seems incredibly gentle, especially for someone who seemed like a drunken buffoon about five minutes ago. *At least he's being nice to me*, I think, *which is more than I can say for Adam.*

"Plus, this party sucks," Jeremy says. "It would make anyone cry."

For some reason, this strikes me as incredibly hilarious and I start laughing like I haven't in weeks. When Jeremy grabs my hand this time, I don't shake him off.

"What do you say we get the hell out of Dodge?" he asks, as he gives me a spontaneous twirl. "Have an after-party at my place?"

My eyes land on Adam and Lizzie making their way to the exit, and then on Stephanie, now talking to someone near the bar. I wave to her and mouth that I'll call her tomorrow.

"Why the hell not?" I say.

Jeremy's house, nestled high in the Hollywood Hills, has a view not only of L.A. County and the Valley, but also of the roofs of houses belonging to Keanu Reeves and Leonardo Di Caprio. As I look at the incredible view, an altogether bizarre thought occurs to me.

Roughly translated, it's that I'm probably not an alcoholic.

Suddenly, everything becomes incredibly clear. I never actually enjoyed drinking all that much—it always made me feel kind of achy and tired. But I allowed Tommy and everyone in rehab to convince me that being a coke fiend and an alcoholic were one and the same. But I could see now—Christ, any sane person could surely see—that they weren't. They were entirely different. And I'd spent the past six-and-a-half months in meetings with people that, now that I thought about it, seemed incredibly insane. Justin was really the only person I felt connected to and he had distanced himself from Pledges altogether. Why had I allowed these militant sober people to influence me so much?

Of course, I've been listening enough in meetings to have heard people talk about how this might happen to me—how one day my "disease" would probably try to convince me I wasn't an alcoholic. But if I didn't actually suffer from the disease, it couldn't be my disease convincing me of anything, could it? Besides, who the hell believes that diseases can talk?

The only person who could answer this, the only person who'd understand, is Justin. With Jeremy inside checking his messages and e-mails, I pull my BlackBerry out of my bag and speed-dial Justin.

I'm sorry. The mailbox for the person you are calling is full. Please try again later.

It's that damn recorded voice lady, the one who always sounds so harsh and yet calm, a voice that couldn't ever be in the midst of a crisis or important quandary because she's not real. Suddenly, I'm having a hard time trying to figure out what is. And since Justin is one of these utterly modern creatures who uses his cell phone as his home phone, there's nowhere else I can try him. I could call Stephanie, I think, but I know that try as she might, she won't ultimately understand. And for some reason, I'm just not in the mood to hear Rachel's opinions right now. "They" say that when you want to drink, you're supposed to call someone in the program before you do. And I had tried, I tell myself. I did exactly what they told me to.

"So, baby, what do you say—I've got a 1995 Chateau Margaux that I could crack if you're game," Jeremy says as he joins me out on the balcony. I detect the distinct scent of Drakkar Noir that wasn't there before.

"Jeremy, I have to tell you something and it's going to sound a bit crazy," I say, looking down at the infinity pool.

"I like crazy." If a voice could leer, his now is.

"I don't actually drink. I'm sober." He looks at me confusedly, so I add, "I went to rehab."

"But—"

"I faked doing the shot that night at the Roosevelt," I say, and he crinkles his forehead as he clearly tries to go over that night in his mind. "Water looks exactly like vodka when it's in a shot glass."

"No way," he says, looking bizarrely intrigued. "But why?"

"Well, I used to be really wild and crazy," I say. "Holed-up-by-myself-at-home-not-able-to-stop-doing-coke crazy. I was completely out of control and I lost my job and was generally a real asshole. Then, just as I got my shit together, I was given the chance to write a column documenting my wild and crazy life, and it was too good an opportunity to pass up. So I do the column, culling all my information from my old life, and—"

"Act the part when you have to," he says, nodding approvingly. "That *is* crazy, baby. I like it."

I smile, relief over having gotten this off my chest flooding through me. "You don't think I'm completely out of my mind?"

Now it's Jeremy's turn to smile. "Oh, I do," he says. "In a great way, though." He turns to walk back inside. "So, what can I get you? I have cranberry juice and Perrier so I could make you a—"

"That's the thing," I interrupt. "I haven't had a drink in six and a half months, and I'd like to now."

"But I thought you just said—"

"I said that I was a coke fiend. It's the people at my rehab who have been telling me that means I'm an alcoholic, too."

He looks at me carefully. "I've always heard that those people like to go around calling everyone alcoholic," he says.

I nod. "They do. All of which is meant to say, yes, I'm game for splitting that bottle of wine."

Jeremy looks me over, then nods. "Great," he smiles. "Let me go get it."

* * *

The first thought I have when I sip from the crystal goblet and feel the bitter and familiar-tasting liquid coasting down my throat is, *Is this what all the fuss has been about? The rehab and the slogans and the meetings and the incessant talk about feelings has all been about this—this liquid?* And, feeling even more empowered, I take another sip. It tastes . . . fine. Nice, even. Not like the first drop of water after having been stranded in the desert for six and a half months—not even close. *Clearly*, I say to myself, *if I were really an alcoholic, this moment would feel monumental.* But to me, right now, it just feels like I'm drinking something.

"This is nice," I say, smiling at Jeremy. I've never been able to tell the difference between Trader Joe's $9.99 wine and the kind that people save for eons because it's such a great vintage or whatever and this has always made me slightly self-conscious. *If I were an alcoholic, surely I would have studied wines and gone to tastings and whatnot,* I tell myself as Jeremy blathers on about why the wine's particular year is so crucial.

We move to the living room, where Jeremy gets out a photo album and starts pointing out pictures of him with Al Pacino, his mom, his brother, and what looks like all the current and former Lakers Girls. And it all feels very sophisticated—the wine drinking, the multimillion-dollar mansion, the photos all gathered in green leather binders. If I were at Adam's, I think, we'd probably be drinking out of cans and sitting on his futon couch.

"My God," Jeremy says, as I sip from my wine and examine a photo album page dedicated to a film festival, complete with pictures of Jeremy with indie darlings like Aaron Eckhart and Catherine Keener. "I can't believe you thought you were an alcoholic—I mean, you're barely sipping your wine."

"I know," I say, glowing with this latest revelation to add to my arsenal of information about what a good decision it was to drink. I take another small, delicate sip to emphasize the point.

I walk outside to smoke and Jeremy joins me a minute later, bringing a freshly opened bottle of wine which seems weird, seeing as there's no way we could have possibly finished the first, but he's telling me some story about how when he was an assistant at ICM, he had to take his boss's dog's stool sample to the vet, and I'm so riveted by the concept of such a demeaning job that I forget to even ask about the bottle.

We continue to drink the wine and I blow smoke rings and talk—about my life, my column, my feelings on various and sundry topics—and Jeremy mostly listens, piping in occasionally or laughing. It's starting to feel a little like a performance I'm giving and he's watching but neither of us seems to mind. *I forgot how theatrical I can get when I drink*, I think, as I spontaneously decide to recite dialogue from *Grease*, which I saw about 199 times during my formative years and thus can recite verbatim, complete with Australian accent for Sandy and New York accent for Danny.

Later, we're in the living room and it occurs to me that I might be buzzed because Jeremy seems to be holding my hand while I'm talking, and I don't seem to be snatching it back. When he leans in to kiss me, I get the distinct whiff of bacteria breath, and this—not the fact that he's about to kiss me—is what makes me wake up and push him slightly to the side while I straighten my skirt.

I think it's around the time when I light my first indoor cigarette—he's given me free rein to smoke wherever I want to now—that I see Jeremy reach into his pocket and pull his hand out with his fingers folded over as they clasp something.

"I don't feel bad about giving you the wine," he says, and I think that this seems like an oddly serious comment to be making at this point, seeing as we've mutually decided I'm not and have never been an alcoholic. "But I do feel a little bad about the Ecstasy."

I look at him, confused, thinking for one brief, horrifically wonderful second that he's dosed the wine with Ex and I've thus just done drugs without it having been my fault, when I glance into his previously clasped hand and spy a slew of small white pills gathered there.

Is that Ecstasy? I've done it a bunch of times, but I've usually been so drunk or wired by that point that I don't really remember what it looks like.

"Well, my problem was with drugs," I say, regretfully. "I mean, I was addicted to coke, and that's a drug. So doing a drug is out of the question, right?"

I'm not sure if I'm asking a rhetorical question but it doesn't really matter because by the time the sentence is out of my mouth, I've already grabbed a pill and gulped it down with the wine. I look at him as he swallows one himself, and want to feel guilty for having just taken a step down the proverbial rabbit hole, but that age-old I-just-took-drugs feeling kicks in and I feel only excited, like I'm about to take a trip where my head will leave me alone for a little while. And then I think, *Well, since I've already taken one and clearly blown this whole sobriety thing, I may as well take another one. If I'm going to go out, why not go all out?*

So I swallow another pill and light another cigarette and wait for that feeling of deliriousness to start rushing over me. "I don't feel anything," I say to Jeremy as he puts U2 on the CD player.

He looks at me. "You're sweating bullets," he says. "Trust me, you're feeling something."

I feel my forehead and notice that it is uncharacteristically moist but I don't do drugs to sweat, I do them to feel good, and since when does sweating mean I must be feeling good? At my senior prom in high school, my boyfriend and I took Ecstasy and didn't tell the other couples sharing the limo because we thought they would judge it. But trying to hide the high I was feeling over dinner took its toll on me, and my trip turned decidedly negative. When we got to the after-party and the two other couples found out what we'd done, they spontaneously decided they wanted to do Ecstasy, too—and they all had an amazing time. I remember sitting on a couch trying to figure out why exactly I couldn't seem to communicate with anyone while watching one of the girls, who'd never touched drugs before, jumping up and down and shrieking, "I feel like I'm dancing on a cloud! This is the best I've ever felt in my life!"

I watch Jeremy open another bottle of wine, feeling convinced that his Ecstasy sucks. "Can I see those pills again?" I ask.

Jeremy smiles and pulls another one from his pocket. "Open up," he says, and even though the act seems overly intimate, almost invasive, I want the pill too much to care. My jaw falls down, he pops a pill in my mouth, and I take another swig of wine.

Pretty soon after that I feel extremely animated so I start scrounging around his CD cabinet looking for music that I can dance to. But when Jeremy mentions that he has a sauna, that seems so thoroughly interesting that I immediately insist on seeing it. *This house is like an amusement park*, I think as I bound up the stairs after him, realizing that the thought doesn't make much sense and wondering why I'm so excited about a sauna when I grew up with one.

Turns out I don't so much want to take a sauna as just see it, and once I've seen it, my mind has moved on to something else. A cigarette! Another glass of wine! Maybe a drink-drink? Maybe we should go out? My brain leaps from one possibility to another, attempting to land on the perfect plan of action that will keep my high alive. And then I think of Adam and what a crazy liar he must think I am and the thought feels so sad and overwhelming that it seems like it might take over my entire body and mind.

"I think I'd like to take another," I say to Jeremy as we leave the bathroom with the sauna.

"I don't know." He looks slightly concerned. "This is pretty strong stuff and you've had a lot already." I can read his face perfectly: Girl says she's sober, then goes off the wagon and now appears to be going on some drug binge, which will probably end with a 911 call.

"Look, I can handle my drugs—trust me," I say, and hold out my hand. It feels uncomfortable to be having to ask someone for drugs. When I did coke, I was almost always the provider.

"Let's split one," Jeremy finally says, and he breaks a pill in half. As we go down to the kitchen for more wine, it occurs to me that I don't really like him at all, and I don't even mean romantically. As I swallow my half of the pill, I wonder why I'm even spending time with someone I wouldn't want to talk to for ten minutes at a party, and that's when it occurs to me that this entire night may well have been a massive mistake.

After a few more cigarettes, I realize I'm a little tired so I lie down on one of his overstuffed velvet couches. "I think your Ecstasy kind of sucks," I say, as I tuck one of his Oriental rug–covered pillows under my neck.

"Trust me, this is the best shit in town," Jeremy says, pulling a pillow of his own from the other side of the couch under his neck and mimicking my position. "My guy is the go-to guy for everyone who works on the Fox lot."

I guess I close my eyes for a while because when I open them, I feel groggy and confused. At first I don't remember where I am and in the second where I do, I feel even more confused—especially when I realize that Jeremy's lips are on mine and we're kissing.

"Oh, God," I say, pushing him away and sitting up. He smiles at me and I notice that his pupils are enormous. He trails a finger on my leg and even though I hate it when people do that and I'm fairly convinced he's taking complete advantage of me, I still feel bad when I move my leg away. When I gaze around the room and see empty wine glasses filled with cigarette butts, CDs scattered all over the floor and my favorite Theory jacket crumpled in a heap by the deck door, I'm suddenly overwhelmed with a nearly paralyzing emptiness that I haven't felt in over six and a half months.

"I should probably go," I say, walking over to my jacket and picking it off the ground. "What time is it?"

Jeremy glances at his silver Rolex. "Three thirty," he says. "Come on—don't even think about going home. I can't drive in this condition."

"I'll call a cab then," I say, like it's the most normal thought in the world, even though I can't actually remember the last time I called one. Do we even have cabs in L.A.?

"You're being silly," he says, standing up and walking over to me. "You should just stay here."

Now, I don't know if it's the fact that his pupils are making him somehow resemble what I think the devil might look like or if I just need to get as far away from this experience as quickly as possible but I reach for my bag, pull out my BlackBerry, dial information, and ask for Yellow Cab. Every city surely has a Yellow Cab?

"Amelia," Jeremy says, as—Eureka—the operator connects me. "You can stay in one of the guest rooms. We don't have to do anything."

Something about the way he says that utterly convinces me that I won't be left alone no matter what room I'm in. I don't know if the drugs are making me paranoid or if I'm having some kind of clairvoyant vision but I don't have any interest in finding out. "What's your address?" I ask and he reluctantly says it. I repeat it to the Yellow Cab receptionist and hang up, feeling like this is the smartest move I've made in hours.

And then Jeremy suddenly seems overwhelmed with concern—or at least paranoia. Or perhaps disappointment that he shelled out almost his entire supply of E and several expensive bottles of wine and isn't even going to get laid for his efforts. "Look, I feel sort of bad about all this," he says, following me outside, where I pick up a nearly empty pack of Camel Lights I'd left on his patio table.

"Don't," I say, but my voice is cold. Now that I've decided I'm done, I want him out of my face. "I make my own decisions. There's nothing to feel bad about."

He hands me one of my plastic 7-Eleven lighters. "You know, I don't think this is anything we need to tell people about," he says, and I feel like I can suddenly read his paranoia, which is telling him that a *Variety* story on the hotshot movie producer who coaxed a sex columnist out of her sobriety with drugs could be imminent.

I nod just as I see the taxi pull up outside.

"Bye," he says, pulling me in and giving me a kiss on the cheek, like this has been a perfectly lovely and appropriate evening. "I'll call you."

I start walking toward his front door, realizing that I seem to be having some trouble walking without falling. I want to say, "Please don't," but I don't have the balls. When I get to the door, I turn around to look at him one last time. "You should probably get a new drug dealer," I say, and then I leave.

When I come to at about three in the afternoon, I expect to be borderline suicidal, but I actually feel strangely calm. I sit up in bed, knocking a sleeping cat—who'd been meowing with unabashed vigor a few hours earlier but had clearly given up and decided to catnap it on my shoulder—onto the floor. Last night is incredibly clear in my mind: saw Adam, felt rejected, relapsed. *I've fucked everything up*, I think, as I reach for a cigarette. *Why the hell am I not hysterical about it?*

Deciding not to smoke, I get out of bed and wander into the kitchen, where I have some toast. While my head doesn't seem to be reeling as much from the experience as I'd think it would, my stomach is convulsing in what feels like somersault after somersault.

As I force toast down, I remember how Tommy used to say that a relapse starts long before you take a drink. When did mine start—when Justin told me he was using? When I climbed into the life-size champagne glass? When I faked doing a vodka shot? I guess there's no way of knowing. Then a thought pops into my head: *Clearly, I can't drink without doing drugs.* Somehow this feels like an immense relief because now I don't have to wonder. In rehab, people kept calling alcohol the "gateway" drug because as soon as they drank, the gate for doing drugs would open. But since I tended to do coke first and drink later, I hadn't had many alcohol gateway experiences.

Looking back over the night and realizing, with bizarrely amazing recollection, that I'd easily consumed a couple of bottles of wine myself, I start to wonder if maybe there's something to this concept of my being an alcoholic, too. Riding back in the cab earlier this morning, I'd toyed with the idea of not telling anyone about my little Ecstasy and alcohol escapade, thinking that I'd just keep going to Pledges and still celebrate a year's sobriety in six months. Apparently, people do that—they go out and don't tell anyone and smile about how well their sobriety's going—but they usually end up relapsing in a far bigger way as a result.

I realize that if I leave the house without showering or even brushing my hair, I can make the Pledges afternoon meeting. I probably look like death but since going to a meeting can help me escape that, at least for the time being, I allow necessity to trump vanity. *Making progress already*, I think as I slide a bra on under the wife beater I slept in and step out the door.

"My name is Amelia and I'm an alcoholic," I say, expecting the people in the room to all swivel their heads in unison over the fact that I've finally surrendered to using the word "alcoholic" over "addict," but everyone just does the smiley Hi-Amelia thing.

"I relapsed last night," I say, and I see the whisperings that start up whenever anyone mentions the word "relapse." When Vera drank, I remember leaning over to Justin and saying, "I could see this one coming from a mile away," so I feel like I deserve whatever it is anyone's saying. I realize my heart is beating incredibly fast, which seems strange to me, since I've shared a lot in this room and haven't felt nervous talking in front of the group since my first day of rehab. "I didn't really believe you guys when you said that being an alcoholic and a drug addict were the same thing," I say and I notice a couple of people nodding with compassion. "So last night, after being blown off by the guy I like, I decided to go have a glass of wine with the guy I don't like." Several people laugh and, while I'm surprised that anyone could find humor in my fuck-up, at the same time it makes me feel like I belong. I've definitely shared things here that I've known were funny, and felt completely validated by the laughter it's gotten, but I haven't ever really talked about anything sad or wrong or that makes me feel bad. In fact, I've heard people laughing at other people's hardships around here and wondered how things like having been suicidal or institutionalized could be so uproarious to other people—let alone to the person sharing, who always seems to join in the hilarity. But somehow, now that I'm the one talking, it makes sense: what I'm saying is illogical and basically crazy. And for some reason, in this room filled with people bobbing their heads and laughing, that seems okay. "Three and a half hits of E later, I realized I'd made a horrible mistake," I finish and most of the room guffaws. I break into a smile—I can't help it. "So I guess . . . I don't know . . . I guess that's it. I don't know. And you guys seem to." Everyone claps.

As the sharing in the room continues, people pat me on the back and women start writing down their numbers and passing them to me on pieces of scrap paper. As I tuck the phone numbers into my purse, I realize that I'd completely stopped reaching out to people here. When I was in rehab, I bonded like crazy with Justin and Robin and Vera and Peter and Joel and everyone else. But these days, with Justin and Robin both long gone, Vera always relapsing, and Peter and Joel only hitting the meetings every now and then, I've stopped. I now see that from the day I moved out of Pledges, I've essentially been acting like I was cured. Rachel always told me not to show up at meetings right when they started or leave right when they ended but I hadn't really listened. Looking around the room, I realize that I don't really know any of the other alumni sitting there—some of their faces are familiar and I know a few of their names, but I've tended more to look at them as audience members during my funny or profound shares than people I might befriend.

When the meeting ends, I decide to stand in line to thank the main speaker, something Rachel has always suggested but I've never done. It always seems so much like waiting in a receiving line at a wedding, where you're only going to be able to say something the person before you already did. *I'm probably just thinking about myself too much* floats through my head as I wait in line.

I tell the woman—who looks like your average Valley housewife but had shared about her heroin addiction, multiple marriages, and former life in porn—how grateful I am to have heard her, and she gives me a hug. I feel tears stinging my eyes as we embrace and, while the tears aren't, of course, surprising, the reason for them is: they're tears of comfort and relief, not the more familiar ones of self-pity.

Different people come up to me as I make my way out of the room and I realize, with shock, that it's twenty minutes after the meeting ended and I'm still here. As I'm hugging this girl with nine months of sobriety who tells me she "related to every word I said," I see someone I hadn't even realized until this moment was in the meeting, and my heart starts racing like an IV of cocaine has been injected straight into it.

"We need to talk," Rachel says, and I nod.

"You need to start making friends at Pledges," Rachel says, looking at me sternly. We're sitting at one of the plastic tables outside a burger stand near her apartment in Culver City after leaving the meeting. There's something about her that seems almost angry—a sort of schoolmarmish drone has replaced her typical singsongy lilt.

"I have friends at Pledges," I say. I look up at her. "I have you."

She looks me straight in the eye. "I'm not your friend," she says. "I'm your sponsor."

I feel a bit like I've been pummeled in the gut but don't want to show it. "Okay, Miss Serious. I'll make some new friends."

She still doesn't smile. "Amelia, this *is* serious. It's about life and death. And sometimes I think you treat recovery like it's an accessory—it helped you get your shit together and made you better and now you can go about pursuing your fabulous life again." She picks up a fry and dips it in ketchup. "But it doesn't work that way. You can't show up at alumni meetings when you want, smoke cigarettes outside, and pretend that everything's going to be wonderful and easy now that you're getting famous." She shoves the fry in her mouth, chews, and sighs. "It's not about incorporating this into your life; it's about incorporating your life into *this*."

I want to object and defend myself but I see she has me so nailed that there's no use in fighting her on it. Since getting out of Pledges, I've basically neglected everything I was taught in there—about how my day-to-day happiness and serenity depended on getting out of myself and being of service to other people, about going to meetings and connecting with the people there.

"Being sober has to be your primary purpose in life or you don't stand a chance," she says. "Do you get that?"

"Well . . ."

"My point is this: if you're really committed to doing this right, I'd be honored to keep working with you. I think if you set your mind to doing this the way it's suggested, there's no limit to the kind of serene life you could live. But if you want to half-ass it, I don't really want to be a part of it."

There's a tiny pause. "I want to do it." When I say it, I realize I've never felt more certain of anything.

"That means sitting down to write about your resentments and fears and being willing to go apologize to the people you've hurt because of your disease."

Every time she's brought this up before, I've somehow diverted her attention away from it—usually by telling a funny story. I'd assumed that I'd been so sly that she hadn't even realized I'd been purposely distracting her. Writing all this stuff down and having to face my entire past has always sounded wholly unappealing but somehow, right now, I look at it in a different way. *I've been waiting a long time for people to ask me who I'm pissed at*, I think. *Possibly my whole life*. "I'll start today," I say.

"And it means trying to live your whole life according to sober and honest principles."

I nod.

"And that includes your job."

I look at her as she polishes off her fries.

"Are you saying I have to quit doing my column?"

She balls up her empty wrappers and tosses them into the nearby trash can—a perfect shot.

"I'm saying that you have to try living your life according to sober and honest principles. In the same way that no one can diagnose another person as an alcoholic, no one can tell you what that should mean to you. It's for you to decide."

"Rachel, I want to do this."

She picks up her keys and stands. "This is a lot to hear all at once. Why don't you think it over and call me later."

"But—"

"Call me, Amelia," she says, as she starts to walk away. "I love you."

At first I'm sort of pissed. Who the hell is Rachel to suddenly transition from cute, bubbly girl with a pixie haircut to a hard-edged slave driver? But when I get home and crack open the Pledges book for the first time since leaving the place, I start to realize that everything she talked about today is right from this book. And at some point I'd known that. What the hell had happened to my memory?

I continue reading and notice a sentence in the book that talks about how short our memories seem to be when it comes to changing the way our brains work, which is why going to meetings every day, or at least as often as possible, is so important.

The more I read, the more this book begins to make sense, and the guidelines start to sound like the ideal way to live a happy life. *I never had any guidelines before*, I think. I mean, sure, I've heard things like don't lie and cheat and steal, but this other stuff, about looking for my part in every resentment I have, sounds almost like the exact opposite of the way I've been living. *Resenting someone is like drinking poison and expecting the other person to die,* I heard someone say in a meeting once. Another person chimed in that "expectations are re-sentments under construction," and everyone laughed, including me. But now I'm really beginning to get it. Most of the things I'd spent most of my life pissed about—my parents not doing something, friends not being supportive, people not loving me enough—came about be-cause I had expected so much from them.

Armed with that epiphany, I take out a notebook and start listing all the people I'm pissed at. As you can imagine, it's a long list. I've heard people suggest that a good way to start is to write down every single person you've ever known because chances are that you resent them for something. And for me, that seems highly likely.

So I start by listing Mom and Dad, then friends from grammar school—these petty slights I've carried with me over the years—and move on to my life today. I take out old photo albums, dig up old ad-dress books, and even join classmates.com to jog my memory. When I start to write down why I resent them, I realize this project will take hours, if not weeks. But I want so much to have my slate cleaned, to get this all out on paper and face who I really am. The more I write, the more I see that I've already spent too much time in my life upset and angry.

The pen I'm writing with starts causing an indentation on my right pointer finger and I'm lighting about my twentieth cigarette since I started writing when the phone rings. When we first started working together, Rachel had suggested that I not screen calls because when someone's calling, it's probably the interruption I need, whether it feels like it or not. I'd nodded but continued screening, always mak-ing sure I answered when she called so she wouldn't know.

"Hello," I say, not even glancing at caller ID.

"Sweetie?" I recognize the voice immediately.

"Hi, Nadine," I say. "What's going on?" I don't feel that anxiety I always feel when I talk to her—that I have to be so fabulous, so Party Girl, so "on."

"What's going on with you?" she asks, sounding alarmed. "What are you doing home on a Friday night?"

I glance at the clock: 9:30 P.M. I'd absolutely lost my sense of time and space and feel shocked that somehow day ended and night started without any acknowledgment on my part. I'd left Rachel at about noon. Had I actually been reading the Pledges book and writing for over eight hours? And was it really Friday night? I had no idea.

"I'm just home," I say. "Reading, writing." I glance at one of my cats, who's asleep next to me. "Playing with my cats."

Complete silence on the other end of the phone line.

"Nadine? Are you there?"

"Oh, yes, sweetie. I'm just surprised, that's all. Not exactly the image I have of our Party Girl on a Friday night."

"It happens," I say. "More often than not."

Again, Nadine doesn't say anything. She never asked me what happened with Ryan Duran and I never offered up any information. I have the distinct impression that I'm devastating her, which feels wrong but also strangely necessary.

"Well, I was just calling to let you know that we've booked your *View* appearance for the week after next," she says. "And also, I have some very exciting news!" Her voice is now about four octaves higher than when she first started talking. "I know there's been a lot of talk about companies buying the rights to Party Girl and making it into a movie or show. But a little birdie told me that the VP at Ridley Scott has come to Tim with a solid offer. Honey, they want to make it into an HBO series for next season!"

"Really?" I ask. I know I should be thrilled—this is what everyone in Hollywood and beyond fantasizes could happen with what they write—but I feel bizarrely unaffected.

"Sweetie, you don't exactly sound excited."

"I am," I say, trying to muster as much false enthusiasm as I can. "That's terrific." I can't remember the last time I used the word terrific.

"Of course, since only a few columns have come out, they need to wait and read the next couple," she says. "But he said—his exact words were, 'If she continues to do what she's done so far, I can't imagine why we wouldn't make the deal.' Sweetie, they'd want to make you a consulting producer! And you could even be *on* the show. Tell me, have you thought about acting? There's no reason you can't be Party Girl *and* an actress."

Something—or rather everything—about this conversation suddenly starts giving me a headache and I know that all I want is to be off the phone and lying down.

"That's great, Nadine," I say. "I actually have to get back to what I'm doing but thanks for calling to tell me that."

"But sweetie—"

I hang up.

30

I spend the next week writing down my resentments, only taking breaks to go to Pledges for meetings. By now, I'm on the last section, where I write down the part I played in each resentment—whether I had overly high expectations or was being competitive or said something nasty before the person yelled at me. It's starting to become incredibly surreal to remember details about all these things that I'd somehow forgotten or repressed. Yet owning up to my part doesn't feel shameful; it's actually a relief because it makes me believe my future can be less messy.

"You don't need to do it like a speed demon," Rachel says when I tell her that I'm almost done. "Most people take months. Some people take years."

"I know," I say. I'd heard as much. But for some reason, as soon as I started writing, some compulsion deep inside kept propelling me forward at this rapid-fire pace. I didn't even know if I could stop. It's like I sensed that if I didn't take action now, my perspective might change again and I didn't want to risk forgetting how important it was again.

It was hard to believe what I was learning about myself—essentially, that, except for my grandfather, who used to call me stupid for no particular reason, I played a part in every single resentment I had. I'd either had expectations from people that weren't met or done something to provoke whatever I was now angry about. Kane, for example, couldn't have screwed me over if I hadn't acted completely inappropriate and unprofessional in the first place. Even my grandfather and my parents, whose transgressions against me, I'd always felt, were almost too numerous to mention, were just doing the best they could at the time. If I was too young to have played a part in what they did, my part today was that I was continuing to hold on to the resentment.

I go to a Pledges meeting and share about all the realizations I'm having, and for the first time, I'm not saying things that I hope will get a laugh or demonstrate how articulate I am. I finally understand what people mean when they say that talking about things in a group helps them to make sense of their emotions. And if they were right about that, wasn't it possible that they were right about a whole lot of other things?

Finally, a few days later, I sit in Rachel's fern-filled apartment and read her everything I have—an entire hundred-sheet notebook's worth. And then I read some more. And smoke. And read some more. She nods and smokes with me, occasionally taking notes on a yellow legal pad.

"You must be bored stiff," I say when we're getting into our fourth hour.

"Not at all. Remember, you're being of service by allowing me to hear all this."

People with the most sober time at Pledges talk a lot about being of service and how listening to someone else talk about their problems takes them out of their own heads, and how almost all the problems we alcoholics have are the same—most of them related to our over-sized egos—and how they find themselves giving suggestions that they probably need to hear themselves. To be honest, I've assumed that most of them are full of shit. But I'm looking at Rachel and, since she's a teacher and not an actress and Pledges is always telling us how important it is that we work a program of "rigorous honesty," I assume she's telling the truth. So I keep reading and reading and reading, until after the sun goes down and my last page has been turned.

When I'm done, Rachel presents me with a list of my defects, and even though it includes words like "selfish," "self-seeking," "manipulative," and "dishonest," for some reason it doesn't make me feel at all bad about myself. It actually makes me feel hopeful that I may be able to conquer the kind of relationship problems I've had my whole life, since long before I took my first drink.

"You haven't been bad," she says. "Just sick." She tells me to go home, read through the first part of the Pledges book, and think about these defects.

"It's that easy?" I ask. "I just think about them and then I'm done?"

"Done?" she asks, laughing. "More like just getting started."

31

"Amelia, we already went through this—on our hike, remember?" Stephanie says, blowing dust off her keyboard. "You don't have anything else to apologize for."

I'm sitting in her office, bizarrely nervous considering I'm sitting in front of someone who I know loves me unconditionally. It's my first time in the building since the day I fled *Absolutely Fabulous*, and I know that that's where I'm going next.

"Please, just listen," I say. And then I tell her that although I already apologized to her for being selfish, I haven't changed my behavior at all—I'm still always calling her in the midst of a crisis and then abandoning her as soon as it's over. I finish by saying, "I haven't been treating you the way I want to be treated, and I want to start doing that now."

Stephanie looks completely shocked. "Amelia, I don't know what to say," she says after a few seconds of silence.

"You don't have to say anything," I say. "Unless there's something I can do to make up for what I've done."

She shakes her head. "Can I hug you now?"

I nod and we both stand up and embrace. As we hug, I tell her I love her and notice that she's crying. "You're foul," she says and we both laugh.

Next, I go upstairs, walk straight into Robert's assistant's office and ask if it's possible for me to speak to him. His assistant, Celine, looks terri-

fied, like I may be on the verge of pulling out an Uzi, but Rachel had
told me that I wasn't allowed to react to anyone's behavior during this
apology tour. I was just supposed to be loving and take whatever was
dished out.

"Um, hang on," she says, scooting quickly out of her office and just
as speedily into Robert's. As I stand there, Brian walks by, his head
down as he reads a fax.

"Brian," I say, and he looks up. "Can I talk to you for a minute?"

Not looking terribly surprised, Brian nods just as Robert opens his
door, so we walk in and take the exact same seats we had the day I was
fired. I waste no time—launching directly into how sorry I am for
being such a self-absorbed, entitled prima donna. I apologize for acting inappropriately with the people I interviewed, for not respecting
the people above me and the rules, for having a sense of entitlement
borne purely out of insecurity, and finally for doing coke at work. I end
by saying that I thought I deserved to be fired and then something entirely unplanned escapes from my mouth. "I'm actually really grateful
it happened," I say, "because it helped me get to where I am now."

"Well, I never . . ." Robert says, and then lapses into the muteness
that seems to be his trademark. But for the first time since we met, he's
actually looking at me with kindness.

Brian glances from Robert to me and then breaks into a smile. "I'm
proud of you," he says.

The rest of my apologies go as well as can be expected. I call Chris, ask
if we can meet for coffee and, at the Coffee Bean and Tea Leaf on Beverly, explain that I took out my own shame about my wild behavior on
him and couldn't ever be direct with him about it. I also apologize for
mocking him and Mitch in my column. He nods, informs me coldly
that he still thinks I'm a bitch, and all I can do is say, "You may be
right." Rachel had advised me to use those words if I ever felt like I
was about to react negatively to someone while I was apologizing.

I show up at Chad Milan's office and his assistant at first tells me he doesn't have time to see me. Just as I'm getting up, though, Chad wanders out to the hall and says he wants to hear what I have to say just to satisfy his curiosity. I end up telling him—here in the halls of CAA, with about a trillion suits wandering by every millisecond—about my addiction and recovery. Rachel had said that I didn't need to go and explain that I was an alcoholic to every last person I spoke to—that, in fact, it could be considered a cop-out because I might try to use that as an excuse for my behavior—but for some reason, this is how I explain it to Chad. I add that this in no way makes me feel like I'm entitled to some kind of get-out-of-jail-free card but I just wanted him to know that I think he's a nice guy and deserved to be treated better. He doesn't exactly throw his arms around me, but he doesn't have me escorted out of the building, either.

I drive over to Holly's office at Imagine but a serious-looking, bespectacled brunette is sitting where Karen used to. I ask if Holly's available and the girl—who introduces herself as Samantha and explains that she's a temp—says that Holly's in meetings at Universal all day. So I sit down in the waiting room and write Holly a note, apologizing for bailing out on the job and for not giving it the energy it deserved, and adding that she should call me if she wants to discuss the matter further. I put the note in an envelope, along with her keys, that I leave with the temp.

Rachel had made it clear to me that I should make every effort to apologize in person but if there were people I couldn't get to or felt too uncomfortable to see, it would be okay to e-mail them or write a letter. And since Justin's voicemail is full, I send him an e-mail saying that I'm sorry for acting like his relapse was some personal slight against me, only calling him when I needed him, and essentially abandoning him the minute he told me he wasn't sober. I also ask him to call me whenever he wants to because I'd like to say these things to him in person.

I call Rachel to tell her about the apologies I've made and she says

I'm off to a great start. I know that I have far bigger and more terrifying apologies to make—to, say, Mom and Dad—but that I don't have to do them now. Rachel says I'll know when I'm ready.

As Rachel and I talk, the other line keeps ringing and I notice Nadine's 212 number on my caller ID. She's been trying to schedule this trip to New York for me to be on the *View* and I can only put her off for so long. So, even though I'm not remotely sure I can keep doing the column, I say good-bye to Rachel, then click over and tell Nadine I'm sorry I haven't called her back but that I can go to New York whenever she wants me to.

"Fantastic, sweetie!" she trills. "They'd love to have you on tomorrow so how about the red-eye tonight?"

Looking around the apartment, I see that it's in complete disarray, and realize that it doesn't matter. *I'm tidying up what's inside, not what's on the outside*, I think as Nadine calls me back and tells me that she's made my reservation and I have a few hours before the car will come get me and take me to the airport.

After packing, I sit down to make my final apology for the time being—to Adam. Like with the others, I want to make it simple, direct, and absolutely devoid of motive, so I write him an e-mail saying I'm sorry for criticizing his date when I saw him and for generally taking out my frustration on him because he wasn't doing what I wanted him to do. I add that I appreciate his questioning me over why I'd do something for a living that I didn't believe in because it was helping me to look at my life and my actions in a new way. As I send the e-mail—Rachel and I had decided that it was okay for me not to make this apology in person because, face to face, I might try to manipulate and cajole him into asking me out—I realize that I don't actually want anything from Adam anymore. My feelings for him are still there, but if he doesn't want me, I now see, there's really no point in my pining for him. It's clearly not meant to be, and one day I may come to understand why. The feeling that he has to be my boyfriend is simply gone, just like that. Then I realize something even more shocking: my desire to use cocaine and drink is also gone. I've heard people in meetings talk about how their urge to drink or do drugs had suddenly been removed and I'd always gazed at them somewhat skeptically, but I guess I'm now living proof that it can happen. As I sit here thinking about how serene I feel, a wonderful idea occurs to me, so I make a call asking someone to meet me in New York.

Who have I become? I wonder as I walk down my driveway to the waiting Town Car. As I get inside, I realize I don't really have the answer to that yet.

32

"You're something else," Joy Behar says after she takes a sip from her coffee cup. "Getting together with two groomsmen. Kissing girls during Truth or Dare. Picking up on a guy at a bar while you were on a date. Most women would be hanging their heads in shame, but you—you're going around getting rewarded for it. Now why do you think that is?"

The *View* producer went through all the questions they were going to ask me in my dressing room, so I already have my answer ready. I glance at Tim, who's sitting with John and Nadine in the studio audience, and offer, "Maybe other people are doing the same thing and they're relieved someone is actually being honest about it?"

Some audience members laugh and a few of them applaud as Elizabeth Hasselback squints her eyes at me. "Do you think you represent society's movement toward a more brazen attitude toward sexuality, as some people have said?"

I give Elizabeth a Nadine-coached response about how I'm just being myself but if people want to call me the poster child for a movement, then it's fine by me. As I continue to field questions from Rosie, Joy, and Elizabeth, I deliver all the appropriate quips and answers but I'm distracted because I know a big moment is coming soon. It seems terrifying but at the same time completely appropriate and I suddenly know that everything's going to turn out fine.

And then, before I know it, the moment is here. "What are your plans for the future?" Rosie asks, looking up from one of her note cards.

"Actually," I say, leaning forward, "my plan for the near future is to be thoroughly honest."

All four of their heads spin toward me, since this is when I was supposed to mention the plans to make Party Girl into a TV series. Before anyone can say anything, I say, "And that means telling all of you that I'm not, in fact, a party girl."

"Come again?" Joy says. I hear people start whispering to each other.

I glance at Tim in the studio audience and say, "I used to be one—big time—but thank God, that's behind me now."

Rosie tries to interrupt me but I just keep talking.

"The thing about it is that my life wasn't cute and sexy and funny, the way I make it sound in the columns. It was actually rather soulless and empty—I was always trying to avoid my real feelings by creating drama and crises or just escaping through chemicals, which really only made me feel worse."

In the audience, Tim stands up but then, clearly realizing there's nothing he can do, sits back down.

"So you've been living a lie?" Joy asks.

"Well, yes and no," I say, amazingly calm for someone who's in the process of upsetting a number of people. "Everything I've written about did happen, and a lot of it did seem amusing and entertaining at one point. But I wasn't so much free and loose as I was just out of control."

"Why have you been writing the column, then?" Elizabeth asks, looking perplexed.

"I've been thinking about that a lot lately," I say. "And I guess the answer is that I wanted to feel special. I could just be another struggling freelance writer, slugging it out with everyone else, or I could be celebrated—albeit for a part of me that I put to rest. And I chose to be celebrated." I gaze out at the studio audience. "Wouldn't anyone?"

A heavyset woman in a flowered sundress nods and Joy makes a gesture to a producer that they should cut me off. Before that can happen, I say, "I may be a fraud, but I'd like to introduce you to someone who's not—someone who's living the life because it's who she is and not because her self-destructiveness brought her there."

I glance down at Charlotte—aka Tube Top girl—who's sitting, as planned, in the farthest audience seat to the right.

"Want to come up here, Charlotte?" I ask as I hear a producer backstage shout that they need to cut me off. But Charlotte stands up and removes her Marc Jacobs wrap, suddenly the very picture of sexified youth in a halter dress, thick belt, and dainty heels. Joy shakes her head while the other three cohosts sit there eagerly, waiting to see what will happen next. As Charlotte walks onto the stage, her tanned and muscular legs sauntering confidently toward us, I marvel over how ripe she is for this opportunity and how much publicity Nadine and Tim will surely get over my dramatic departure and her sure-to-be stunning takeover. I walk over to give her a hug, then turn back toward the women.

"May I present the real Party Girl," I say, nudging Charlotte toward them and then walking off the stage. I remove my mic from my shirt and place it on a shelf filled with other microphones in front of the green room. As I walk down the hall toward the exit, I hear a producer say into a headpiece that they're going to bump the next guest so they can see how this story plays itself out. I smile as I continue into the green room, stopping only to pick up my bag, which contains my ticket back to L.A. My BlackBerry beeps that I have a text message, so I pull it out as I make my way from backstage into a hallway. Glancing at my BlackBerry, I see that the text is from Adam and it starts with the line *Always trust your first impression.*

As I take the elevator down to the ground floor, I read the rest of what he wrote. *Just saw Hasselback almost lose her lunch, thanks to you. She wasn't the only one. Any chance you can forgive me for buying into the hype instead of trusting my first impression?*

I smile as I put the BlackBerry back in my bag and exit the building. Nobody chases after me, and, casually as can be, I hail a cab and ask to be taken to JFK.

ACKNOWLEDGMENTS

I cannot conceive of what rough road *Party Girl* and I might have traveled had we not been lucky enough to be discovered by the tenacious and devoted Pilar Queen—who guided me through every step of this process.

Thank you as well to Maureen O'Neal and Jenny Brown at HarperCollins for always being so respectful and encouraging, and to Suzanne Wickham, Chase Bodine, Gregg Sullivan, and Megan Beatie for doing all they could to get the *Party Girl* word out.

Without a doubt this book would not have existed had Melanie Bromley not made a deal with me that we'd send each other one thousand words of the novels we planned to write every Sunday. Thank you as well to Brendan Smith, who helped motivate me when Mel's career interfered with our plans. I look forward to buying both of your novels one day soon.

Thank you to Andrew Brin, Mike DeLuca, Alec Shankman, and Vanessa Grigoriadis for reading the manuscript early on, not to mention being the kind of friends who offered to do so—and did it with the kind of expedient enthusiasm that a sensitive perfectionist like myself demands—without having to be asked.

Bottom-of-my-heart thanks as well to Melissa de la Cruz, who consistently told me, "Don't worry—it will all happen" with the calm confidence that must come from cranking out five-plus books a year, and to Rachel Resnick—both of whom passed along the wisdom, advice, and encouragement of seasoned pros; I only hope to be as gracious with other aspirants as they were with me.

For general support, encouragement, friendship, and love, my thanks as well to Nicole Balin, Becket Cook, John Griffiths, Phil and Sierra Mittleman, Jeannie Sloan, and Alexis Tellis. For keeping the technological aspects of my life running smoothly, thanks to Joel and Ivy-Anne Sigerson and Eddie deAngelini (the most talented non-designing website designer I'm lucky enough to somehow employ).

For giving me or leading me to the kind of breaks that have allowed me to write for a living over the past decade, thank you to Laura Gilbert, Steve Reddicliffe, Todd Gold, Sean Smith, Jen Furmaniak, Chris Napalitano, Michael Soloman, Amy Sohn, Stacy Morrison, Vicki Larson, Lew Harris, and Andrew Essex.

For financially aiding this struggling writer during the times that were lean despite the help of those listed above, I have gratitude for Steven and Ned David.

For keeping me sane and healthy throughout this process, Gordon Kernes (neck), Alex Katehakis (mind), Colin Kim, Allan Avendano, and Grace at Olympic Day Spa (body), Thom Knolles (breathing), and the pool at the Standard Hotel.

For love, guidance, and help trudging the road at just those moments I needed it, thank you to Bill W., Sammy H., Carrie W., Candace B., Amber V., Rachel L., Susannah B., Justin K., Roger K., Peter M., Leslie K., Richard R., and the 10 A.M. Bliss 1 and 2 crew (Dufflyn L., Michael D. B., Philip M., Alex D., Denny P., Mark D., Christian S., Rob G., Leslie S., and everyone else both at the table and not).

And finally I'd like to thank my mom, Gail, who not only dedicated her first book to me but also made me want to write (I still remember the awe I felt as a child watching her fingers flit over the typewriter keys without her having to glance down) and hasn't yet disowned me—even though it's meant having to put concerned Momness aside in order to swallow *Playboy* layouts, reading graphic sex and drug scenes, and telling people that her daughter writes for "non-girlie" magazines, too.

Also, I never would have made it through even the first draft had it not been for the fact that I promised myself I could eat Trader Joe's Sweet, Savory & Tart Trek Mix—the best, and most addictive food on the planet—as I wrote. Thankfully—or I'd weigh double what I do now—I'm now in recovery from that addiction, too.